FAVORITE
DEAD GIRL

Jerry Kuznik

NOTEBOOK
PUBLISHING

First published in 2019 by Notebook Publishing,
20–22 Wenlock Road, London, N1 7GU.

www.notebookpublishing.co

ISBN: 9781913206277

A CIP catalogue record for this book is available from the British Library.

Typeset by Notebook Publishing.

To my wife Pamela

PART I:
LIFE INTERRUPTED

"Because I could not stop for Death —
He kindly stopped for me —
The carriage held but just Ourselves —
And Immortality."
—*Emily Dickinson*

"I looked Death in the face last night
I saw Him in a mirror
And He simply smiled
He told me not to worry
He told me just to take my time."
—*Danny Elfman*

"I promise not to kill myself tonight, if you let me tell you
EVERYTHING.
After all, I am your favorite dead girl."
—*Pamela Vasquez-Kuznik*

RITES OF SPRING

They gathered one night on the eastern slope—wandering souls, men of oak, soiled by mud, by gravel and glass, their arms and their clothing splattered in blood—lost souls chained to the stretch of asphalt that stole them out of their suburban dreams.

It was March 19th, the day before the Vernal Equinox—a season foretold to avenge their fate. "Harness the violence of all of the elements—drunkenness, courage, foolishness, lust. Gather them up from the valleys below and like 'hooks in their jaws' draw them up into our lair." Candles danced in the cold night air as spirits chanted a dark invocation. A priestess shrouded in long dark robes—bearing the scars of a fateful decision, her body outlined in flickering light, sockets replacing her once dark eyes—stretched forth her arms in the midst of the masses.

A victim of the canyon herself, witnesses claim that she not only murdered her young husband's mistress but disposed of her body in one of the creeks. Leaving the scene, her car lost control on the hairpins—her body and spirit avenged in the same rocks and water.

"Lost Eyes" lifted up her head to the hills as spirits sang in an ancient Chaldean tongue, then raised her arms to harness their power. "Reverse the winds that blow in the spring, the breath of the desert, a plague of locusts." Chanting arose in harmonic convergence—a plainsong from the abode of the damned—the ground quaked in nefarious spasms. "Send for me the soul of a woman; young and beautiful, dressed all in black, Pisces Moon and Scorpio Venus, illusions of her own immortality, a doubter of God, locked outside of His 'hedge of protection.' Her soul for mine! Her eyes for my own!" She lifted her head as the warm canyon wind sent torches dancing in a circle of hands—dark empty sockets glowing with fire, her face a bruised and blood-stained pallor— shadows answering down from the hills.

FLASH DELIRIUM

A warm eastern wind awakened the canyon from an early spring slumber. Later that night, two cars entered in through its gates, and the narrow black snake lined down the middle in broken white stripes awoke to receive them. A young engineer—a round of golf, then too many drinks, his prized black Z-28, a final call home to his wife, "Don't wait up." His engine revved as the car swung out onto the road, throwing gravel from under the tires. A few miles later, he was up in the hills—sharpening turns, popcorn under his left front wheels, the canyon yawning below on his right. "Come on, Ed, keep it together."

A group of teens stopped in Olinda Village, then drove on out to a make out point in Sleepy Hollow—the driver robed in the horns of Pan after shedding his Robin Goodfellow garb. They drank their purloined *Bartle's and James*, exchanging soggy half-eaten gummies between familiar clove-stained lips, while Pan and his mistress stole behind an old barren oak. The wind picked up and rustled the branches. Shadows bent into shifting shapes closing in all around them. Startled, they rushed back to their car.

***

The popcorn soon gave way to a long and steady washboard rattle before disappearing into a thin yellow line that broke in erratic waves through the windshield. He drifted in and out of a swoon as his car swung back and forth between lanes.

"Where's Pam? Get Pam!" Pan's mistress called out, then shut her inside the backseat next to her cousin.

"What's happening? Where are we going?"

"The fuck out of here!" Pan replied, lifting the pair of phony wax horns from out of his hair.

"What's the matter? She wouldn't put out?" Pam snarled at him, her eyes boring holes through his rear-view mirror.

"Shut up! Would you just shut up?"

"Come on, cuz", Susie spoke up. "That's no way to talk about your BFF."

"BFF? More like BFFB, as in best friend fucking my boyfriend!"

"Pam, that's enough! We've got to get out of here. Someone was back there I swear. Look, I'm sorry, we're sorry. But right now we all need to just leave."

The car made one last sweeping turn before rejoining the highway—tires screeching the last few yards. The engine roared then slowed to a hum, pistons and pavement marching in tune, tread marks swaying along each curve, bobbing and weaving in a seamless ballet.

His eyes flickered open then closed for a moment. Distant lights dotted the hills like needle points on a black velvet curtain—plants bending up toward the light guided by some unseen force—his mid-life trope, a guided missile, a blood-red "Z-28" on the hood.

"Why don't we put on some tunes?" one of the boys said from the back, "Pam, how about that tape?"

"What tape?"

"The one you that you lent to Trey last week. He did give it back to you, right?"

"That's some creepy ass shit." Pan's mistress complained then started to giggle.

"Then you should like it." Pam said as she handed it forward, "Bitch."

"You're the bitch, bitch!"

"Ladies, knock it off!" Pan's voice now rising in anger as he pushed in the tape until it clicked in the deck. Speakers began to throb all around, the pulsating rhythm driving them forward into the dark, swooping and swaying around every curve, crashing together in a cacophonous march. A sudden hard left, then a valley of oaks—the tight hug of trees reaching out from each side, branches posing like skeletal fingers, dancing and leering over the windows, spiders reaching out for their prey.

"Marty, slow down!" a terrified shriek arose from the back, piercing the Horusian cadence.

"I can't." A small frightened voice croaked out between quivering lips—lungs contracted, chest heaving, filling up with an inaudible scream. The engine breathed in heightened gasps, tires tossed along black asphalt waves, a curtain of darkness concealing the light, a wayward flare hissing on through the night, a silver bullet locked on to its target.

The screeching of brakes and the crashing of metal—shards of glass fractured the light like a shower of mirrors then fell to the ground in a crystalline sea. Bodies scattered on the canyon floor. Spirits rising against the darkness—others still barely clinging to life. One of the bodies slowly stood up then staggered forward through vapor and glass, bones protruding her black leather jacket like spokes on a wheel. Far down the road, she could see her shadow, lying face down dressed all in black, a pool of blood surrounding her head. A figure began to emerge from the trees, a burial shroud stretched out in her hand.

"Pam. Pam!" Susie screamed into the darkness, stumbling toward the phantom in black as she unfurled her robe across the young girl's body. "Pam! Pam! Please help me find Pam!"

Lifting her hand up to her shoulder, the phantom spoke without raising her head. "Don't worry about her, child, that one is dead." Then, rising up to meet her eyes, Susie noticed the scars on her face—her matted hair embedded with gravel, sockets where her eyes used to be.

"I told you, she's dead! She's dead, and I have her with me!"

HARVEST NEW MOON

Everything about that night was wrong. It hadn't rained since the sudden storm late last month dropped snow into the surrounding hills. Weather forecasters stared at their millibar charts in stunned disbelief. "I've never seen this so late in the year. Shit, is it September or April?"

"Ninety-one degrees today—ninety-fucking-one, can you believe it?" a tall man in a neatly pressed suit then looked toward the camera. "Three, two, one, you're on."

"A ridge of high pressure will dominate the weather this weekend." The tall man smiled then waved his arm in a long sweeping motion back toward a map like a game-show host revealing a prize. "Winds kicking up across the canyons." the smile now running away from his face, "very unusual for this time of year."

The switchboard blinked in solid red lights. "Got another one—two more being sent to Canyon, another arriving at Placentia-Linda." Pushing his hair back under his cap, he sipped his coffee and slid back in his chair. "Bad accident on Carbon Canyon, both drivers killed on impact. There's another being lifted to Western, this one's bad, really bad. Doesn't look like she's going to make it." A young voice crackled in through the headset. "Roger that, headed to Western right now. Geez Kyle what the fuck's going on out there tonight?"

***

A sickle of stars marched up in the sky—the head of the lion joined by the bright-orange beating heart of Arcturus. The sky was dark without any moon, warm winds blowing on a midnight-blue canvas, a ribbon of lights wound through the hills in broken, yellow, serrated bands.

"Medical emergency, north Orange Freeway. Marine stationed over at Pendleton." A crackle of static then a moment of silence. "Dead at the scene, 10-9, driver is dead at the scene." Tearing his receiver off of his head, the young man wrung his hands through his hair then exhaled a prolonged coffee-soaked sigh. "My God, will this night ever end?"

DEATH WISH

The alarm pierced through the mid-April morning—a throbbing red glow of numbers spurting blood like arteries from a still-beating heart. Behind the curtains, the sun began to warm the horizon in orange shards of feathered clouds that outlined tall black silhouettes of palm trees yawning over a sea of outstretched serrated roof tops.

"Shit." Susie grunted, then, throwing off a thin white blanket, reached toward the night-stand and frantically groped for the button to mercifully end the clangorous din. "Fuck it!" she murmured ripping the chord out of the wall, then turned over and went back to sleep. Within minutes she could hear the shrieks—wave upon wave of anguished wails, bright red lights no longer flashing, an orange glow came through her window and covered her walls in long twisted shadows. She jumped out of bed, rubbed her eyes, and threw open the door. At the end of the hall, a warm yellow blaze leaked out from each side of the door, pulsating against each wave of sobs like a monstrance set on an altar of sorrow. Fists clenched at each of her hips, she steadied herself and marched forward into the halo of light.

"What the hell's going on in here?" Susie growled. Her dark eyes narrowed to conceal her rage.

Pam turned her face from against the mirror, her fair complexion flushed in red, her dark brown eyes awash in tears. "I hate it!" she cried. "Why God, why?"

"What are you talking about?" Susie inquired.

"This!" Pam turned again toward the mirror, pointing to a bright red pimple positioned between her cheek and her lip. "And it's the last night of the play! Everyone's going to notice! God, I hate myself right now!"

"You're making a big deal out of nothing! No one's even going to give a shit."

"That's easy for you to say! You're just an usher, I'm one of the leading actors!"

Susie paused as if smacked in the face, took a deep breath, then set her hands on both of her hips "Well, maybe the *real* Tatania also had a crater face!"

"Fuck you! You bitch! Leave me alone, you fucking dike!" With a rush of fury, Pam turned and pushed Susie out into the hallway, closed the door behind her, and returned to her place in front of the mirror.

Within moments there was a faint knock at the door. "Pam? Pam?"

"Go away!"

"Pam, open up, I have something that will help. Open up, *please*?"

Pam turned around and slowly opened the door, but Susie pushed her way inside, squirted a dollop of shaving cream into her hand and pushed it directly into Pam's face. "Here, this ought to make that zit go away!"

"Give me that, you bitch!" Pam reached over and grabbed the can out of Susie's hand, then began to cover her entire body with white menthol foam. Soon the entire bathroom looked like some sort of Halloween prank—the sink and mirror awash in Noxzema, Susie and Pam writhing from wall to wall like a pair of exotic female wrestlers. Suddenly the door burst open and both girls stood in silent terror as their father's eyes locked onto them like a bear awakening out of his slumber. "Both of you girls are grounded!" he bellowed as the walls shook under the weight of his voice.

"But, Dad", Pam protested, "it's the night of the cast party."

"I don't care what night it is!" her father erupted. "You get your asses straight home after the play!"

"Yes, Daddy," Pam sheepishly answered, her eyes staring down at the floor.

"Oh, and before you leave, you better get all of this shit cleaned up!"

As the last door slammed in succession behind him, Pam shot one final glare at Susie. "It's all your fault— fucking, bitch!"

"Uh, my fault? Susie shot back, then turned around one last time before closing the door. "By the way, you better start cleaning this up. We've got to leave in less than an hour."

"Damn it!" Ron slammed his hand on the dashboard as a sea of red lights rushed up to greet him as he began his commute on the westbound 91 freeway. Ducking and weaving like a broken field runner charging through a formidable line in solid bright colored jerseys, he aimed his Camaro into a fast closing space up ahead. "Assholes!" he shouted, then leaned on his horn as the car beside him lurched forward and cut him off—a jolt of brakes sending ripples of hot black coffee out of his cup and on to his dark-blue monogramed Dickies button down. "Shit!" he exclaimed, shaking his free arm toward the driver's side window then wiping his hand on his pant leg. "I've never seen it this bad on a Friday." He let out a sigh, leaned back in his seat and turned on the radio. He tapped along with the music, then started thinking again about the two girls. Was he being too hard on them? Pam was his baby, the one who would greet him each day when he came home from work, cherubic face aglow with delight at the sight of her daddy. She was the youngest, the "miracle baby" as her mother had put it, the one she'd had after her doctor had told her that she couldn't get pregnant again. Yet, on September 14, 1970, there she was— dimpled cheeks, soft brown curls caressing a glowing Gerber baby face. Then there was Susie—the tom boy— his ex-wife's niece whose mother had left her for life on the streets, the petulant rogue whom he raised as his own. "Those two never did get along." He mused. Pam—always the girly-girl, Barbies and dresses. With Susie, it was cars and sports. Now in high school, boys had become their primary focus—especially for Pam whom he worried was growing up way too fast. *I'll talk to them when I get home tonight*, he thought, knowing they would probably have their sentence commuted by Saturday morning.

Both Pam and Susie got off the bus in the high school parking lot. "Later, bitch." Susie snarled as she rushed past Pam, brushing against her as she hurried away.

"Hey, Pam!"

"Erika!" How's my BFF?

"Chillin'. Ready for the play tonight?"

"Sure. All except for this thing on my face."

"Shit, Pam, no one's even going to notice!"

"You sound just like Susie."

"Perish the thought!"

Both girls stood and laughed for a while, then Erika suggested some make up.

"I tried that already." Pam stopped her mid-sentence. "No dice."

"Then use some of this." Erika smiled as she pulled a small tube from out of her purse.

"What is it?" Pam shrugged.

"The stuff I use. It's for those days when even *I* need a little help looking perfect."

"Thanks!"

"What are BFFs for?" Erika smiled, tossing her long blonde hair over her shoulder. "And Pam, you *do* know that stuff about Marty and I," she paused, tilted her head, let out a breath, then took a moment to regather herself, "it's all bullshit, I swear!"

"Promise?"

"Would I lie to my BFF?"

"Okay, pinky swear."

"Fuck that!" Erika snickered, brushing her off with a wave of her hand. "We're how old now? Come on let's get to class."

Ron didn't like what he saw on one of the lathes. "Look, Charlie, you've got to wipe off the chuck every time that you put a new part on, or this happens." He held up a thin metal disk and pointed at a series of nearly invisible scratches like broken vessels on a smooth, metal, circular orb.

"Got it, boss." Charlie apologized then gave the chuck an extra wipe while Ron was still watching.

"We don't take short cuts around here. If these parts are no good, I'm shuttin' it down."

"Hey, Ron." Oscar pulled up a chair in the breakroom as Ron began to peel on orange. "Rough morning so far?"

"Yeah."

"Charlie again?"

"Nah, Charlie's a good guy, just doesn't always do things the way that I taught him." Ron paused, took a sip from what was left of his coffee, and leaned over to Oscar. "Actually, it's the girls."

"I hear ya. I raised three of my own."

"Yeah, but your girls didn't fight all the time. Neither did my two oldest, Marie and Veronica, and my son Ronnie never gave me any trouble, but Pam and Susie," Ron stopped to finish his coffee, "I need to sometimes separate those two."

"They got along fine when I was there."

"They put on an act. This morning they were going at it in the bathroom—shaving cream all over the place."

"TMI, Ron! TMI!"

"Hey, fuck you, Eddie! Get back to work!" Ron waved off his eavesdropping coworker and turned back toward Oscar. "I put them both on restriction this morning."

"Yeah, but if I know you, you'll let them off by tomorrow. At least Pam will talk you out of it."

"You're probably right. Especially if I get lucky tonight."

"Going out dancing again."

"Yup, right after work I'm going to get ready to go to the Foxfire."

"Ladies beware!"

"For sure!"

Ron glanced at his watch and got up from his chair. "Well, back to the lathes."

The day moved slowly as Pam kept staring up at the clock. Ten minutes till lunchtime, then it was Mr. Moore and Theater Arts and getting ready for the night of the play. When the bell finally rang, Pam got up from her seat like it was a fire drill. As she walked out of the Science building, she could see Erika waiting for her outside the cafeteria.

"Hello, Tatania," she greeted Pam with a truncated curtsy.

"Good to see *you*, Hermia."

"*Hernia*?" Trey chuckled out loud as he walked up beside the two girls.

"Piss off, Trey!" Erika replied in a mock Brummel brogue.

"See you drama queens at the cast party tonight?"

"If you're lucky." Erika snorted. "Later, Trey."

The two girls walked up to the counter, grabbed a snack and a bottle of Martinelli's, and went to sit down.

"Hey, wasn't *Midsummer* set in Athens?" a tall boy with shaggy blonde hair walked up to remind her as he sat down at the next table over.

"Uh, it's Shakespeare, Mike." Erika countered somewhat bewildered.

"Well, maybe they speak with English accents in Greece—just saying."

"Hey, Pam, hey, Erika."

"Hey, Paul." Pam waved over to where Paul was sitting down next to Mike.

Erika waived, then turned back toward Pam. "Great, we get to sit right next to the 'God Squad.'"

"So, what are you ladies doing tonight?" Paul inquired.

"We're both getting drunk—*piss drunk*! Then we're going to get laid and afterward maybe smoke some weed." Erika mocked as she lifted a fake joint up to her mouth and took a long drag from her finger and thumb.

"I've got to go home right after the play." Pam lamented.

"Grounded?"

"Yeah."

"For what?"

"Being a bitch!" Erika broke in.

"Well in that case, Erika, *you* would be grounded for life!" Pam shot back.

"Syke!" Paul gave Pam a quick high five, finished his drink, and got up from the table.

"Seriously, Pam, you should really consider giving up your life of sin and commit yourself to following God."

"Oh no, here comes the sermon!" Erika said as she got up from her chair. "Well, it's been nice, but I've gotta run. Hey, Tatania, I'll see you in class." Pam watched as Erika picked up her drink and walked to the door humming the tune of *Amazing Grace*.

"Look, Paul, unlike *most* people, I at least try to be a good person." Pam responded.

"Well, at least *some* of the time." Mike corrected.

"Besides," Pam continued, brushing him off, "how do you even *know* there's a God? Maybe heaven and hell are just what you make of it right here on earth?"

"And how do *you* know that there isn't?" Paul questioned.

"Well," Pam retorted, getting up from her chair, "if there is a God, let Him *prove* it to me!"

Erika entered the theater from the back door and walked into the green room where Marty was rehearsing his lines. "Well if it isn't my Lysander!"

"No, it's Puck." He corrected.

"Lysander." She said again and again as she pushed her body against him, and their lips locked together. "Lysander... Lysander..."

Several minutes passed and all was silent. Teenage lovers caught up in the moment. Class was still ten minutes away—a lover's eternity shaded by curtains. Kisses and moans, a hand on her waist sliding down lower, a creak of the door, then a thin beam of light growing brighter and brighter, intertwined bodies, now fully enveloped, glared in the spotlight. Turning her head, she could see a shadow, eyes glowing bright like the sun.

"Marty, Marty," it began to call out as the shadow moved closer then stopped for a moment to size up its prey.

"Pam? My God! Pam, what are you doing here?" Erika stared back in shocked disbelief.

"Same thing as you. Rehearsing my lines." Pam walked slowly in their direction, then, taking a breath, her cold, icy stare locked onto its target. "She was a vixen when she went to school—and though she be but little, she is fierce." Then turning her eyes in the direction of Marty—the boy who she had dated all year, the one who her mother had arranged for her to marry someday. She plucked the wings of her unfaithful imp. "O me, you juggler, you canker-blossom, you thief of love!"

"Pam, honey, I can explain." Marty now trembled like a sinner standing before heaven's gate.

"No need to explain, Marty. Erika, you always were a little tramp. I should have expected this much from you. But, Marty, *you* are so full of shit."

"Wait, Pam, can we just talk?"

"Talk? No, Marty, I never want to *see* you again. As a matter of fact, I wish you were dead!"

GOOD GIRLS

Ron slid his card into the clock, waited for the click, then walked out the door. "See all you turkeys on Monday!"

"Have a nice weekend, Ron." Oscar waved as he got into his car.

Ron turned left on to Artesia, waiting for each light to change before it became the 91. In less than an hour, he would be home, take a shower, and be off to the Foxfire where friends, booze, and scantily clad women awaited.

He stood alone in the halo's haze, curtains poised, ready to shower down in front of him, a crowd of parents, teachers, and friends set to erupt in cascading rounds of ovation. With all of the lights dramatically dimmed, a faint blue glimmer surrounding his body, Puck stood there alone, wings spread before him, a crown of horns adorning his head. "Take my hands if we be friends, and Robin shall restore amends." The lights disappeared as the auditorium fell into darkness. Then the crowd rose to their feet, clapping and shouting as the curtain descended. As waves of applause began to subside, the lights reappeared above the stage as the actors arrived in pairs taking their bow—Helena, Demetrius, Lysander, Oberon, Tatania, Hermia, and finally, Puck. As Pam and Erika stood at the back of the stage ready to join hands and walk out under the lights, Pam squeezed Erika's fingers together, one last reminder of her betrayal until she let out a long, stifled moan. They stood in the light—a sea of hands and smiling faces, Mr. Moore beaming from the left of the stage. They turned to each other for one final glance as the blue light between them turned hot to red. As Puck stepped forward for one final bow, Pam looked on from behind the curtain and sarcastically murmured, "Else the Puck a liar call, so, a good night unto you all."

As the throngs pushed forward out of each door, the cast members arrived to greet them in front of the theater. "Pammy, you were amazing!" her cousin gushed, taking a hand in both of hers. "And your friend over there, she looked so beautiful!"

"Yeah, she was all right." Pam shrugged.

"I see." her cousin replied, her brows arched in surprise at her expression of shade.

"Anyway, you'll need to come see our new place sometime, cuz." Pam spoke up and quickly changed the conversation. "It's not Yorba Linda, but it's pretty cool. I even have my own room."

"Yeah, I'll need to get out there sometime. Give everyone my love."

"Love you, cuz!"

"Love you too, Pammy!"

"You did pretty good there, girl." Trey said as he stole up behind her.

"Thanks, bro!"

"By the way, you going to the cast party over at Randy's?"

"No, I'm grounded. Going straight home."

"Is your dad waiting up?"

"No, he's out for the night."

"Well, it's only 8:30, and besides, I need to give you your tape and it's over at Randy's."

"What do I do about Susie then?"

"Bring her with."

"Trey, I don't know."

"Come on, Pam. We'll have you back before your dad even knows you were gone."

"All right then, but first let me go and get Sue."

A long plume of fragrant steam followed Ron out of the bathroom as he wiped the lather off of his face and stepped into the neatly pressed clothes laid out on his bed. He combed his hair, brushed his teeth, put on his jacket, then reached for the bottle of cologne on his dresser. One dab on each side of his neck, then a splash in each hand as he clapped them together and rubbed them up and down on his body. A final glance in the mirror, then a puckering smack that rang in the room as he shut the door. "If you want my body, and you think I'm sexy, come on sugar let me know," he sang to himself in a melody of off-key assurance. "If you really need me, just reach out and touch me..." he paused for a second adjusting his pants at the crotch, "come on sugar tell me so." He locked the front door behind him, indiscreetly humming the chorus, then made his way out to the car.

***

As Pam walked inside the living room, Marty and Erika were already sitting down on the couch, his hand sliding up and down on her back.

"Hey, Pam." Marty looked over and said, then picked up a glass from the table and took a long drink.

"Hey." Pam mumbled, then turned away into the kitchen where Susie was standing.

"You girls want anything to drink?" Randy inquired as he walked inside from the garage.

"How 'bout a couple of wine coolers?" Pam replied, then handed one over to Susie when Randy got them from out of the fridge.

"Thanks, Pam." Susie replied extending her hand. "And by the way, you did really good tonight."

"Yeah I thought so." Pam nodded.

"Look, Pam, I'm sorry about all of the shit that went down this morning. Just so you know."

"Me too." Pam conceded. "Here's to not fighting." Then she raised her bottle and clinked it against the one that Susie was holding.

"Here's to not fighting." Susie paused for a moment. "Unless of course you piss me off!"

"Ah, ladies, getting all mushy like schoolgirls." Trey walked up and handed Pam the tape that he'd borrowed. "Anyway, I'm glad that you both decided to come."

"Hey, Pam why don't you and Susie come outside for a smoke." Randy emerged with his arm around Cindy who leaned against him giggling to some inaudible lark.

"Sure," said Susie as she took Pam by the hand and led her through the sliding screen door.

"So, you're Pam's sister?" Randy asked Susie as he handed her the joint in his hand and exhaled deeply into the air.

"We're cousins." Pam broke in. "We just live together."

"Then how come I never see you together at school?"

"No real surprise there, Randy," said Susie taking another long hit, then holding it deep into her lungs. "We also manage to avoid one another at home."

As the evening wore on, the crowd started thinning out, young actors exchanging one final embrace, car doors slamming, engines racing off into the dark. Pam went inside to use the bathroom then returned to where Susie, Randy, and Cindy were standing.

"Hey, Sue." We'd better get going." She said looking down at her watch.

"Shit, it's already ten?" Susie looked back to Randy. "Pam's right. Technically, we're both on restriction."

"I was going to ask you to crash over here since my parents won't be home from Vegas till Sunday. Marty and Erika aren't going home until tomorrow."

"Yeah, I bet," said Pam. "I hope you don't let them fuck on your couch. Your family might catch something."

"Pam!" Susie's eyes bore against her. "Please don't start anything tonight."

"I didn't start it!" Pam retorted. "You don't get it. Erika is a skank, not to mention a backstabbing bitch!"

"I get it, Pam." Susie agreed. "I could have told you that all along. But as they say, every dog has their day, sure as every turkey has its Thanksgiving!" Then they all high fived and started to laugh.

Just then, Pam and Susie turned to see a tall slim shadow emerging from a dim yellow haze moving slowly toward them. As she got closer, Pam could make out the long blonde tresses of hair sweeping over each shoulder.

"Erika?"

Ron walked through the lobby and reached out his hand for the security guard to stamp. Pulsating waves throbbed from each of the speakers and shook the walls as he made his way into the club and took a seat at the bar.

"Hey, Ron." The bartender nodded over to where he was sitting.

"Hey, Mooch."

"What are you having?"

"The usual, Scotch and soda. Single malt. The good stuff."

"Hey, Ron, you're looking sharp tonight."

"Hey, Tony. Good to see you! Your old lady know that you're here?"

"Ah, she doesn't give a shit where I go. Besides, she's up in Fresno with her mom."

"I get it, so while the cat's away..."

"Exactly!"

"Well, if it isn't the man in black." A short, balding, middle-aged man walked over and stood directly in front of Ron and his friend. "And what's with the 'stache? Just get back from robbing a train?"

"Fuck you, Phil!" Ron shot a punch into his arm, took one last, long swallow out of his glass, then set a hand on each of their shoulders. "What do you say we go rob some cradles?"

"Pam." Erika spoke in a hushed, careful tone. "Trey sent me over to ask if you needed a ride. He's had a few too many."

"I'd rather walk!" Pam shot back.

"Come on, Pam, Marty pleaded as he slowly walked up to where Erika was standing. "Erika told me that you and Susie were grounded. We'll get you back before your father gets home."

"How did *she* know that we're grounded?" Pam shrugged, "and that my dad would be getting home late?"

"Randy told us." Erika interrupted.

"And I think Trey let him know that your dad was going out for the night." Marty added.

"Fuck, those idiots!" Susie broke in. "I barely know them and they're spilling my guts. I'm going to tell Randy off at school on Monday."

"No need to wait until Monday. He and Cindy are coming with us." Marty informed them.

"Come on, Pam?" Erika gave one last final plea. "I'll sit in back. We don't even need to talk to each other. We'll drop you off then come right back here." Erika looked over at Pam with puppy dog eyes, before cheerfully glancing back over at Marty.

"Okay then." Pam finally agreed. "You ready, Sue?"

***

Ron set his eyes on a woman with long dark hair as the band returned back onto the stage. "Watch this, guys." He said has he slid off his chair and walked over to where she was sitting. Soon they were both out on the dance floor together.

"Looks like Ron isn't going home alone." The two men looked at each other with jealous approval.

"Seldom ever does," Mooch said as he picked up their glasses.

Four girls and two boys squeezed into the small white rear-engine sports car as Marty turned the keys and took down the roof as a warm breath of spring blew through his hair. "Gotta take Cindy home first." Marty assured Susie and Pam. "Then I'll drop the two of you off."

"Here it is, house on the right." Randy told Marty as two lanes narrowed between rows of white fences.

"Drop me right here." Said Cindy as they got to the driveway. "I'll go in through the back."

"Good night, honey." Said Randy as he pulled her closer, pressing her wine-cooler stained lips against his.

"See you on Monday." She said, getting out of the car then staggering up the long winding driveway, she walked around to the back of the house. Marty waited for the upstairs light to go on, then drove forward into the night.

***

Ron took off his jacket and set it on the back of his chair. "You guys watch this for me while I get my lady another drink. Oh, by the way, this is my new friend, Lena." He introduced Tony and Phil as she held out her hand. "It's *Reina*," she corrected.

"Sorry." Ron said, pushing a glass in her direction. "I had a sister-in-law named Lena—really pretty just like you."

Her expression softened as she took her next installment of the *quid pro quo* and sat down next to Ron at the bar.

Marty turned right onto Imperial then crossed back over the freeway.

"I sure could go for some gummy bears." Erika spoke up from the back.

"There's a Seven-Eleven up ahead." Said Marty. "I'll stop over there." A few minutes later Marty returned, both hands empty.

"They didn't have any."

"There's an AM/PM on Placentia and Chapman." Why don't you try over there?"

"Shit, Erika. We've got to get Pam and Susie home."

"It's right on the way, dear. Will you do it for *me*?"

Marty parked the car then walked back the same way he came, cursing under his breath. "They looked at me as if I was from outer space!" he bemoaned. "Look, Erika, that's two places already. I'm going to Pam's."

"Marty." Pam spoke up. "I know a store over on Valencia, north of Imperial. I've bought them there before. Can we at least check to see if it's open?"

"All right, but that's the last place I'm going." Marty put the car in gear, made a hard left and sped out of the lot. Soon the lights disappeared on either side of the road as streets checked off their names all around. "Goodness, Pam, how far is this place"?

A few more miles then her eyes lit up. "Right there." Pam pointed over to him as he jerked his car to the left, pulled in the lot, got out of the car, then disappeared through the door. Outside, the winds began to pick up as sepia toned road signs, painted in white mission fonts, danced together like a legion of pixies on Walpurgisnacht.

"Sure is dark out here tonight." Randy observed. "Were the hell are we?"

Pam looked out the window and stared outside as an old faded landmark swayed in the breeze, its letters rang out with a cautionary Dantean threat—*Carbon Canyon Road*—that drew them in like moths to a flame.

The music resounded out on the floor as the lights swirled all around up above. Ron took his lady and gave her a spin then guided her back into his arms. They stopped for a second as the music faded when Ron leaned into her and asked, "So, what are your plans for the night?" Before she could answer, he saw two women quickly approaching, unsmiling faces bending in anger, eyes like shards of burning coal set directly upon him.

"Veronica. Ginny. What are you doing here? Excuse me a second." Ron turned aside leaving Reina standing alone, taken aback, then walked up to his ex-wife and middle daughter. "I'm a single man now, or did you forget?"

Veronica cut him off. "There's been a bad accident. Susie called from Placentia Linda."

"Come find me later." Reina said as she turned around and walked off of the dance floor.

"I'll be right there." Ron motioned over, then stared straight ahead.

Veronica took a deep breath then gathered herself. "She said she doesn't know what happened to Pam, but she thinks..." she now began to choke back sobs, "she thinks that she's dead!"

"That's impossible!" Ron stood up straight. "Both girls are at home! I grounded them this morning! I know they would never disobey my wishes! Both Pam and Susie are good girls!"

"You grounded them then came over here to pick up on some little tramp like the one you were with!" Virginia shouted at him, her hands now clenched together with rage, veins protruding out from her neck.

Ron stood alone, lost in the crowd. His eyes froze in terror, his voice choked inside him as his heart began to beat like a drum inside of his chest. He walked outside without saying a word, bowed his head, and got into a double-parked car waiting to drive them all to the hospital.

NOT MY BABY!

P am's dead! Pam's dead! Oh my God, Pam's dead!" cried Susie, as Ron, Virginia, and her boyfriend David entered the ICU, Veronica walking in behind them. Her arms were hooked to a series of tubes that hung from bottles over her bed.

"She's still in shock." The head nurse told them as she put a hand on Virginia's shoulder. "Is this your daughter?"

"She's my niece." Virginia said in a slow somber voice. "What happened?"

"There was a bad accident on Carbon Canyon."

"My God, I told them to stay away from that road!" Ron spoke up. "People get killed out there all the time!"

Virginia glared back at Ron then turned again toward the nurse. "Who else was in the car?"

The nurse swallowed hard then led the four of them out into the hallway. "Your niece is going to be all right. She's sustained several broken bones and a lacerated cornea, but she's going to recover." She stopped for a second, looked at the ground then steadied herself. "The driver was pronounced dead at the scene. Both drivers actually. Four others were badly injured."

"Who was driving?" David inquired.

"The boy driving the car that the girls were in," she stopped for a moment to clear her throat, "the boy driving the car was a Mr. Martin Haag."

"Marty! Oh God, not Marty!" Virginia broke out in uncontrollable sobs, her knees buckling, sending her crashing down onto the floor.

"And Pam? Is there any word on what happened to Pam?" Ron frantically questioned.

"There were two others taken to Canyon. And a young lady airlifted to Western." The nurse looked at them for a moment, let out a breath and continued. "How old is Pam?"

"She's fourteen." Answered Ron as Virginia, now sitting down in a chair, chest heaving, wiping her eyes with a tissue, stuttered under a hail of sniffles. "Long, dark hair, very pretty."

"The girl at Canyon is blonde and the one at Western I'm told was in her early twenties."

David squeezed Virginia's hand. "We've got to get to Western, honey!"

"I can arrange a patrol car to take you." The nurse informed them. "Wait right here."

"Dave, can I have you send Veronica back to the house in case Pam is still there?"

"Damn it, Ron!" Virginia said as she broke out in a new round of anguish. "Didn't you listen? Both girls went out together! So much for your damned restriction!"

"Calm down, Ginny." We need to stay calm and cover all bases," Ron assured, grasping at one last hopeless chimera. "Pam and Susie have never gone anywhere together before. Besides, Susie's still in a state of shock. She could be thinking of somebody else."

"And what if she's not? What if our daughter is dead because of *you*? You, selfish bastard!"

"Here you go, Veronica." David reached in his pocket and turned over his keys. "We'll be at Western. Please let us know."

Sirens wailed into the night. A shower of red and blue lights spiraled all around at each side of the car. Virginia held David's hand like a lifeline that kept her from falling into a yawning abyss. Ron sat silently and prayed for a miracle to a God he no longer even believed in.

Branches of eucalyptus trees scattered across the complex like broken limbs strewn throughout a concrete battlefield. A phalanx of palms shading corrugated rooftops danced all around her dropping their seeds. She opened the door, turned on the light, hushed the dog, and climbed up the stairs. "Pam? Pam? Veronica shouted, each inquiry growing louder and more frantic as she moved toward the door. "Pam!" she finally burst in and threw on the light. "Oh God! Oh no!" she buried her head in her hands and wept out loud. A neatly made and empty bed, posters hanging all around on her wall, perfumes and make-up sat under a lighted vanity mirror, stuffed animals looking down from the shelves that answered her cries.

Sirens blared as the patrol car pulled into the lot. "Thanks, officer." Ron said as he got out of the car, the lingering smell of Jameson Scotch concealed by a stick of

Dentyne. Virginia and David got out from the back, still holding hands and walking slowly in through the door. "Pamela Vasquez." Ron told the security guard as he marched into the ICU.

"You family?"

"Yes, I'm her father and this is her mother," he said, looking back at Virginia, her shoulders still shaking beneath David's arm.

"Hold on a minute."

Ron paced back and forth, while Virginia began quietly sobbing.

"It's okay, it's okay," assured David calmly stroking her head.

After several minutes, the door burst open and the guard gave them all a "visitor" tag. "Right this way." He said as he led them in through the door.

A doctor met them as they walked between faded walls of green and gray, white smocks and a pungent alcohol vapor that breathed in and out through the vents, fluorescent lights flickered above like convulsions of a perpetual morning. He led them down to a room at the end of the hall then cautioned as he stood at the curtain. "This may be difficult," he warned. "Let me know when you're ready."

"Are you sure that it's Pam?" Ron hesitated. "The nurse at Canyon told us that the girl was in her early twenties. Pam's only fourteen."

"Mr. Vasquez." The doctor replied waving him forward. "Why don't you come in and see for yourself."

***

A skeletal blue tower of metal, the hum of machines, a row of red lines rising weakly in time then retreating back to a thin dark plane. Numbers blinking above each panel, a steady Morse-code melody of cascading loops and pulsating beeps like a graveyard of dying video games. A white sheet draped like a burial shroud covered the body. A highway of tubes dripping their poison into its veins. Ron reached over and lifted the edge to reveal a face that he knew belonged at least partly to him, head swollen and covered in gauze leaking blood from each sterile pore—oxygen keeping her body alive. As he leaned in close, he could still make out her beautiful face. Cheek bones set high under deep brown eyes dusted with the dew of heaven lighting the edges of an awakening smile. A dimpled chin, soft, full lips, and a single zit that set above them like a stamp of identity. His heart raced in terror as his body grew numb. He pulled the sheet back up to her chin, drew the curtain and staggered back to where Virginia was standing, then bowed his head and closed his eyes to assuage the flood pouring out from his chest. "Ginny," he whispered. "Ginny, it's her."

Virginia ran forward, threw open the curtain, looked inside and let out a scream that enveloped the room in sheaves of primordial terror. "That's not my baby! That's not my baby!" she wailed, then collapsed to the floor.

PART II:
BETWEEN TWO WORLDS

"I thought I was going to see God or reach an epiphany or to levitate or something. But I never did."
—Douglas Coupland

"I remembered a few things about waking. I remembered the sense of surprise as dream life and waking life swapped primacy, and the way in which the most tangible and deeply involving dreams could bleach entirely away."
—Alex Garland

"Imagine that on the day that you're grounded all your friends come over and play right outside your bedroom window. You can't quite make out what they're saying, but you can faintly hear them once in a while, calling your name."
—Pamela Vasquez-Kuznik

OUT OF HINNOM

An engine fire broke out against rows of crumpled seats and lit the night like a tiki torch, illuminating a corpse-strewn arena with fallen bodies of teenage gladiators. A chest fully impaled on a wheel, a tall blonde body strewn over a hood, a wandering phantom, bones protruding through dark leather sleeves, a figure in black laying face-down on the side of the road, and a severed head tipping back and forth between broken rows of bright yellow lines. Shrieks arose from the back of the sports car as a tower of flame arched against a slender physique still pinned inside and unable to move. Sirens screamed out into the canyon as emergency vehicles raced to the wreckage and encircled the scene on either side. A helicopter orbited above them, descending in a circle of light. The shrieks grew louder as sirens froze and fire-fighters uncoiled their hoses. Rotor blades beat like drums in the Valley of Hinnom drowning out each of the young boy's screams. Two men ran out from the back of the chopper, loaded the phantom onto a stretcher, covered her body in clean white linen, and pushed her back inside through the door.

"Dammit, Brian, we're losing altitude!" the copilot shouted, as the aircraft struggled its way up over the hills, swaying side to side in a warm gust of wind. "Never seen a downdraft this bad!"

"Downdraft? Hell! This ain't no downdraft!" the pilot answered. "It's like something is trying to keep us from leaving!"

"Pam! Pam! Stay here with us!" A circle of shadows surrounded the bloody white sheets that lay over the stretcher and entombed it's still beating heart kept alive by a highway of oxygen tubes. Her fading body started to quiver as if transfixed by their inaudible plea.

"Full collective, let's get her climbing!" the pilot instructed, pulling up firmly on the collective lever to his left as a curtain of darkness loomed in the window. "Max manifold pressure—redline it! Let's go! Let's go!"

"Come on honey, you're gonna make it," a paramedic whispered, taking a hand in both of his as her head began to slowly shake back and forth. A jolt of turbulence, a rush of warm air, a sudden downward thrust, the canyon had now become the horizon, a destination, and likely tomb.

"Shit, Brian, we're going down!"

"Hold max rate of climb!" the pilot commanded again, his voice now rising into a panic. "Pitch forward, get the airspeed up! You hear me? *Hold it!*"

The chopper pitched, then turned hard left as the mountain again appeared through the window. With both hands engaged, the pilot watched as the speed finally increased, and the chopper fought the turbulence, beginning a long, slow ascent into the darkness. As the craft began to gradually steady, he let out a breath and raised his eyes briefly to heaven.

Breaking over the black canyon walls, an expanse of concrete opened beneath them, a welcoming sea of flickering lights. The 55 freeway rolled out like a red carpet between lighted rows of dark velvet sheaths.

"Damn, Brian, I almost thought we weren't gonna make it!" The copilot glanced over, his hands still shaking.

"I know, Travis." The pilot agreed, revealing a small silver cross he wore under his shirt. "I was praying the whole time. Praying, and also pissing my pants!" He took a breath and called in their flight. "Western helipad, Bell helicopter eight-five-hotel-charlie, ten miles east, requesting emergency touch down."

A voice hissed in his headphones, bringing a sense of familiar calm with it, "Bell 85-hotel-charlie, maintain heading, fly altitude 3000, call with visual, Western."

"85 hotel Charlie, maintaining heading, 3000, will call with visual." After a few minutes of calm flying, Brian breathed a sigh of relief, "Western helipad, Bell-85-hotel-charlie has helipad in sight."

"Bell 85-hotel-charlie, clear to land." The voice crackled in over the speaker.

The chopper set down at 1CN1 as a team of paramedics rushed to the stretcher like a squad of medics on Omaha Beach. A bloodstained sheet flapped in the breeze as the lifeless body that lay underneath disappeared beneath the crimson lights that spelled out the words EMERGENCY ROOM.

"Hey, Brian." The copilot looked over before setting the rotors in motion for takeoff. "The little girl back there, do you think that she'll make it?"

The pilot thought for a moment then finally answered. "That's in God's hands, Travis. But you know," he continued, "it sure seems like there's something inside her that *wants* her to live."

MAGIC KINGDOM

I don't know how I got here—lush green fields like hanging gardens above a rocky abyss, voices of children singing and laughing, a large stone fortress off in the distance, a clock staring down from the loftiest peak of its towering gables, an analogue face punctuated in dark Roman digits but without any hands marking the time. I didn't feel any pain. Weightlessness maybe, but not any pain. I have to admit there was a moment of terror when serpentine hands took hold of my ankles and refused to let go. But then there was this still, small voice. Was it that of an angel? I don't know. I'd heard that everyone has a guardian angel, but I never believed it. I wasn't raised in a church-going family. Anyway, this voice spoke to me and promised that I would be all right. Then another one mentioned God and Jesus until the hands finally let go, their shadows falling out through a glass and metal door. Next thing you know, I ended up here. But where is *here*? And who are *you*?

I had forded the banks of a river—shallow and green, its waters stirred by a set of oars. A tall gaunt figure with rough unkempt hair and piercing gray eyes led me aboard a shallow rust-colored skiff. There were two oarsmen on either side who referred to him by the title of "Captain." Leaving the marsh, we sailed downstream as the river forked into three different branches. We took the one on the right or the "path of cleansing" as the captain announced, then instructed his servants to row much faster to escape the current that carried a fleet of much larger vessels down streams to the left. Soon we were surrounded by lush green hills like the ones I would see from my backyard each winter as it turned into spring. We docked along the outer banks, as the captain lifted me out of the boat and walked me to a small waiting cottage. As we grew closer, the air turned cool with the encroaching night fog of jasmine and white evening primrose as windows glowed through a whisper of oaks.

"You'll be staying here for a while." The captain informed me bringing a hand up to my shoulder, his eyes peering directly into my soul. "See to it that you get some rest." I was too tired to ask any questions. I collapsed onto a large brass bed that folded out under a tall wood beam ceiling, pulled up the covers, and drifted off safely to sleep.

I may have been dreaming, but a calendar page appeared on the wall. Looking closer I could make out the word "April" and a year "1970." A still life photo of orange groves spread out underneath that led up into the side of a hill. Directly beneath it was a circle of red around the number "1." I thought for a moment then remembered that my father had told me this was the day when my mother had learned she could no longer get pregnant. Since they already had two little girls and a young boy— his junior, his "Ronnie"—it was welcome news. They went out that evening, had a few drinks, came home, and threw away all of their condoms. Five and a half months later, a daughter—the youngest of three, their baby, was born.

On the evening of September 14, my father had driven home from work, showered, and sat down to dinner. Minutes later, he was speeding down the 91 freeway as a Harvest Moon lifted its bald orange head above the Anaheim Hills. At 11:55 PM, his third daughter was born—my "miracle baby" as my mother had called me. The problem was, I still needed a miracle to even survive. I spent the next four months in an incubator as my small frail body learned how to breathe on its own. In mid-January of the following year, my parents were finally able to carry me home.

"Pamela, we'll call her Pamela." My father announced. "A beautiful name for a beautiful girl!"

The first memories I had of our Anaheim home were the loud explosions each night around nine when all of my siblings rushed outside as the sky erupted in a shower of light. The "booms" I would call them.

"Mommy, were do they come from?"

"The Magic Kingdom," she'd tell me. "The place where all of your dreams come true."

"I want to go there!" I'd tell her as I traced each color as its ember rained back down to the earth.

Years later, my Uncle Bill got a job in one of the restaurants and would sign us all into the park every weekend, then a few years later, the magic had stopped. Daddy would be gone all day and Mommy would leave for work before he got home. When they were together, they were always fighting, something about her "drinking too much," although I never did understand what that meant.

Mommy working out at the drive-in meant that we could all go see a movie whenever we wanted. My father put the kids in the back, then hid the concessions under our blankets. "There's no way I'm paying a dollar for popcorn!" he'd snarl. "Cheaper just to make it at home." I usually fell asleep in the back and my father would carry me into my bedroom and put me to sleep. "Next time we go, can we just leave the baby at home?" my brother would protest. "All she ever does is talk all the time!" "That's enough, Ronnie!" my mother would say and threaten to backhand him if he didn't be quiet.

Sometimes, when my daddy got home, he'd eat his dinner then take me shopping when my brother and sisters were gone with their friends. Sometimes they got pretty angry with me. Years later, I learned that if anyone even talked to my dad when he was watching TV after work they got smacked and sent to their room. But I was his baby. I sat in his lap as he pulled up his tray, turned on the TV and sat down to eat.

"Who's that? What's he doing? Why did he just shoot that man?"

"Because he is the bad guy, princess." My father would say. "And that's what happens to bad guys."

Sometimes Daddy was gone "doing some work on the side" so I hardly ever got to see him. When Mommy got home, I was already in bed, and on days when I was allowed to wait up, she would come home smelling like what I was told was tequila. Those were the days she got pretty mean. One night, I got up and I watched her slap my sister Veronica right in the face. My oldest sister Marie went into the kitchen, peeled me an orange and sent me back into my room. "Nothing to see here, Pammy, get back to bed." But I didn't believe her.

Before long, I didn't know what to believe. One thing I knew, was that I was the favorite. I never got in trouble for anything, and if I did, my brother and sisters would get it instead. It wasn't long before I believed that there was nothing that could ever hurt me.

The movies stopped when my mom got a job at the grocery store. Sometimes there were nights where she'd never come home so it was up to my sisters to raise me.

One day, my sister Marie came home crying. "I don't want to go to another school! All of my friends are right here in Anaheim! I'm not going to move!"

"But you'll make new friends." My father told her. "Besides, you'll get to have your own bedroom all to yourself." She had cried while my daddy put all of her things in boxes then piled them up into the garage. That summer, he got us registered in our new schools. Marie and Veronica would be going to Troy—Marie as a sophomore, Veronica as a freshman. Ronnie and I went to Mabel Paine. Ronnie in fifth grade, while I was in Kindergarten. My mommy seemed really excited. All of her bosses lived up in the "hills" and she would soon be joining their clique.

It was a hot summer day when the moving vans came. We got in the car with both of our dogs and pulled out of the driveway. After a left, then another when we got to the light, we drove down La Palma then got onto the freeway. The summer breeze blew in through the half-opened windows as we exited on Imperial Highway.

Within minutes, we were up in the hills and on our way to our new home in a place they called Yorba Linda.

GRACIOUS LIVING

The hills tumbled like golden waves on a distant shore as orange groves released their fragrance into the air. Modern, sprawling, ranch style homes sprung from tree-lined streets on carpets of green surrounded by white picket fences—a lifetime removed from the bruised, stucco, graffiti-stained bungalows where my father grew up. Twenty years after his own father died, leaving him to raise his siblings in a converted garage, he had signed his name on the deed of trust that gained him admission inside the velvet ropes of success.

"Three-seventy-five a month! Holy shit, Ginny, how are we going to do this?"

"We'll find a way, Ron." She held out her arms and let out a sigh. "Just look at this place! Don't worry, honey, we'll make it work."

There were no vacations that summer. No trips to Disneyland for that matter. Movie nights were gone as well. But my father found ways of keeping us busy. He put a small "dough-boy" pool in the back yard, then took a large piece of plastic from inside the garage, laid it out on the grass, sprayed it down with a hose, then invited us all to come on outside and play on the "slip and slide." My sisters and I slid right across as the cool stream of water carried our bodies down the make-believe runway out into the grass. "This is fun!" I giggled then took another plunge on the mat.

"Hey, Ronnie, it's your turn!" My father waved over as my brother stood in the doorway.

"I don't know, Dad." He hesitated before kicking off both of his sandals and walking out on to the grass.

"Come on, bro, it's fun." I insisted. "If your baby sister can do it..."

"Yeah, come on, Ron." Marie taunted flapping her arms like a pair of wings. "That is unless you're a chicken—cluck, cluck, cluck..."

Clenching both of his fists at each side of his waist, Ron glared out onto the grass, then summoned one last rush of courage and charged out across the lawn like an unguided missile. As his feet hit the plastic, both of his legs slipped out from beneath him, his body briefly suspended between water and sky before it fell like a stone back down to the ground. His face now awash in both water and tears, he got up and glared at my dad. "You're always doing things to hurt me!" he cried, then ran through the door and into his room, put on his records and banged on the drums. Two years later he got a guitar and started a band—go figure.

That summer I also began making friends with all our new neighbors.

"Hi, I'm Pam!" I said pointing at my father who was mowing the lawn. "I live over there with my mom and my dad, and my sisters Marie and Veronica, and my brother Ron. Do you have any kids I can play with?" Sometimes they'd invite me over for dinner and my mom would have to go looking for me. Sometimes I would walk down the street to the Nixon Library, other times I was at my friend Kelly's. Her father had made her a little doll house in the backyard where we'd spend the afternoon watching TV and playing with all of her toys. Her father was gone most of the time and when he got home, he'd buy her anything that she wanted—bicycles, Barbie's, records, clothes, you name it. We sometimes talked about getting married one day and the kind of man that we'd choose for a husband. It was no surprise that she told me that the man she would marry would be "somebody just like my daddy."

Her dad also had a movie collection that he kept in a small shack in the backyard. One day, his wife found all of his movies and her father moved out a short time later. After a while, her mother left too, and I never got to see Kelly again. Then there was this old man who lived all alone on the corner. We were sure he didn't like kids. When one of our balls rolled on to his lawn, he'd open the door and shoo us away. One day, he picked up Marie's soccer ball and my mom had to go over and get it. I used to think he was just being mean, until I learned from my mom that his wife had recently died and that they didn't have any children.

"The old bastard probably killed his wife," Marie asserted, "and buried her body somewhere in his yard."

"Yeah, I bet he even eats children for dinner!" Ron spoke up. "Pammy, maybe *you* should pay him a visit."

"That's enough, Ron!" My mom stared him down from across the table. "He probably just wants to be left alone."

One time, his trees had been covered with toilet paper. I had watched as he picked at each strand with a rake, cursing under his breath. I wanted to ask if he needed some help, but I was too little, so instead I had a better idea.

"What a beautiful thought!" My mom hugged me when I told her about it. "I'll have everything ready for you tomorrow. And Marie, I better not find any of *our* toilet paper missing!"

The following day, I walked across the street with a large plate of food and a slice of pie in a small cardboard box and knocked on his door.

"Who's there?" He growled.

"It's Pam, your neighbor."

"Well, I'm not buying anything today."

"That's fine sir, I'm not selling anything."

"Then why are you here?"

"I brought you dinner."

He walked over and unlocked the door. "You brought me *what*?"

"I brought you dinner. Here, there's soup, salad, steak, and a baked potato. I even brought you desert."

"Why would you want to do that for me?" He responded somewhat perplexed.

"Because I care."

Then he opened the door and stepped out on the porch. "Well, I guess you're the only one around here."

"Then maybe I can start a new trend."

He put a long bony arm around one of my shoulders then took the plates from my small outstretched hands. "You really are a sweet little girl. What did you say your name was again?"

"Pam. My name's Pam."

"Pam, I'm Fred. You tell your mom that I said, 'thank you.'"

I took him dinner every day for the rest of the summer until I started school that year. After school I would visit my friends, so I only got to see Fred every once in a while. Sometime later, an ambulance pulled up in his driveway and I never got to see him again. He used to tell me stories about him and his wife—how they'd moved down from Reedley to Yorba Linda when it was a small agricultural town and worked for the North Orange County Fire Department until he retired. He and his wife lived in his house ever since the tract had been built. He never had kids because he "couldn't" then he got too old and just wanted some "peace and quiet." He would have been married fifty years next Valentine's Day if his wife hadn't died. They intended to celebrate in Hawaii. Maybe that was where the ambulance took him.

Toward the end of August, my mother and father were planning a huge Labor Day party. Our family, our neighbors, and all of my mom's friends from work were invited. My dad invited his friends Oscar and Tony and his brother Bill as the DJ. Most of my mom's family didn't want to come—something about "Ginny showing off her new house in the hills with the money she got from our father," or something like that—I didn't understand at the time. Anyway, it was a blast. My friends and I mostly hung out in the pool while my brother and his friends stayed in his room and listened to records. Marie and Veronica helped my mom with the food and the drinks while my father proudly stood at the door welcoming everyone into "his" new home.

I didn't recognize most people there. My mom introduced them as "friends" from work, but aside from her boss and a few other managers, they were mostly part of some acting troupe that she'd recently joined. They were all pretty drunk—drinking and dancing, twirling each other around in the living room. I took off my swimsuit, got into a dress and decided to join them.

"Who's this little angel?" a middle-aged man with a beard inquired, putting a tobacco-stained hand on my arm.

"That's Pammy, my baby." My mother told him, walking over to take my hand. "Pammy, shouldn't you be outside with your friends?"

"Let her stay, Ginny." He pleaded. "She's a beautiful girl. Have you ever thought about doing commercials?"

"Maybe someday when she's older," my mother broke in.

"Well here's my card when you decide that she's ready," the man answered then walked outside to grab a drink. I really didn't know who he was, but the whole thing sort of gave me the creeps. I was glad that the Lopez's had decided to come. It turned out that Nick was the chief of police. My father had decided he'd better "get in good with those guys if we want to have parties." His son Jim was friends with my brother and his wife Karen invited us over to swim in their in-ground pool. When Karen's brother Roger moved in, Marie even started going over to visit. I was starting to think that she had a crush. Roger was already in his twenties. He was tall and tan with long blonde hair and a beard that made him look like one of the Beach Boys. He would come over and do all their yard work since Nick was too busy being a cop. Pretty soon, my sister and him were always together, hanging out, talking, and working on cars.

"I wouldn't be surprised if those two get married one day," I told my mom.

"Slow down, Pammy," my mother commanded. "She just completed her first year of high school."

The following week, the alarm clock ended that magical summer. My mom got up early and made us all breakfast before handing us our lunches in half hour shifts—my dad first, then Marie and Veronica, and finally Ronnie and me. My mom walked me out to the edge of the sidewalk, gave me my bag, then hugged me and whispered, "You be a good girl at school now, Pammy. I'm sure you are going to make lots of new friends." Then she kissed my forehead and walked back in the house. When I turned around, both of our dogs were staring at me through my bedroom window. I raised my hand for one final good-bye as tears ran down both of my cheeks. Next thing I knew, a big yellow bus pulled on to the street, red lights flashing, the sound of brakes like air rushing out of a deflating balloon, a door opening up in front of me, and a lady smiling and waving me in.

"Good morning, miss." I smiled and curtsied. "My name is Pam. How are you doing today?"

"I'm doing fine, honey." A lady about my mother's age with short blonde hair turned around in her seat. "I'm Miss Barbara. Come in and sit down."

As I walked inside, I could hear someone calling my name. "Pam! Pam! Come sit here," she said, slapping the empty half of her seat with her hand. It was Katie, a girl I had met at the riding stables.

"Katie!" I said as I walked over and sat down next to her. "Whose class are you in?"

"Miss Davis," she said.

"I have Miss Milhaus. But I'll see you at recess?"

"Yeah," she said. "Maybe we can even go riding together some time?"

"That would be great." I told her. "Come find me at lunch."

A few minutes later, we got out of the bus and some nice old lady walked us into our homeroom. The day went well, the teacher liked me, and I made lots of new friends. I told my mom when I got home "I love my school, Mommy!" Then an hour later my sister Veronica walked in crying.

"I wish I could go back to school in Anaheim!" She said through a series of sobs. "Seriously, I was scared the whole day. There were girls who dressed in next to nothing, and guys were talking about smoking and drinking and trying to get in our pants."

"I'm sure that they're not all like that." My mother broke in.

"They were." She sobbed. "I want to go back to St. Joseph's!"

"Well you can't, honey. You're just going to have to get over it and make the best of things."

Things had gone better for my sister Marie. "My first day and I was already invited to a football game! Is that cool, or what? Hey what's wrong with Veronica?" She asked as she heard the sobs coming out of her bedroom door.

"She's taking some time to get used to things." My mother assured.

"Stop being such a FRESHMEN!" she looked in her room and laughed. "How's Ron and Pam?"

"Ron's over at Jim's. He didn't say much so I guess it went well. Pammy had a great day at school!"

"Coolness." Marie walked into the kitchen, grabbed two sodas, and walked out the door. "Going over to see Nick and Karen. Be back in a few."

"Say 'hi' to Roger!" I giggled as she looked over at me and left in a huff.

That whole semester, life went by in a blur. When I wasn't in school or reading, I was over at Katie's. On the weekend, we'd go out to her stable and visit her horses. The hills around us had long since died, their summer dress unchanged since we moved, rolling brass waves beneath a pale blue sky.

It was December and my dad still watered the lawn every day when the sun went down and Christmas lights blinked on all around. At night, there were packs of coyotes, scrawny and gaunt, yellow eyes glaring at passing cars and riders on horseback, scattering down from the nearby hills for a feast of roadkill. By January it still hadn't rained, and at night it got really cold, much colder than Anaheim. Sometimes the grass would frost over until all of the green had turned into brown.

"Daddy, everything around here looks dead," I'd complain, as I stared outside at the burnt rolling hills.

"A dry winter this year, I guess," he answered, shaking his head. "Not just us but the whole state. Remember that river we drove across when we went out to Vegas? It no longer reaches the ocean, just dies in the sand."

"That's sad," I lamented.

"That's sad, but its life," he said with a sigh. "Sometimes it rains, sometimes it doesn't. You can't always predict the seasons."

THE HILLS HAVE EYES

My first year of school had ended and on the last day, I handed Miss Milhaus a card and told how her how much I was going to miss her.

"My dear, Pamela," she said as she hugged me, "I'm going to miss you too!"

Ronnie and I made perfect grades, my sisters not so much. Marie hung out with the jocks in school, then spent most of the summer with Roger. Things were going better for Veronica too. Her grades weren't that good, but she was now making friends and a lot of boys wanted to date her. But that's where my mom stood her ground. "There'll be no dating until you're sixteen!" she warned. "Unless he thinks he can outrun my gun!" I thought she was kidding, but knowing my mom, I could never be sure. I was in first grade now and Katie and I were in the same class. She was always talking about her horses. She said that her dad was going to teach her to ride them. I asked if he would also teach me. "I don't see why not?" she said. "You can ask him when you come over this weekend."

Friday night was the football game, and my sister Marie wanted to go. My mother told her that is was fine as long as she was home by eleven. I guess she forgot to mention that a couple of guys from school were taking her. They pulled up in an old white pickup and blasted the horn. "That's my friends, I gotta go," she said as she walked out the door.

"Who you guys playing?" I called out after her.

"Scummy Hills!" she shouted back. "See you later!"

After dinner that night, my mom and dad sat in the living room each reading a book. Every now and again, my mom would put down her book, take a long drink of wine and light up a cigarette.

"I'm going to bed, Ginny," my father announced, then kissed my mom on the cheek and walked into their room. I got in my pajamas, pulled up the covers but couldn't sleep.

Ten became eleven, then eleven turned to twelve, yet there was still no sign of Marie. Sometime after one, the front door burst open and my sister walked in. She smelled like beer and my mother and her got into an argument. "I don't want to talk about it!" Marie finally shouted, then walked into her room, slamming the door. The sound of her crying, muffled sobs were hushed by her pillow. After a while, I heard the door open and the gentle hum of my mother's voice.

"It wasn't my fault, Mom! It wasn't my fault!"

"I know, honey, I know," I heard my mom say as she rocked her back and forth in her arms.

"There were two of them, Mom, and one held me down, the stadium lights had all gone out, and no one could see what was going on behind all the bleachers," she said, choking back sobs. "That's when it happened. I remember the gravel under my back, and rows and rows of steel beams looking down at me from above. I wanted to scream, but they covered my mouth."

"Don't say a word to your father," my mother whispered. "I'm going to take care of it. Do you remember their names?"

"Derek, the tall one was Derek, and the other one I think was Brad."

"Derek and Brad," my mother confirmed. "Are you sure?"

"Yes."

"I'm going to take care of it, honey. Derek and Brad will never hurt you again! Right now, we need to go to the hospital. But remember, not a word to your father."

"Yes, Mom."

I heard the front door close, then the sound of my mother starting her car. I sat up in my bed and looked out the window as lights disappeared at the end of the street, then spent the next hour sitting up in my bed wondering how my sister got "hurt."

Marie didn't go to school that Monday. My mom sent her down to San Diego to stay with her aunt until she got things all "straightened out." After school, I went over to Katie's, Ron was at Jim's, and my sister Veronica was supposed to be staying with some of her friends, except that she changed her mind and came home instead. I know that she must have been really frightened because she still recalled each vivid detail when she told me about it after she moved. When she got there, all of the lights were out, and the curtains were drawn in each of the windows. There were several cars in our driveway and lining the street on either side. Some of them she recognized belonged to her aunts. She crept beneath the shade of drooping palm trees that bowed their limbs and concealed her against the side of the house. Stooping down, she kneeled under a row of shrubs, and glanced around dancing swaths of pure white linen. Inside she could feel the presence of evil.

Six women shrouded in black, held hands and chanted in unison. "Earth... fire... air... water... cast their bodies into the pit." A black candle glowed on a five-sided cast iron table strewn with skulls and drawings of demons—shadows danced in the flickering light, a figure arose like a high priestess standing before them, lifted her veil, and pointed her hands up to the sky as waves of reddish-brown hair fell over her face.

"Mom!" Veronica gasped in horror, hiding her head beneath the window.

"Derek and Brad," the priestess intoned, summoning some ancient spirit she called out by name. "They must pay with their lives! The white pickup truck—sever its brakes, undo the seatbelts, roll it over the side of the road—make it all look like an accident!" The chanting rose as the women joined hands over the table. "Powers of darkness, make this so!"

Veronica stiffened, frozen by fear, her jaw slacked open to stifle a scream. She struggled to her feet, braced herself against the one of the shutters, then ran through the gate and hid behind the gardening shack.

"All of my family are witches!" she whispered and panted, her voice seized with terror and dread. "My mom and her sisters—all of them witches!"

One by one, the cars peeled out of the driveway, and my mom went into the kitchen to start making dinner.

I got home right after my dad and Veronica walked in shortly after. "What's the matter, my dear?" My mother asked as she looked at my sister. "You look like you've just seen a ghost." My mom sat down, poured some wine, and served us our dinner. The meat was skewered on kababs set down over a bed of curried brown rice. There were vegetables in a rich brown sauce, kale and spinach mingled with bay leaves. It was something we had only once before at the Anaheim house about a month before we'd moved.

"Delicious, Ginny!" My dad gave her a "thumbs up" sign before wiping his mouth. "What do you call this again?"

"Carne cabrito," my mother answered, then turned to my sister, a wicked grin moving over her face. "I killed it myself!"

The next day it was raining. It seldom rained that time of the year. But there it was, coming down in buckets. My father's car pulled into the driveway and he covered his head with a paper so he wouldn't get wet. He opened the door, wiped both of his feet, and hung up his coat.

"Ginny, you are not going to believe this." He let out a breath, put down the paper, and sat down in his chair. "Two boys that go to school with Marie and Veronica— killed last night on Imperial Highway."

"What?" I said, as I covered my mouth.

Veronica emerged from the kitchen and looked at my dad in disbelief. "Two boys from Troy?" Her voice shook as she spoke.

"That's right," my father explained. "Going too fast, rolled their truck, thrown out on the street—dead just like that."

"That's awful!" I shrieked. "Their poor families! Mom, did you see it today on the news?"

"Didn't need to," my mother said as she turned and walked out into the hall, then glanced back over in my direction, "I already knew." My mother excused herself and went into her room.

"Where are you going?" I hollered.

"Calling Marie," she calmly explained. "I'm driving to San Diego to get her tomorrow. I already spoke with Katie's mom and she'll be picking you up from school. Is that clear, Pammy?"

"Yes, Mom," I answered, knowing I didn't dare say anything more.

The next day after school, Katie and I ran outside to the parking lot to where the crossing guard was standing ferrying a line of kids across Plumosa Drive and into the waiting arms of the new housing tract that had been recently built right across the street from the school.

"Hello, Mr. Stevens." Katie waved over as he turned to greet us.

"Hello, young ladies." He waved back. "Waiting for the bus to get here?"

"No," I told him. "Katie's mother is picking us up."

"I see," he said. "Looking forward to the weekend?"

"Oh yeah!" I exclaimed. "Katie's dad is going to teach us to ride horses!"

"Look, Pam," Katie said taking my hand in hers and walking me out toward the edge of the street, "you can see the stables from here. Right down there, right across Bastanchury."

"You girls be careful now," Mr. Stevens cautioned then walked back to the crosswalk and sat down in his chair.

"My favorite horses are Shadow and Blossom," Katie explained. "One is white and the other is a real dark brown."

"Let me guess, the dark one is Shadow."

"Yes, yes. Shadow is mine, but you could ride Blossom."

She crept even closer to the edge of the street until both of her feet had left the gravel and were out on the pavement. "I wonder if I could see them from here."

"Katie!" I shouted. "Katie get back!"

From the corner of my eye was a blur of white, the blast of a horn, and a screeching of brakes as I ran to pull her out of the way. There was a sickening thud, then a rush of hot air sweeping over my body. The smell of rubber hung in the air as blinking red eyes stared back from under a long sloping hood, winked for a moment then disappeared altogether. I rolled myself over onto the gravel as Mr. Stevens ran from his chair.

"Oh my God! Are you girls all right?" he screamed as he ran to the street waving his arms to stop traffic.

That's when I saw her. Eyes gently closed as if in a dream. Her chest slowly heaving like an expired balloon, a trickle of blood leaking out from her nose, and a tiny red stain on the street. Soon the police were there and then a stream of flashing red lights. An officer put his hand on my shoulder, directing my body away from the street. I started to cry, and he held me there as the paramedics leaned over her body then lifted it onto a small metal stretcher.

"Are you all right, little girl?" he finally spoke. "It looks like you got scratched up pretty bad."

"Where is Katie?" I started to scream, before my screaming turned into wails. "What did you do with my friend Katie?"

He just held me and said nothing as waves of bodies closed in all round us. A car stopped and slammed its door. A flood of tears and a cry of anguish. A mom's broken heart. The car started and followed the ambulance until sirens disappeared in the hills. Horses whinnied and neighed in their stables as a whisper of wind rustled the trees, the fading light of the warm autumn sun, all of nature grieving together.

The policeman gave me a ride home. I spent the next week locked up in my bedroom, then the nurse spoke with me and my mom when I went back to school. At night, I wanted to pray, but I didn't know if there was even a God who would listen. My father always told there wasn't, but I wasn't sure. If there wasn't a God, then was there a heaven? Were there horses in heaven? I thought for a moment, then closed my eyes and bowed my head.

"Dear God," I said. "If you are real, then please take good care of my friend. And please, dear God, would you let her know how much I miss her."

A while later, the heater started going on at night and I waited outside for the bus in a jacket. Pumpkins and skeletons appeared in our windows as black and orange streams of light swept down from the roof. After school one day, my mom told me there was somebody who wanted to meet me. It was one of her friends, some guy named Carl, she told me that he was a dance instructor. He was tall and skinny, with light-brown hair, and glasses that made him look like a librarian. He was about thirty, but I didn't think he was married. My dad called him "Tinkerbell"—whatever that meant.

It turned out Carl was a really good dancer. Each day after school, my mom took me over to his studio where we'd practice for hours. The week before Christmas, we had a recital. My mom was there in the audience sitting next to a man who wasn't my father.

"Pammy," she said, as she stood up to greet me when I walked off the stage, a bright blue ribbon around my neck. "There's somebody else that I want you to meet."

We had met sometime before, his dirty-blonde beard and the smell of tobacco. This time, he had on a pair of dark glasses and was dressed in a red and orange Hawaiian shirt. My mom introduced him as her "good friend" Dirk.

"Hello, little angel," he said as he held out his hand. "I'm not sure if you remember me, but your mom said that you wanted to get into acting."

"She did?" I said, as he put his dry, calloused hand around mine and gave it a shake, while my mom glanced over and shot me a look.

"Of course you did, Pammy. Remember? *Remember*?"

"Oh yeah, sure," I told him.

"Well I can get you into commercials. That's where it starts," he assured me. "And besides, you're such a pretty young lady, who knows where else it could lead? I've had several girls about your age that I personally helped get into movies."

"I'm taking you over to Dirk's house next weekend," my mother informed me. "You'll be spending Saturdays there."

"I don't know, Mom," I questioned.

"Don't worry," he promised. "It will be fun. There'll be a lot of other kids there too. You can make lots of new friends."

When Saturday came, we drove up to his house in the Rocking Horse section of Anaheim Hills. The outside looked like a medieval castle like the one at Disneyland where Sleeping Beauty was held captive in one of its towers.

"You be good now, Pammy." My mother reached over and gave me a hug, then drove down the long winding road and out through the gates.

When I got inside, there were lots of kids, some my age, but most were older. There were sodas and candy and toys all around. Now and again kids would emerge from out of a room with some adult who was holding a camera.   After a while, Dirk descended a long spiral staircase that wound its way through flickering shards of stained-glass beams and spilled out into the room where all of the children were laughing and playing. He was dressed in a burgundy robe, lined in fur on either side, and a cigar hung out from the side of his mouth.

"How's my little angel?" He smiled, then put both of his arms around me. "You just go on and make yourself comfortable. Next week I'll get you some nice new clothes and introduce you to my photographers. And feel free to take home a Barbie—my gift to you."

I wasn't sure what to make of things. The house was beautiful, and all of the kids seemed really nice, but something just seemed out of place. That's when a pretty blonde girl who said she was twelve, but looked as old as my sister Marie, walked up beside me.

"My name is Chrystal." She said.

"I'm Pam," I responded, holding out my hand to greet her. "How long have you known Dirk?" I asked her.

"About four years," she said. "He's a really nice guy. He got me started doing commercials. There was one for Trident, you know 'four out of five dentists' and all of that shit. Then there was another for suntan lotion."

"I see."

"Anyway, that's how I started. Now he has me doing what he calls 'more grown up stuff.'"

"What 'grown up stuff?'" I asked.

"Well, it's a little creepy at first, but you kind of get used to it," she said, the smile now running away from her face. "Besides, it's how every young actress gets started. Dirk calls it 'paying your dues.'"

"I don't want to go back next week!" I told my mom when she picked me up and drove down through the hills past rows of tree-lined stables.

"Oh, Pammy, you're getting all worked up over nothing!" she scolded.

"I don't know, Mom. Something just didn't seem right over there."

"Look, Pammy, Dirk is a really nice man. He'd never do anything to hurt you. Same with all of those other kids. How dare you even think such a thing!"

"But I don't want to go back!"

"But you *are* going back!" She glared over at me, hitting the brakes to stop at a light. "You don't have any choice in the matter. Besides, I've already signed all of the papers."

When spring came that year, the air was filled with fragrant streams of orange blossoms and coconut oil as waves of chlorine spilled out of swimming pools and onto the pavement. It got really warm early that year and a cold winter sky soon turned into brass. On the news they talked about water shortages and it wasn't long before my dad started timing our showers.

"Hey, leave some water for the rest of us!" he'd shout if I or my siblings spent more than five minutes running the water.

Every Saturday, my mom would take me over to Dirk's and he'd buy me lots of new clothes and stuff then have his friends take pictures of me when I tried them on in one of the rooms. One night he called my mom and the two of them talked for a really long time about agents and things. "She's about ready," he told her. "It won't be long until she's famous."

That day when I got there, he opened the door dressed in his robe. He let me in and gave me a drink, a "Shirley Temple," he said. When I looked around, there was nobody there and both of his dogs were out in the yard locked behind the sliding glass window. "Can I go pet Lady?" I begged as her white-yellow face excitedly panted, and her tail swung wildly back and forth.

"Maybe later," he promised. "Please, follow me upstairs. I have something for you."

"Where is everybody?" I asked as we wound our way beneath the open ceiling until the upstairs walls closed in behind us. He didn't answer but extended his hand and waved me forward.

"Right this way."

There was this really big room painted all in purple and gold. A round brass bed sat in the middle as a ceiling fan spun slowly above it. In the corner was a man with a camera who nodded at me without saying hello.

"Here, change into these. I'll be back in a minute," he said before closing the door.

"Joey, Joey." I could hear his voice out in the hallway. "Come right this way."

A boy walked in, about ten years old, shaggy brown hair, and smelling like dime store cologne. Then he unbuttoned his shirt and stood there before me.

"Pam, Joey... Joey, Pam," Dirk gave us a brief introduction then motioned over to the guy with the camera. "Now you both do what Pedro tells you." Then he turned around and walked through the door. I don't know how long I was in there. The "Shirley Temple" was making me sleepy. I remember we were both on the bed—his trembling hands undoing my blouse. I slapped him at first, then Pedro got pretty angry, so I didn't slap him anymore. His hands smelled like Cracker Jacks and he kept on forcing my mouth open with his tongue. He seemed pretty scared. I was scared too. Sometime later, it got pretty cold, so we pulled up the blankets to cover our bodies then both fell asleep under the fan. Later on—I don't know how long, maybe an hour, maybe two or three, the door opened up, and Dirk came back inside.

"All right you two. Up and at 'em!" Dirk was back in his usual shirt, the kind that looked like a couch somewhere was missing its cover. "You were great. Some real good acting right there! See you next week?"

Neither of us said a word. Then Dirk looked directly at Joey.

"Not you, son. I'm talking to Pam." Then he paused for a moment stroking his beard. "I mean, you can come over during the day, but I'd like Pam to get here around six."

I didn't say anything when my mom drove me home. After dinner that evening, I went straight to my room, closed the door and turned on the TV. The following week it was just me and him. A corner room looking out over the fields—curtains half-drawn and a sea of lights that stretched out all the way to the ocean—a Shirley Temple that tasted different than the one that he gave me last week.

"Ewe, this is gross!" I told him.

"Drink it!" he insisted, then fixing himself, he lowered his head and calmly assured, "just a few sips, it will help you relax."

"Where's Pedro?" I asked.

"Pedro's not here. Tonight, it's just me and you."

He slid his hand along my back, removed my shirt, and started kissing the nape of my neck. At first, I started to struggle, then the room begin to spin all around, and the smell of tobacco was making me sick. I kept my eyes on the ceiling, drawing shapes in the asbestos speckles. Sometimes I turned and looked out the window pretending it was a large screen TV like the one that my father had bought when we moved. I used to sit next to him on the couch each Sunday night when we watched *The Wonderful World of Disney* together. Sometimes I'd see Walt himself—his neatly combed hair and those flannel grey suits, a smile that seemed to look out of place on his otherwise stern and angular face as if it concealed a much darker soul. Sometimes it was Mickey and Goofy or Sleeping Beauty asleep in her castle waiting on her prince to arrive. But sometimes I'd see a thousand bright lights, some white and others a fiery yellow, shining from behind a window. Then a heavy fog began to roll in and lights glowed like a blanket of mirrors. I watched as a horse stepped out of the fog, its coat a glistening white, and then another—dark brown, almost black. I pushed my face up to the window and cried into its murky wet mane. I could hear the horses whinny and neigh, then one snorted, took air into its nostrils, and shook its head back and forth. Then a trailer pulled up shining its lights and a big man in a raincoat got out and whistled as the horses turned and walked up a ramp then disappeared behind two metal doors. I begged him to give me a ride, but he just drove out into the fog.

"Stop crying!" A face staring down from above like a badly aging Peter Lorre. "Stop crying, or I'm going to smack you!" So, I shut up and just stared at the ceiling waiting for it all to be over.

The next thing I knew I was down in his pantry, sipping a tall glass of orange juice while he poured himself a hot cup of coffee. It must have been morning because the light started coming in through the shades.

"Let's skip next week," he finally said. "In fact, let's hold off for a month or two."

"What do you mean?" I asked him.

"It's not you, Pam," he explained, taking a long swallow from out of his cup. "You know that I love you. Don't worry. I'll still take care of you and your mom. I even gave her the names of some other directors. I know someday that you'll be a star."

"What do you mean take care of my mom?"

He finished his coffee, set his cup in the sink, then pushed his face only inches from mine.

"I mean that you need to keep quiet! Not a word, do you hear?" He was starting to scare me. "You remember Chrystal?" he asked.

"Yup."

"That little bitch! Four years now, and I've given her everything. Got her into commercials, modeling, you name it. And how does she repay me? I'll tell you. I'll tell you how she repays me! She finds some agent up in Hollywood and he tells her all this shit about me. Yeah right," he fumed. "It's not like her mom even gave a damn the whole time she was busy cashing my checks!"

He got up, grabbed his coat, and took his keys off of the sink. "Come on, I'm taking you home. If your mom asks any questions, just tell her that we were having a sleep over and that you crashed over here on the couch."

"Yeah, whatever," I told him.

"Well that had *better* be your answer." He pulled out a smoke and held it over a gold butane lighter that sparked to life when he flicked it open. He took a long drag then exhaled out through the window and set his eyes directly against me. "That is if you still love your family."

For the next week or two, I don't remember seeing my mom very much. She was always at work or out with her friends, and when she got home, her and my dad would get into arguments. Most of them had to do with her drinking, but my siblings and I had begun to suspect something else. Sometimes the arguments got pretty violent, my father would say things and my mother would throw something at him. One day, there was glass all over the kitchen and my father was bleeding from a cut on his forehead. "Go away, Pam!" was all he would say when I asked him if he was all right. One day, I was sitting in my bedroom and I heard my mom screaming for everyone to get out of *her* house.

"Ginny, calm down!" my father insisted, putting a hand on both of her shoulders.

"I hate you! You bastard!" she screamed. "Get out of *my* house or I'll call the police!"

"I live here!" he hollered. "Goddammit, I live here! I'm your husband, remember?" He told me later that as he looked in her eyes, it was as if he could see her soul disappear behind two distant brown shadows. Every now and again it came to life and the screaming began all over.

"Husband?" she raged. "I've never even *seen* you before! Get out of my house or I swear I will kill you!"

Soon all of the kids were out in the living room, except for Ron who was over at Jim's.

"Who are these people?" my mother demanded. "*All* of you, get the hell out of my house!"

My sister Veronica grabbed my arm and pulled me back in her bedroom. Her TV was on, like it always was— a black and white set that she'd gotten for her birthday— and she told me to "sit right there" and to "not make a sound." I flipped through the channels until I saw *Three's Company* on. In the living room, I could still hear my mom screaming as a siren pulled up in our driveway and two men in white coats knocked on the door. Next thing I knew, the two men were taking her out of the house, each holding one of her arms. Through the window, I could hear her calling my name. "Where's Pammy? Where is my baby?" she wailed. "Bring me my baby! I need to talk to the baby!"

"Stay right here." Veronica held me down in my chair, covering me with both of her arms like a momma bear protecting her cub. Every now and then, she would turn and glance through the window as both men held my mother down and led her through an open door and into the windowless part of their vehicle. Then there were the sirens again, shrieking one last cry for help as they finally disappeared down the street. I just sat there, glued to my chair, the one that Veronica sat in to put on her make-up beneath the glow of a lighted mirror that stood on her dresser. My face was pressed against the TV as I imagined myself being pulled inside through the glass to be with Jack and Chrissy and Janet.

When my mother got home, her and my dad were no longer speaking. She'd make him his dinner then get dressed to go out. Sometimes she came back and sometimes she didn't. Things went on like that for a month or so, before the day that my dad got the letter that she wasn't coming home anymore.

ASHES AND SNOW

It was the last day of my first-grade year and I had Miss Barbara drop me off at the library. "Don't worry, I'm getting a ride," I assured, her knowing it was a little white lie. Later that day, when I got home, both of my sisters were sitting down in the living room. I knew that something was terribly wrong.

"Pam, you had better sit down," Marie insisted. "Our father has something he wants to tell us."

"Am I grounded?" I asked, knowing that I had been coming home late every day.

"Just sit down!" she commanded. "Ronnie will be here any minute, then Dad said that he wants to talk to us all as a family."

When I looked in her eyes, I could see that she had been crying. Every now and then she'd rub her fingers against them then look straight ahead at the door. In the kitchen, I could hear my father pacing back and forth and the sound of papers shuffling together, then the shuffling stopped, and he'd sit down and let out a sigh.

"Hey guys," Ron said, as he walked through the door.

"How was school today, Pammy? Hey look there's a booger!" he said, pointing at the mole on my face as I lifted my hand to wipe it away. "Ha, you fall for it every time!"

No one said anything, except for Marie who told him to shut up and sit down. Just then, my father walked in and pulled a letter from out of his pocket. He held it up inches from his face then squinted an eye to the cursive ink, trying to figure out the parts he could share.

"I found this on the table when I got home from work," he began. "It's from your mother." He let out a long deep breath then lifted his head. "She said that she's going to be leaving. She told me that it's nobody's fault and that she just wants to start a new life."

"So, where the hell is she?" Marie interrupted.

"She said she's moving to Alaska with her boyfriend," my father continued.

"Boyfriend?" Veronica said with a dumbfounded stare. "What boyfriend? You're not supposed to have boyfriends when you're married!"

"Well that's pretty fucked up!" Marie interjected. "She's leaving us to move to Alaska?"

"Is that all she said?" I wondered aloud as I looked at my dad, his face still frozen in disbelief.

"Just one final thing," my dad, said as he turned over the second page of the letter. "P.S. I'll send for the baby."

"Over my dead body!" Marie objected. "There's no way that Pam is going to Alaska with Mom and her fucking new boyfriend!"

"I may not have any choice," my father bemoaned. "She's still her mother. But I promise, I'm going to get a real good lawyer. She's not taking my family from me!"

I could see his eyes beginning to water, but then he forced a smile and folded the letter back into his pocket.

"Well," he said, "it looks like it's only the five of us now."

He smiled again, then turned and walked into his room. All of us just sat there in shock. There were so many things that we wanted to say, but we knew that it wasn't a good time to ask.

That Fourth of July, my father took us to see the fireworks at Bradford Stadium a few miles from our house. The lemon-yellow summer sun slid behind rows of bleachers, as wispy high feathers of clouds dusted the edges along the horizon. Soon, the sky was exploding all around as flashes of red, white, and yellow splattered against a deep blue canvas of stars. Then there came one final eruption as the Star-Spangled Banner rang out through the night.

The next day, it was nearly a hundred degrees when my father took me to Brea Mall to buy sweaters and gloves. "It's not that bad during the day, but I hear it gets pretty cold at night," he reminded me.

"But, Daddy, I don't want to go!" I protested.

"It will only be for a while," he assured. "You'll be back in time for the start of your classes.

That morning, I carried a suitcase, as my dad pulled another larger one behind him—our two free hands locking together as we walked through the airport. We held each other by the tall bright window as the plane with the Eskimo face on the front stood waiting outside to take me away.

I took a seat by the window and leaned my head against the glass, crying softly to myself. As the engine revved and wheels began to turn toward the runway, I could see my father waving good-bye. "I love you," I whispered, pushing my head back into the seat. Soon we were out over the ocean and everything soon faded to blue. The next thing I knew, there were towering mountains dressed all in green and white at the top and somewhere below them what looked like a city nestled somewhere between the mountains and water. "Flight 914, from L.A. to Anchorage all clear for landing," The pilot announced. "At this time, I will ask everyone to remain in their seats."

"Pammy!" My mom ran up to greet me as the passengers got off the plane and spilled out into the lobby. Standing next to her was a man I had never seen before who my mom introduced to me as her "friend."

"Pammy, this is Larry. Larry, this is my daughter, Pammy."

I held out my hand but said nothing. "You're going to love it here." She finally said. "We have a farm and lots of animals. Give it a chance."

My mother and he both grabbed a suitcase and soon we got into his truck and left the city for a dairy farm in the small town of Palmer—wherever that was. All around was a sea of green with Christmas trees here and there poking out from the ground. Within minutes, there were no other houses and only an occasional car passing us by on the other side of the road. Every now and again I'd see a few cows and fluffy white clouds like bales of cotton playing tag with the sun. I felt really small as if swallowed up in another world—a place I only read of in books. There were castles and dragons, crumbling walls of feudal estates, knights dashing through lush green fields, riding atop their trusty old steeds, gleaming swords in the noonday sun, damsels locked inside of a tower, helplessly waving a hand out the window.

I drifted in and out of a dream as the truck pulled onto a small narrow street that led us between two iron gates. In the distance, there were other houses, each with long and pointed roofs that prayed like hands against the sky. On one of the corners was a small grocery store and on the other side was a gas station. The man in front of one of the pumps waved over to us as we passed. We took another right at the light, one of only three I recall, then pulled up into an asphalt driveway and parked the truck in a wooden garage.

"Here we are!" My mom reached over and grabbed a suitcase, while her boyfriend got the other from out of the trunk. "Isn't it beautiful?"

I said nothing.

"Look it's so peaceful up here. And look at the size of this farm! You won't see anything like this in Orange County."

"It's the middle of nowhere." I shrugged. "There's nothing but cows."

"It's a dairy farm, honey." The man spoke up. "Those cows over there, each one of them belongs to me."

"Larry and I will be staying out here until his family can sell it." My mother informed me. "Then we'll probably be moving back down. Honey, why don't you take Pammy inside to her bedroom? I can't wait to see the look on her face when she sees what you got her."

At the end of the hall, a door opened into a cerulean kingdom of high blue ceilings and endless green fields reaching out into towering snow-covered peaks. Now and then, a cloud passed over, like a dimmer switch, and merged them together in shades of gray. At one side of the room was a color TV, and at the other was some sort of contraption that looked like a typewriter with some kind of screen. Unfolding out from beneath the window, a large white headboard and a mattress adorned with Disney princesses, magic wands, and glittering wings. The closet was filled with bright colored outfits and stuff for me to wear when it was cold. But it wasn't cold—at least not today. It was still about seventy when we walked outside after dinner and the man introduced me to all of his cows.

"That one's so sweet!" I said, pointing to the one with black and white mottles who stood against a white picket fence swishing its tail.

"Go ahead, you can pet her," he said. "She's very gentle. We call her Cecilia."

"That's my mom's middle name." I told him. The man said nothing, just nodded his head.

"But she's getting up there. We're no longer able to use her for milk."

Each morning, I walked outside to the fence and she greeted me there. "Hi, baby girl," I'd whisper, her deep brown eyes staring back into mine. Then we would just stand there together, and I'd sing her the songs I remembered from *The World of Disney*. At night, I would sometimes stare out my window and see her standing outside by the fence. One night, around midnight, my mother came in and pulled down the shades as the twilight strained along the horizon.

"You better get to sleep now, Pammy, Larry and I are taking you into town to go shopping tomorrow. And when we get home, Larry's going to teach you how to use your computer."

"My what?" I asked her.

"Go to sleep, Pammy," she said, as she gave me a kiss on the cheek and tucked me in bed.

When the door closed, I sat up and looked at the window. "Good night, baby girl." I murmured. "I'm sorry I won't see you tomorrow."

The next morning, my mom got me ready to go down to Anchorage, while her friend talked with some of the guys who worked on the farm. "Be there in a minute," he said when he saw us walking out of the house, then got into his truck next to my mom and turned the ignition.

"Who were you talking to?" I asked him.

"Ah, just some guys who need to take care of a few things while we're gone," he told me. "Don't forget to buckle your seatbelt."

Soon, we were out on the Old Glenn Highway, as we drove with the sun at our back. Before too long, we could see the city unfolding against the roadside glaciers and deep endless sea.

"Where are we going?" I asked my mom.

"The Great Alaska Mall," she told me.

"Is it like the Brea Mall?"

"It's different, but nice," she answered. "Honey, we're not in Orange County."

When we got there, we went into all of the stores and my mother's friend told me that he would buy me whatever I wanted, pulling out a little gold card that he kept in his wallet. When I spent the next hour or so looking bored and not saying anything, she finally started making suggestions.

"Look at that dress over there, Pammy," she exclaimed, waving over the lady who stood at the counter. "This would look so good on you!"

"I don't know, Mom." I said. "I'm getting hungry."

"Well you must want *something*," my mother's friend said. "I have two teenage girls of my own and I can't seem to buy them enough."

"Well, I'm not for sale!" I told him. "I want to go back and talk to my cow."

"Pammy, that's no way to talk to your new daddy!" my mother scolded.

"That's not my daddy!" I objected. "My daddy's back home in Orange County!"

"I give up," my mother said to her friend. "Let's just go get something to eat. Maybe she'll change her mind later on."

"I'm not so sure of that, Ginny," he said. "Maybe it was too soon to bring her up here."

We sat down in a little café and I drank hot chocolate and picked at my lunch of halibut tacos and "reindeer fries"—whatever that was. After that, we shopped a little more and my mom finally talked me into letting him buy me a shirt and a little Eskimo doll. When we finally got home, I went straight to my room and collapsed on my bed. It was something like three in the morning when the sun woke me up through the window. I put on my robe and walked out to the kitchen to get some milk. There was an empty bottle of wine on the table and two half-empty glasses standing beside it. There was also an ashtray filled with crushed out cigarette butts, most with lipstick stains on the filter. My mom and her friend were still in bed, so I opened the door and walked outside. "Baby girl," I whispered. "Baby girl? Where are you?" They must have moved her inside of the barn, because she wasn't where she usually slept. Just then, I heard movement then the light flickered on inside of the kitchen.

"Pammy, what are you doing out there?"

"Nothing, Mom."

"Well get back in here and get back to bed!"

"Sorry."

The whole next week I couldn't find her, and I mostly just stayed in my room reading some of the books that I'd brought. One morning, when I got up, my mother's friend was out in the field while she was in the kitchen making us breakfast. Neither of us said a word to each other. When he came in, we sat, and we ate, then she got up and collected our plates.

"Pammy, Larry is going to show you how to use your computer." She told me.

"It should be fun," the man broke in. "I can teach you how to play lots of new games."

"That's nice," I said.

"Your mom said that she's going to be cooking something special for us tonight, right Ginny?"

"Sure, honey." She said, as he walked with me into my room.

We spent the next few hours shooting at aliens and protecting the earth from falling asteroids. I did really good, or maybe he was just letting me win. In the kitchen,

I could tell that my mother was drinking as she always started to smoke when she drank. One time, I could hear a glass break on the floor and the sound of her swearing. Then, after a while, she finally walked into my room.

"Pammy, go get cleaned up. Dinner will be ready in less than an hour."

"Smells great, Ginny!" the man told her, as he got up and walked out of my room.

I went into the bathroom and took a shower then got dressed in one of my new outfits. Then I went over and looked out the window again before I went out into the kitchen. There were candles and glasses and a bottle of wine that her friend had uncorked. My mom had him pour some into a glass and set it before me.

"What's this?" I asked her.

"Larry and I decided you can have some tonight." She paused for a moment then finished her glass. "My, don't *you* look pretty!"

"Thanks," I answered.

We started off with a salad, then my mom brought in some vegetables and au gratin potatoes, while her friend carried in what looked like a roast. We sat and ate, as the sun sank behind the mountains and slowly covered our bodies in shadows. My mom kept pouring glasses of wine and took a long drink with each bite of her meal. Every now and then, I took a sip from my glass and pushed the food around on my plate. After a while, my mom stood up, turned on the light, and stared straight at me.

"What the hell's the matter with you?" she said, only inches away from my face.

"What do you mean?"

"The whole night, you've sat there and said nothing, and you hardly even touched your food."

"I'm sorry," I said. "It's just that I'm worried."

"Worried about what?" she asked me. "Your father and sisters are doing just fine. So is your brother. Besides, Larry and I have done everything here to make you feel at home."

"It's just," I lifted my head and struggled to speak. "It's just that I'm worried about my cow."

My mom sat down, threw up her hands, and poured herself another drink. "You tell her, Larry."

"Honey," he turned around and looked into my eyes. "Do you know what happens when dairy cows can no longer give milk?"

"No," I said. "I don't know what happens."

"Well what happens is..." he started to answer but my mom cut him off.

"I'll tell you what happens." She glared at me from across the table. "What happens is that we just *ate* your damn cow!"

I got up from the table, my face awash in a flood of tears, then ran straight into my bedroom.

"Just let her go" my mom insisted, when her friend got up and tried to follow me.

I stayed there for the next few days, sometimes reading, but mostly crying. Every once in a while, the man would come in and ask if I wanted to go for a walk or play a few games, but I just told him that I wanted to leave. Then a few days later I got my wish as my mom told me to start packing my bags.

Back home, I spent the next few weeks trying to leave everything beneath those midnight suns and white glacial peaks. When school started that year, Carl would pick me up around three and take me down to his studio where we'd dance together for hours. Pretty soon, he started talking about me someday becoming a professional dancer. With my mother gone, my sister Veronica did all of the cooking, and Marie's friend Roger came over and helped my dad in the yard.

About a week before Halloween, it got really hot, then the winds started coming down from the canyons. That day when I got home from school, there were herds of coyotes racing against the blowing dust, their eyes aglow with the instinctual knowledge of a fire raging not too far away. Pretty soon, we could all smell the smoke. At first, it was a warm glow of musk like the first breath of autumn blowing the summer back out to sea, then the smoke became darker and covered the sky. When my father got home, he told my siblings to start packing and bring the dogs inside and that we may need to leave if things got much worse.

We were all watching the news, as my father went up on the roof with a hose. Carbon Canyon State Park was fully ablaze, and thirty homes were already lost in Sleepy Hollow. Our city was under a voluntary evacuation, and cars were beginning to line the street as fire engines raced in the other direction. From our window, I could see a ring of fire slowly creeping down from the hills. Outside was an oddly warm breeze fueled by the malevolent flames. I could not look away, like Icarus scorching his wings on the sun's gallant beams, or Fabius peering up into the Alps as Hannibal's army of elephants thundered down on his legions, death and destruction never looked so amazing.

That morning when we woke up, our entire street was covered in ash. I walked through our front yard, thinking about how each small flake could have been somebody's home, like tiny whispers of ruin and loss picked up by the wind and dropped by my window. Or they may have been the remnants of trees that had stood for decades against fires and floods until the day that their time had finally come. I thought of the birds that twisted nests inside of their branches to one day raise their small young family now flying for their lives to escape through the smoke. I bent down and raked the grass with my hands, grabbing a small fistful of memories before releasing them back into the wind.

Later that year, it got really cold and dark. One day, it started to hail, pellets of ice piling up like snow outside my third-grade classroom window. All of the kids ran outside, scooping up snowballs into their hands and sliding across pools of slush. When I got home, I grabbed one of my coats, put on some gloves, and tried making a snowman in our front yard from the pellets that hadn't already melted. Later that evening, my dad made me hot cocoa and I tried not to think of Alaska as I took long sips from out of my cup. He made a fire and we all watched TV. That was when he told us that my mother was moving back in before Christmas.

A HOUSE DIVIDED

One particular day when I came home from school, the TV was on and red and green candles were lit on the table, sprinkling the room in a delicate fragrance of myrtle and rose. In the corner, a tall Douglas fir stood cloaked in a blazer of blinking white lights and covered in ornaments. A white and gold angel sat at the top and spread her wings out over a sea of neatly marked boxes, each one bearing one of our names. In the kitchen, a light was on and the familiar aroma of chilaquiles hung in the air.

"Veronica?" I called out. "Veronica, is that you?"

For a while no one answered, then I saw her walk out of the bathroom. She had on a long red dress that let out a trail of perfume behind her. As she came down the hall, she blotted her lips and fluffed both sides of her hair with each hand. "Mom?"

"Well, hello stranger!" she said. "You expecting someone?"

"No." I said. "Well, maybe Veronica. Anyway, I thought that you left us."

"Oh no, silly!" She looked surprised. "I'll be staying here for a while or do you forget that this is *my* house."

"You mean yours and *Dad's*?" I corrected her.

"Of course. But half of it still belongs to me. Besides, don't you want us to have Christmas together?"

"Sure," I said not knowing whether I meant it or not.

For the next few months, things were sometimes pretty weird. My mom would make our lunches for school then have dinner ready when we got home. Then there were days when she'd do the dishes then go back into her room to get ready. Then the doorbell would ring, and my father would answer. "Oh, Larry. Won't you come in? Ginny will be ready in a few minutes. Can I get you something to drink?"

My sister Marie would sometimes joke, "I'm not so sure that I'd take that drink if you know what I mean." Sometimes it was my dad who went out and my mom would stay in her room with a pack of smokes and a bottle of wine. Those were the days that really scared me. I remember her always yelling at Veronica. Sometimes, they would get into fights and then I'd hear my mom start to beat her, sometimes with her hands and sometimes with a shoe. It was all over stupid stuff really, not washing the dishes or forgetting to make the bed or whatever. It wasn't until I got older that I figured it out—Veronica looked *just* like my mother, especially now that she had grown up.

Sometime, right before summer, Marie had something she wanted to share. Roger stood beside her holding her hand.

"What, you're graduating with honors?" my father joked.

"Very funny," she laughed, then looked over at Roger and burst into a wide toothy grin. "Roger and I are getting married!"

All that summer my mom sat in her room, sitting under her sewing machine, working on dresses. Sometime after I went back to school, she called me and my sisters over, gave us each a hanger, and told us to go to our rooms and change. The dresses she made for me and Veronica were a lightweight tropical coral chiffon that hung just below our knees, while Marie's was an ivory A-Line Princess that swept to the ground in layers of sequins.

"It's beautiful, Mom!" Veronica said as she lifted the edge and twirled around, flexing her knees. I told my mom that I never wanted to take mine off, while Marie said nothing, she just stood there and cried.

The wedding took place in a small church in Fullerton, and my mother and Veronica did all of the cooking. I asked my dad if I could invite Carl so we could show off some of our dance routines, while my mom invited a few of her acting friends. Marie and Roger both looked so happy— the "tom boy" and "beach boy" my father would call them. My family watched me dance and everyone said, "look at the baby, she's going to be a professional dancer someday." Later that evening, my father tied two metal cans to the back of my sister's Volkswagen as the happy new couple drove down the street. I waved back until I felt a hand come down on my shoulder.

"Pammy, this is Mrs. Haag," my mom said as a short skinny lady a few years older than her reached over and extended a hand. "Her son Marty is taking some classes at the Acting Academy on the weekends, and I thought that it might be something you'd like." Knowing my mother, this wasn't a question, but a place that I'd soon be spending my Saturday's. "I'll think about it," I answered. "Nice to meet you, Mrs. Haag."

"You can call me Elizabeth, dear," she said. "Nice meeting you too."

That night when we got home, I asked my mom if Dirk was going to be in those classes and I remember that she got pretty angry. "I don't want to talk about Dirk!" she warned me.

"Why?" I asked. "What happened to him?"

"Dirk is dead!" She said as she looked directly into my eyes. "Somebody said a bunch of shit about him and so the cops started poking their noses around. Then one day they found him and..."

"And what?" I asked.

"And so, one day they found him outside with a gun in his hand and a hole blown right through the side of his head—brains splattered all over the trees."

"I see," I answered but knew that I better not say nothing else.

The first Saturday after the New Year started, I was in my first class.

Later that spring, I became an auntie when my niece Sarah was born. Marie and Roger still lived at home, and my mom spent most of her time working at her boyfriend's store. When Sarah got older, I offered to babysit, and soon I was no longer just an auntie but a second mommy as well. When I wasn't babysitting, I was at school, or acting, or dancing. Veronica was usually out with her new boyfriend Steve, and my mother was helping the man she was dating at the store he had opened off of Imperial. Sometimes, after work, she'd bring home a bag of fresh fruit—guavas, mangoes, pomegranates, and things I had never heard of before like plantains, jicama, and Chinese pears.

For the next few months, he picked her up in the morning, and they'd usually be gone all day. Then, sometime around the first day of my fifth-grade year, his car stopped coming and my mom would still be asleep in her room. Sometime later, I found out that the store had been closed and that the man had moved back to Alaska for good. My mom would spend most of her time drinking until the day that she went out at night and ended up going to jail. My dad got her out, but she still had to go to meetings each week. It was at one of those meetings that she met her new boyfriend, a man who had a really big home up in the hills and six children of his own that he lived with after his wife had moved out and left him.

One day, during my seventh-grade year, my mother came home and told me that my cousin Susie would be living with us. What was even worse, was that we would be sharing the same room. My mom broke the news to my dad.

"Ron, we need to do *something*!" she said.

"Don't tell me your sister's drinking again!" he answered.

"Drinking *and* walking the streets! Ron, Susie literally has no mother."

"As you wish," was all he answered, then he turned and walked out of the room.

Not only did Susie and I not get along, we literally *despised* one another. For starters, we were polar opposites, her the tomboy and me the girlie girl. Since she was a month older than me, she'd sometimes try and boss me around when we were both younger, but now I wasn't having any of that. "Just stay over there on your side of the room!" I told her the day she moved in. A short time later, when Marie and Roger moved out, Susie moved into Marie's old room and spent most of her time with my sister Veronica. I missed having Sarah around, but at least now I had my privacy. Not to mention, my parents had just got me a phone and I was already talking with some boy who lived next door to my mother's new boyfriend. One day, my dad found out and was *pissed*.

"Good lord, Pam, how old is this guy?" he said throwing both of his hands in the air.

"Oh, Clark. He's nineteen," I answered.

"Nineteen? *Nineteen!*" he fumed then walked out of the room.

By this time, my mom had already moved in with David, so Clark and I would see one another whenever I'd visit. That summer, his family invited me to go with them on vacation. I could tell that my father wasn't too happy about it, but he didn't try to stop me. When summer ended, Clark had to go far away for school, Humboldt State, or someplace up north. We both kept in touch for a while, but then just as quickly drifted apart.

My eighth-grade year, I was really coming into my own. I wore my hair longer around my shoulders, and I had begun to master the art of flirtation, pulling on one of my long dark curls, batting my eyes, and letting out a short playful giggle. I had dressed mostly in leather and the training bra that I wore the previous year was already a C-cup. Furthermore, I was no longer Pammy, but *Pamela*. In fact, I never let anyone call me "Pammy" again, not even my family. "It's *Pam-e-la*," I would tell them with an emphasis on the "e-l-a." Of course, *Pam* was okay, but that was strictly among my friends.

My last year of junior high, most of the boys had crushes on me, but I had long since outgrown them and was now dating high school seniors. On weekends, we'd go and hang out at *Cloud Nine* or *Studio K* at Knott's Berry Farm. You had to be eighteen to get in, but that didn't matter if you knew the right people.

That year, my mom got Veronica a job at Albertsons and soon she was dating some guy she worked with. It didn't take long before her and Don were talking about marriage, then my mom started talking about it as well. Only this time it wasn't Don and Veronica—it was *my* marriage that she was talking about.

"Pammy, you remember Marty?" she said.

"That's Pam-e-l-a!" I answered.

"Well, anyway, me and his mother have been talking a lot, and since you both are in acting, we thought that you would make a really nice couple."

"Shit, Mom, I'm only thirteen!" I snapped.

"Watch your mouth Pammy, uh, *Pamela*," she said, correcting herself. "It wouldn't be until you were eighteen and graduated from high school."

"We'll see," was all that I said. "Look, I gotta get ready to go out. We'll talk about it later."

Don and Veronica tied the knot that summer, three months after their first son Andrew was born. The wedding took place in our backyard, it was so hot that day, that the cake started melting.

"What the hell is she doing in white?" My dad asked my mom as he got ready to walk her down the make-shift aisle he'd laid out on the patio the night before.

"Shut up, Ron!" she retorted, then turned toward my sister. "Don't you look beautiful, honey!"

That year, I was starting high school, while Ronnie was going to Fullerton College. The day I registered for classes, I got a call that same afternoon.

"Yes, this is Pamela." I said when my mother gave me the phone. "I see. Awesome! Oh my God, thank you!" I squealed.

"Mom, you are not going to believe this," I said, as I put the phone back in her hand.

"What is it honey?" she asked.

"I just made Drill Team, Tall Flags, *and* Dance Production! Not bad for a freshman, huh?"

I couldn't wait for school to start. "Troy High School will always remember me," I'd say to myself. I guess in a way I was right about that.

It didn't take long for me to make friends. Within a month, I was hanging out with all of the cool kids. I remember that most were in Drama, but there were a few in my English and Math class. There was Dexter and Jason, Diane and Lisa, not to mention the Queen Bee herself—Miss Erika Tracy! Erika was the tall pretty blonde that all of the guys wanted to date. But she was also a tease and not to mention, kind of a bitch, or "Ms. Bitch" as she used to remind us.

Erika, Lisa, Diane and I were all "Madonna-bees" dressed in leather and denim, a black see-through top, and lots of crosses—the Catholic ones with the body still on them.

I would also see Marty each day in class, not to mention on Saturday mornings. Pretty soon we started dating and sometimes he'd come over for dinner. My friend Erika called him a geek, but then again, she called everybody a geek. Then there were my friends Trey and Randy who were both a year older than me. Trey would sometimes give me a ride in the Jeep that his father got him that year for his sixteenth birthday, and Randy would usually just tag along until the day he met Cindy, then the two of them were always together. Erika, Diane, Lisa, and Jason lived just down the street in Placentia, and sometimes I would go there to visit.

"Look, bitch, this ain't Yorba Linda!" Erika hissed the day that I noticed her place "looked really small."

"We call it Sissyland," Jason confirmed.

"Yeah, Jayce, after all the sissies like you and Dexter," Erika taunted.

The odd thing was, after the divorce papers finally went through, I ended up living with my father and Susie in one of the Sissyland condos. My mom moved out of David's house and lived with my brother in a two-bedroom apartment somewhere down the street. My mother and David were still dating, but decided it was better living apart. My mother asked me who I'd rather live with.

"By now, you realize your father and I will not be living together anymore," she told me. "So, you need to let me know right now who you'd rather live with. So Pammy, who do you love more, me or your father?"

I'm not sure that she ever got over me choosing my dad, but that was where all my friends were living, and besides, I didn't want to switch schools since I was already doing so well at Troy. On the other hand, my brother Ron had a car and a job and didn't want to leave my mother alone. But I was her baby and from what I heard, shortly after I moved in with my dad, my mom started drinking again.

It wasn't long after we moved in, that I had to learn all the lines for the play. I was Tatania in *Midsummer Night's*. And that led me to where this all started. What did you say your name was again?

"Virgil," he told me.

He looked like an ancient professor with a long white tunic and a scroll that he carried wherever he went. His hair was combed forward like Julius Caesar, and a laurel wreath hung neatly over his whitening locks.

"Shit, how long have I been asleep?"

"Time is not something that we keep over here," he answered. "It may have been days, or it may have been years."

I'm not even sure that I slept the whole time. I had seen two of my friends looking in through the window trying to get me to come outside. They were telling jokes and asking when I'd be back in school.

"Come on, Pam, you've got to get up. We'll be doing *Merchants of Venice* and you should be Portia, since you're already a rich bitch and all." Then he held his head and started to cry before the nurses came to take him away. "Come on, Pam, we're counting on you!"

"Trey!" I called out but he couldn't hear me. "Trey!" I tried to shout through some invisible barrier that held me inside.

Sometimes, my family came to in see me and my father often fell asleep in the chair next to my bed until my mother and David walked in and he ended up leaving. I was really sad when my mother would come. She would always bring me some flowers that she put in a vase on the nightstand, then she would just sit down and cry. The same with Veronica who sometimes came after work when Don was at home watching the baby. I could hear their voices and sometimes even feel their pain, but I couldn't respond. It was like I was locked inside of a tunnel.

"This does not surprise me," Virgil responded in a hushed, patient tone as if he had seen this movie before. "Those who are here cannot cross over."

"But where am I?" I asked. "And when can I leave?"

"That's all up to the chief commander," he said.

"Chief Commander?" I asked.

"Of course. The Lord of the Universe. Some call him God, while others choose to call him by name."

"What's that?" I pressed him.

"That would be Jesus, the Christ, the living Lord of the Universe. I never knew him when I was alive, but now I just do whatever he says."

"So, this is your home?"

"Yes."

"Is it heaven or hell?"

"Neither," he said. "But it's as good as it gets. I live up there on the hill," he added, pointing somewhere out in the distance. "We call it the Citadel. There's lots of people who live there with me, some of them I'm sure that you'll read about in school one day. Good people, all of them—it's just that, we didn't..."

"Didn't what?" I asked.

"We didn't believe," he finally said. "Where he lives, I cannot go, but maybe you will be able someday."

"You mean someday, I can meet Jesus?" I asked him.

He didn't really give me an answer but moving his hands over his scroll, he read a verse inscribed next to one of the millions of names all carefully engraved in some ancient text. "This is not your final home. In fact, most people on earth never come to this place."

"Then where do they go?" I inquired.

"I'd rather not say," he answered, shaking his head. "But you are one of those rare exceptions whose day of reckoning has not yet arrived. In other words, it is not your time."

I wanted to ask him what he meant by "it is not your time," but he suddenly disappeared from my room. The next thing I knew I was standing aside the water's edge where the same old man with the scraggly beard, his eyes still fixed in a fiery glare, put down his craft and hoisted the sail. He said nothing, just waved me on board, and I went back through the trees before we sailed into a deep impenetrable fog. Every now and again, I could hear their voices, some familiar, some not, but the voices grew louder the farther we went.

When the fog finally lifted, I was laying down in a bed and I felt somebody holding my hand. Light from a window came into a room where all of my family was standing, some crying, while others were praying. Then I heard my mother's voice, soft and gentle, like the voice I'd heard when I was a baby and she'd rock me to sleep.

"Oh, Pammy, I love you," she said over and over. Then my father joined in "Hang in there, baby."

I leaned over as far as I could as the mist began to shift under the light. I tried to breathe, but the tube sticking out of my throat made it impossible.

"Doctor come here!" I heard one of the nurses say. "I think that... I think that she's starting to breathe on her own!"

"You're crazy!" The man who I believed was the doctor shot back, the sound of his clipboard smacking the table. "I just checked her this morning. Nothing's changed for more than a week."

"But she's moving," the nurse pleaded with him. "Please, come over and see for yourself."

"She is! She is!" My mother spoke up. "I think she can hear us!

The doctor sighed loudly into the air then I heard him walk to my bed. "Oh, Pammy we love you! We love you!" My mother repeated over and over as the doctor lifted the edge of the mask from over his mouth. "Can you hear us, Pammy? Please give us a sign."

Then the doctor now speaking in a low and monotone voice started to ask me a question.

"Young lady. If you can hear me right now, please lift your right hand."

The room went silent all around as both of my parents stood by the bed. A minute passed by without a response, so the doctor repeated himself. Still there was nothing. After a few more tries, the doctor tore off his mask and looked at my parents.

"Mr. and Mrs. Vasquez," he said in a soft empathic tone that seemed rehearsed by so many years of seeing the worst. "I know that you both love your daughter, but I need to caution you against getting your hopes up." When he heard my mother starting to cry, he softened his tone. "What I'm trying to say, is that this young lady was seriously injured. We had to remove over forty percent of her brain. I promise we're doing all that we can, but there's still a chance."

My mom cut him off. "A chance of what?"

The doctor paused to collect himself then took a moment choosing his words. "There is a chance that even if she survives, she will always remain a vegetable."

"Doctor, you don't know Pam!" My mother said in a voice I remember hearing when I was a child right before she ended up smacking someone. "Pam is a fighter! She wasn't even supposed to be born—she spent the first four months of her life in an incubator, has lived through more shit than you can ever imagine! If anyone is going to make it, *she* is the one!"

The doctor just sighed and turned from the side of my bed, then a few minutes later he walked back over and spoke to my mother. "Listen ma'am. I have an idea. She may not be ready to lift her hand yet due to atrophy in all of her muscles, what do you say we try something else?"

"I'm all ears, doc," my father said while my mother just stood there and sulked.

"Okay. Young lady, if you can hear us, please try opening one of your eyes."

As the doctor was speaking, I felt a hand clasped tightly around one of mine—soft and gentle, yet strong and assured. I remember that hand when I was a baby as it once led me out of a stroller when I was taking my very first steps and walked me outside to wait for the bus on the first day of school. I remember back then that it had a ring around one of its fingers, but this hand didn't have any ring. Yet, I still wanted to squeeze it in mine and pull it up to my lips and never let go. Then the doctor asked the same question again.

"Young lady, if you can hear me..."

I made one final push as a rush of air filled up in my lungs, and a flicker of light started coming in like fractured shards of broken glass. There was pain, each tiny beam like a series of fiery needles, then a wall full of shadows. But I could hear their voices and felt the hand now squeezing me tighter. Then my mom began to repeat after the doctor and the pain started all over again.

"She can hear us! She can hear us!" my mother shouted.

"Of course I can," I wanted to say. "Now will all of you just shut up?"

Then I heard my mother ask me one final question, and when I opened my eyes this time, it didn't hurt quite as bad. It was as if I was standing in a sea of light and the shadows stole away all the glare, each fiery beam swallowed up in their voices.

"Pammy, do you know how much we love you?"

This time I wasn't afraid of the pain, I slowly opened one of my eyes, and then the other, embracing the light and the love that I felt all around me. Then again, I heard the doctor telling my mom that I still had a long way to go, but things looked much better. She let out a huff as if to say, "I told you so." Yet, after eleven weeks in a coma, it was clear to everyone in the room that the girl who had died that night in April had come back to life.

PART III:
BORN TWICE

"And when the Earth shall claim your limbs, then shall
you truly dance."
—*Kahlil Gibran*

"It is worth dying to find out what life is."
—*T.S. Eliot*

"When snatched from the jaws of death, tooth marks are
to be expected."
—*Hal Story, near-death experiencer*

As I walked out through the hospital door, I had soon
come to realize that dying was easy; living again? That
was much harder."
—*Pamela Vasquez-Kuznik*

LOVE YOU MORE

Sometime after the Fourth of July, my father was talking with one of the doctors. They were both complaining about the weather.

"A hundred and seven today in L.A., even hotter up where I live. I thought I was going to melt in my car."

But there I was in a blanket, shivering underneath a vent. I was still unable to speak, so the doctors would ask me "yes" or "no" questions and I would respond by blinking my eyes. The brightness still caused me a great deal of pain, so the lights in my room were kept low and the curtains were drawn to conceal the glare of the sun's fiery rays. That was the way things went at the time, everyone asking me "yes" or "no" questions and I would answer by blinking. I remember my father noticed me shaking and walked up to my bed asking me if I was cold.

"Would one of you please get her another blanket?" my father said as I slowly lifted both of my eyelids.

Later, as I began to get better, the doctors would have me answer their questions with a nod for "yes" and a shake for "no." Then there was the day that my mother came in with David while my dad and Veronica sat on the chairs next to my bed. My father got up to go, then my mom told him to sit back down. "No, Ron, please stay," she insisted. By that time, my breathing was better, and the doctors were talking about moving me somewhere else closer to home.

"Mr. and Mrs. Vasquez," the doctor said, as he put down his clipboard. "We're going to be transferring her to St. Jude's over in Fullerton. We've done all that we can over here. They will be doing all of the physical therapy and speech pathology with her."

"Speech what?" my father spoke up.

"They're going to try to teach her to talk," the doctor answered him.

"Well don't be in too much of a hurry," my father said. "When Pam was little, I couldn't ever get her to stop!"

My mother and David both shot him a look before my father turned back to the doctor. "Well, that's great news. I'm glad to see that she's doing better."

"Well, it is looking better," the doctor cautioned, "but I still don't want to make any promises. She still has got a long way to go."

Later that summer they took the tube out of my neck, leaving behind a two-inch scar and a sudden rush of hot air that filled up my throat like a torrent of molten lava. I wanted to scream, but the sound would not escape from my mouth.

The next morning, the paramedics came and lifted me out of my bed and put me inside a red and white truck. I got really scared when the driver turned on his lights and bright red circles flashed all around me. When I got to my room, my parents were waiting. They told the nurses what kind of music I liked and my favorite flavors of ice cream.

It was there that I spent the next few months learning to talk all over again. At first, I could only make guttural sounds like that of a newborn, then they tried to start me on vowels, sometimes guiding my mouth with latex glove-covered fingers. I don't recall how many times they got bit, but there was no other way of letting them know when I wanted to stop. "Well, it looks like we're done for the day," one of the nurses would tell me, then the other would usually take off her gloves and feed me some ice cream. That would go on for a week or so until the day that I learned the sooner I bit, the sooner the ice cream, and that's when they started feeding me mashed potatoes instead.

They also sent somebody in to work on my hands and to try to get me to sit up in my bed. That also did not go over too well as what little movement I had in my hands was directed in the form of a punch or a scratch at the onset of even the slightest discomfort. Then one of the doctors had the bright idea of playing the tapes that my parents sent them on a little cassette deck beside my bed. Pretty soon I was singing along as best as I could and moving my hands and my feet in time to the music. Then some of the nurses would come in and join me and the whole room was filled with singing and dancing as Prince, Madonna, and Michael Jackson rang out through the hall.

Then one day, sometime around Christmas, my mother and David came into visit. At least I think it was Christmas because she was saying how cold it was getting and that it was "really raining outside." She put a box on the table all wrapped up in ribbons and bows that she told me was "from Santa" and that I could open it tomorrow morning. She stayed for a while and talked to the nurses, then stood by my bed holding my hand. The nurses told her how well I was doing, all things considered, and that pretty soon they'd be having me walk.

"We're going to start slowly," the head nurse assured her. "Then as she gets stronger, we'll get her a walker. Now, as far as her vision's concerned, that seems to be progressing much slower."

"So, what you're telling me then is my daughter is going to be blind?" my mother said to the nurse.

"Mrs. Vasquez," the nurse informed her, "it's still way too early to tell. But don't give up hope. That girl of yours is a real fighter!"

My mom thanked the nurses for all they were doing, then I heard David tell her that my father pulled in and they needed to go. Then I heard my mother put on her jacket and felt her lips against my cheek.

"Good-bye now, honey, we'll see you tomorrow," she told me as she took hold of one of my hands, giving it a small gentle squeeze. "We love you!" Then her and David walked to the door, as my father was making his way down the hall.

The next thing I knew I took a small breath and opened my mouth as far as I could—breathing and gasping together until the words that were held in my chest poured like a flood into my bosom then finally escaped from out of my mouth. "I-I-I..." I stammered and stuttered taking in one last gulp of air, then I pursed my lips until each letter was perfectly formed and rang out all together at once. "And I love you more!"

When my father got there, he ran down the hall to where my mom was lying flat on her back in front of my door.

"What the hell, has Ginny been drinking?" he said as he and David lifted her back onto her feet.

"Not that I know of," David answered. "Here honey, you tell him."

"Ron, you are such an ass!" She said, wiping the tears away from her eyes. "Don't you want to know about Pam?"

"Yes, yes, how is she doing?" he asked.

"Pam is all right," she said as she started to cry all over again. "She said that she loves us Ron! Both of us heard it, sure as we're standing here. She *said* that she *loves* us!"

LONG ROAD BACK

Soon after I had started to talk, for the next few weeks, no one could seem to shut me up. It was like I was making up for all the lost time I had spent with a tube in my throat. Then, when the doctors decided I was ready, I'd be learning to walk all over again. At first, the nurses would help me get into the bathroom, then they'd start taking me down the hall.

I still could not see very well, only the lights that shined from above and the shadows that they made on the walls. Sometimes, the shadows had voices and hands that reached out to pull me back into their lair, like the day that I heard a voice calling my name as one that came from a distant nightmare and a face peering out at me through the glass. "Pam, Pam," I heard it say. "Pam! Pam!"

"How do you know my name?" I asked.

"We followed you here." Then she kept on calling my name. "Pam, Pam."

I started to scream, then one of the nurses turned me around. "She's hallucinating." The other one said. "Get her back into her room and have the doctor start an IV."

When the nurse tried to put me back into bed, I started kicking and screaming before the doctor came in and I soon felt the tip of a cold steel spear slide into my veins.

"No! No! Don't let me sleep! They're going to kill me!"

"Who? Who's going to kill you?" the nurse asked, grabbing both of my arms.

"Lost Eyes!" I screamed. "She's going to kill me tonight in my sleep!"

The nightmares went on for the next few days, until the day they sent in a priest.

"Young lady," he said in a slight lilting brogue. "No one can hurt you. God sent His angels here to protect you."

"But I'm not sure if I even believe there's a God." I shrugged.

"Ah, but He still believes in you and He's not going to let anything hurt you," he calmly assured. "Just say this prayer each night before bed – 'Angel of God, my guardian dear...'"

I said it with him, then again that night before I went to bed. Pretty soon, the nightmares stopped, and I was finally able to sleep.

The next morning when I woke up, my mom brought her sister Loretta with her to see me.

"Come on, Pammy." My mother said as the nurses came in to get me. "Show your aunt how well you can walk."

When I tried to get up, my leg started cramping and I screamed out in pain.

"Will all of you just leave me alone?" I shouted pushing away both of their hands. "Don't touch me or I swear I will kick you!"

"Remember, Pammy, no pain, no gain." I heard my aunt Loretta tell me, and I threatened to kick her as well, until my mom intervened.

"You don't talk to your auntie that way!" she shot back.

"Why can't everybody just leave me alone? Every day its Pammy this and Pammy that! Pammy you've got to try harder! Pammy you've got to ignore all the pain!" Then I looked at both my mom and her sister. "Let me ask you this, how many of you ever smashed open your head on the pavement?"

Then there were days when I felt pretty good and was sometimes able to walk on my own with nurses standing on either side. One day I made it all the way down the hall then turned around and walked back to my room. As I got back, I heard my mom, my dad, and her sister clapping, then the nurses joined in for a round of applause that lasted for minutes.

"You keep this up and pretty soon you'll be running a marathon," one of the doctors said as he came in the room and shook everyone's hand. "My name is Dr. Tamari, Neurosurgeon. I'll be doing the neoplasti."

"A neo *what*?" my father asked.

"A neoplasti," the doctor said. "It's to protect her head while her brain continues to heal. The good news is that she's stabilized enough to where we can do the procedure."

"So, they're going to need to cut her back open?" I heard my mom saying.

"Fuck that idea!" I shouted when I finally began to make out what they were saying.

"I'm sorry, doctor, Pam is still learning how to properly speak," Loretta broke in. "I know that a doctor as nice as you will be taking good care of her."

"Well that is the plan," he said looking more than a little confused. "Look, you folks get some rest. I'll talk to you later."

"See you, Tamari!" Loretta waived as he walked out the door.

When the day finally came, the nurses needed to hold me back down. "But, honey, don't you want to get better?" They asked me.

"No!" I said. "I want to go home!"

Before long, I was in a room with tubes sticking out of my veins and a large clear mask covered my face. My whole body was starting to shake, and the doctor held my arm on the table so that I wouldn't pull out the needle. Then there was a circle of faces that danced all around in the light up above—speaking and chanting, casting their spells, summoning the rod of Asclepius. "Angel of God..." I started repeating. "Angel of God, my guardian dear..." Then suddenly I awoke in my room where my mom and dad and Loretta were waiting.

One day, I woke up and rubbed my hand on the top of my head. "It's gone! It's gone!" I screamed. "*All* of my hair!"

"Don't worry," I heard one of the doctors say. By the sound of his voice I could tell that he was much older, and he spoke in a thick middle-eastern accent. "Yours will grow back!"

The doctors had me on some pretty heavy drugs and for a while I couldn't remember much of anything, but one day, I woke up and heard Dr. Tamari talking to both my mom and my dad using words that neither one of them could quite understand.

"What the hell is an oculus lobe?" I heard my dad saying.

"The primary function of the *occipital* lobe is to control vision and to recognize objects." Dr. Tamari responded. "Damage often results in vision loss, an inability to identify colors, hallucinations, and in extreme cases total blindness."

"I see," I could hear my dad saying while I heard my mother starting to cry. "And the other one that you mentioned, what about that?

"Yes, yes, the *frontal* lobe," he said as he sighed heavily into the air. "That one's more complicated. Common effects of frontal lobe damage are sudden behavioral changes, memory loss, impaired moral judgment, and lack of reasoning. It's like becoming a child all over again."

"Well at least she was always a good little girl." I heard my dad say.

"Shut up, Ron!" My mother snapped back. "Doctor, is there any chance that she'll fully recover? I mean, she's only fifteen?"

"Ms. Vasquez, you just made my point," he answered. "Her age is exactly what works in her favor. No offense, but if Pam was our age, she probably would not have survived the accident. What she needs now is a stable and nurturing environment, the more stable and loving, the better.

"Thanks doc," I heard my dad say as my mom began with a new round of sniffles.

"We'll do everything we can for her," she promised before taking my hand and squeezing it softly. "Isn't that right, Ron?"

"You know it," he said. "Boy, do you know it."

For the next few weeks, I stayed in bed, then the nurses would come in every morning and I started going for walks down the hall. Then one day, my mom came to visit, carrying both a box and a suitcase. "Pammy!" she said. "Great news! The doctor said I can take you back home!"

"What?" I asked her.

"You're going home!" she told me.

"When?"

"Today! Today! Aren't you excited?" Then she opened the box and put a long dark brown wig on top of my head.

"There you go!" she said, sweeping back the long brown curls that hung down in my face. "Just like the Pammy we all remember!"

"But it hurts!" I objected trying to pull it back off my head.

"You'll get used to it, honey." My mother assured me. "You don't want everybody to see all your stitches.

It was April 5, 1986, eleven and a half months after I died, and I was finally getting out of the hospital. There were hugs all around and one last bowl of ice cream, then I walked out the hospital door and into a whole new world outside.

"Where are we going?" I asked my mom as she helped me inside of the car then sat down next to David in the front seat.

"You're going to be staying with Ronnie and me," she said.

"But what about Dad?" I asked her. "Why can't you just take me to Dads?"

"His condo has stairs, remember? We don't want you getting hurt. Besides," she assured me, "I promise to take really good care of you. When you get better, I'll take you shopping and we can get you all new clothes. Would you like that, Pammy?"

"Yeah," I said, "but I still miss my dad."

"You'll still see your father," she promised. "He'll be picking you up on the weekends to take you to breakfast. You'll be seeing plenty of him."

For a month or so, things went pretty well. My mother cooked all of my favorite meals and slept next to me at night in her bed. Sometimes, I would awake from a nightmare and she would get up and caress me until I went back to sleep, stroking the hair that had already started growing back on my head.

"There now, everything's going to be all right," she would tell me. "You have Mommy here to protect you."

Except for the night that she tried to kill me.

That night, she came to bed late when I was already asleep. But I could tell that she had been drinking. I heard her swearing and yelling at someone, even though there was no one else in the room.

"God, why did you do this to me!" she raged, shaking both of her fists at the ceiling. "First it was Loretta's kids, then now look at what you did to my daughter—my baby! She used to be so smart and so pretty but look at her now! You made her into some kind of freak—a retard—a vegetable! How dare you, Goddammit! How dare you! And Marty, what did he ever do to you? It must have been Pam's idea to go out there that night! I knew I should never have had her. If only I would have listened to the doctors and had her aborted, none of this would ever have happened!"

I opened my eyes to see waves of red hair and fiery eyes staring down into mine. She set down the glass she was holding then leaned over to where I was laying as I pushed myself up into the wall.

"And you!" she said, writhing over to my side of the bed like a serpent hissing ominously through the grass. "It's all your fault!"

"Angel of God. Angel of God," I began to cry to myself as I felt her breath up against my neck."

"Your God is not going to save you, you little bitch! You little fucking bitch!" she screamed. "Oh, sweet little Pammy, the good little girl that everyone loved—the girl who could do no wrong, Daddy's little girl! My God how you had everyone fooled!"

Then she started to hit me as her rings began to cut into my head. "You are the spawn of Satan himself! Shiva! Pele! Erebus! Begone, oh you daughter of darkness!"

I tried to hide from her under the covers, but she pulled off the blanket, ripping off patches of scalp still caught in the threads. "You are the reason Marty is dead! It should have been *you* that night instead of him!" She took a minute to regain her breath, then like the eye of the storm held for a moment by an angry vortex of spiraling rage, the beating started all over again. *You* are the reason I drink! I never got drunk until *after* I had you! You little bitch—it's all *your* fault that I drink!"

I don't know how long the beating continued, at some point I passed out on my blood-covered sheets and my brother was holding my mother down next to me. He picked up the phone, then an ambulance came and took me away. Then when I saw him a few days later, he came with my father who took me back to stay at his condo. No sooner did we walk in the door then I asked my brother what had happened.

"You were having a nightmare," he said, "and when Mom came in, she saw you pulling out all of your stitches. That's when we took you to the ER."

I thought about everything that he told me but somehow it all just didn't make sense.

"Are you sure?" I finally asked him. "Because that is *not* what I remember."

Then he looked at me with stern dark eyes and grabbed me by each of my shoulders. "If anyone asks you, just remember everything the way that I told you." Then he lowered his head and spoke in a voice that seemed like a threat. "And don't you *dare* say anything else!"

I was now living back home with my dad and I even had the same room that I did on the day of the accident. Only this time, Loretta was sharing it with me, since my father had asked her to look after me while he was at work. She usually slept on the bed right next to me, but then there were days that my father's door opened, and it was her walking out in a robe. My cousin Susie was also living with us. Her and her friend Michelle stayed in the room right next to mine, so it was like deja vu all over again!

One morning, I got up to go to the bathroom and I heard the door open in front of me.

"Hey, cuz," Susie said.

"Hey, Sue."

"I heard that you got banged up pretty bad. Feeling any better?" She asked.

"Yeah," I answered. "Depends on what you mean by better."

"Hey, you remember Michelle?" she inquired.

"No," I answered. "Why, should I?"

"Her fucking parents threw her out and your dad said she could stay here with us."

"That's fine, I guess. Just make sure she doesn't bother me," I said before walking inside and closing the door.

For the next few weeks, Susie and I never talked about the accident. But there were times when I heard her in the next room telling her friend it was all my fault. Sometimes I awoke to the smell of weed coming in through my window and the two girls giggling inside of their room.

I would ask Loretta, "Hey, would you tell your daughter to knock that shit off. It's making it hard for me to breathe."

"Come on, Pammy, leave her alone," was all she would say. "Besides, it helps her get through all of the shit she's having to deal with."

"That *she's* having to deal with!" I snapped. "What about all of the shit that *I* have to deal with, not to mention my fucking asthma?"

Sometimes, during the day, two of my neighbors, Neil and Jeff, would come over and take me for walks. By this time, I was starting to walk with a cane. At first, I hated it since I didn't like looking like "some fucking old lady" but it felt really good to finally get out. The days were warm, and the air was ripe with the smell honeysuckle that grew in our complex that time of the year. Sometimes, they would take me out in the evening, and we'd walk around by the swimming pool, the pale blue light shining out through the trees. I was still not able to see very well, but the smell of chlorine reminded me of those long hot summers in Yorba Linda when I would hang out at the Lopez's house. Then there was the day I went for a walk and I heard Jeff saying hello to some lady, then as we got closer, I could hear her calling my name in a voice that was barely a whisper.

"Pam!" she said. "How is my BFF?"

"Erika? Is that you?"

"Do you have any other BFF's?" she asked.

"It's just that I can't see you," I told her. "The doctors tell me I'm legally blind. I'm also paralyzed in my left hand. See", I explained holding it up.

"Let me get this straight. So, *you* are legally blind, partially paralyzed, and *I* am now barely able speak?" she pondered. "Well, that's pretty fucked up."

"How did you end up losing your voice?" I asked her.

"The car accident, or don't you remember?" She snorted. "I was sitting right in back of you when you put us all on Carbon Canyon. Crushed both of my lungs and fucked up my larynx. Took four operations before I could talk."

Then Jeff reached up and put an arm around both of her shoulders. "But I still love her!" He said.

"I didn't know that you two were dating?" I told her.

"There's a lot of things that you don't know," she said. "We'll have to sit down and catch up sometime."

"Sure," I said somewhat confused. "Hey, tell Marty I said 'hello.'"

"Marty's dead," she snapped. "He's been dead for over a year or don't you remember? Anyway, I've got to go."

She gave Jeff a kiss on the cheek and turned and walked back to her condo as Jeff and Neil led me back to my door. Then, suddenly, my mother's words all came back to me like a flood. Marty is dead and it's *all* my fault.

I spent most of my days either out at the pool or going to see my physical therapist. She made me a splint to wear on my hand and told me that swimming would also help me to open my fingers and although things got better, I was never fully able to use it—just dangled right there at my side, a placeholder for my *Medic Alert* bracelet. Sometimes I stayed in the pool all day until my father would come and get me for dinner. Sometimes, he took me out to his car and told me we were going to a fancy French restaurant—Jacque in ze box—he would joke. A few weeks later, my dad and Loretta took me for an eye exam—my first since I got out of the hospital. It was then that I learned the extent of my blindness.

"20/800 in both of her eyes." The doctor said as I could hear my father starting to wince. "That's four times worse than legally blind."

"Is there anything you can do for her, doctor?" he asked.

"Yeah, and not make me look like a nerd in the process?" I added.

"Well, we'll never be able to fully correct her, but we can probably get her under 20/200," He assured him then added turning toward me, "And besides, we have lots of new frames so I promise you will not look like a nerd."

I got both a clear and a tinted pair with matching rose colored Cartier frames. Loretta said how pretty I looked while my dad just mumbled about the cost. Anyway, my vision was better, but I still couldn't always make out what I saw. I spent the last part of the summer outside at the pool and when I wasn't swimming, I was up in my room thinking about the world I left behind and how soon I would have to face it again when I went back to school that year.

That day finally came about a week before my sixteenth birthday. It should have been my junior year, but instead I was technically still a freshman. By then my hair had begun growing back, but I still decided to go with a wig. Loretta put it on for me that morning, carefully brushing its highlighted bangs.

"My now, don't we look pretty?" she said.

"Whatever," I shrugged.

Most of my classes were special ed with the exception of Theater Arts with my favorite teacher Mr. Moore. My first day in class, the first one to greet me was a young man named Michael who once tried asking me out until I told him that I was too good for him. Michael was five years older than me and also legally blind. He was finally graduating that year at the age of twenty-one.

"Just do everything that they tell you," he'd say. "And they'll pass you right through. All of the work here is really easy."

Except I didn't do everything that they told me, and even though the work was easy, within a few days, I was totally bored.

"So, who can tell me what two and two equals?" the teacher would ask. "Pamela, can you tell me what two and two equals?"

"Four, of course," I said while rolling my eyes. "How stupid do you think that I am?"

"Now, Pamela. Nobody here thinks that you're stupid," she said in that annoying voice I grew to despise.

Then the next day she asked us to recite the alphabet. "This is such bullshit!" I said as I looked over at Michael who was kicking the letters around in his head while humming that stupid alphabet song. Next thing I knew, I got sent to the office. Things didn't go much better in Drama class either. The only people who would still talk to me where Michael and Trey.

"Hey, Tatania, nice having you back!" Trey said as he gave me a hug.

"Pam is my friend," Michael added. "She's in all of my classes this year, her and Christina!"

It may have well been the kiss of death. Most of the other students shined me; the ones who didn't openly mocked me. "It looks like Tatania is now part of the retard class!" they would say, and they'd all start laughing. One day after class, I stood on the stage and started to cry. Then I threatened to jump off head-first until Mr. Moore ran over to stop me.

"I think this is high enough to break my neck," I said as a stream of hot tears poured down my cheeks.

"Pam, just ignore them," Mr. Moore pleaded. "None of them mean any harm. They just don't know how else to respond."

A few days later I heard a familiar voice ring out through the intercom. I could tell as soon as I heard it that is was Trey. "Attention, Troy High School, I just want to take a few minutes to say, I am still friends with Pamela Vasquez. And no matter what anyone thinks, I will always be her friend. Two years ago, most of you losers would do anything to be her best friend. Now you losers want nothing to do with her. How pathetic! It wasn't Pam's fault what happened to her!" Then suddenly the voice cut out then a few seconds later the principal came on and apologized.

I thanked him when I saw him a few days later after he served his suspension.

"You are the only friend I have left," I told him.

"Come on, Pam, that isn't true," he tried to convince me. "You still have lots of friends around here, they're just afraid to show it."

"What do you mean?" I asked him.

"People fear what they don't know," he said. "It's easier for them to avoid you rather than to confront their own fear."

"Fear of what?"

"Fear of their *own* mortality," he said. "See you tomorrow?"

"Sure," I told him. "Hey, thanks, Trey!"

The next day I ran into Mike and Paul who sat next to Michael, Christina, and I in the cafeteria. Michael had developed a thing for Christina so that took some of the pressure off me.

"I'm so sorry to hear about what happened," Mike said as he put his bag down on the table.

"Don't pity me!" I warned him. "I don't need anyone's pity!"

"It's not pity," Paul interrupted. "We just wanted you to know how good it is to see you again."

"And to remind me that you were right!" I stopped him.

"Right about what?" he asked.

"Right about there being a "god," because he certainly proved it to me!"

"So, you think that God is some cruel tyrant who gets his kicks out of maiming people just to prove his existence?" Mike interrupted.

"Sure looks that way."

"Then why don't you meet us tomorrow in study hall and see for yourself what God is like?" Mike asked me. "I lead a devotion there every day and you're welcome to join us."

"I'll think about it," I told him.

I don't know why, but I started going to Mike's bible study each day after school, it was much different from all those assholes in Drama. For one, I was fully accepted, despite my disabilities. Sometimes they would even offer to pray for me, and I reluctantly let them, despite my own suspicions about them. Not to mention, all of them seemed to genuinely care about me, not because I was on Drill Team or had the leading role in a play, but because as they put it, I was "such a blessing" to them. When I was little, my father had warned me about all those "religious people." He would remind me what phonies they were and that most of them couldn't be trusted "as far as you'd throw them." I remember that I used to believe him, but all I knew was that except for Trey, Michael, and Mr. Moore, they were the only ones who at least seemed to give a shit.

One day after school, Mike invited me to his mother's for dinner.

"Mom, this is Pam. Pam, this is my mother, Ruth," he said as we walked through the door and into the kitchen.

"Nice to meet you, Pam," she said extending not just a hand but a hug. "Mike has told me so many things about you. You are a living miracle, honey."

As it turned out, Ruth was a living miracle too. Her first husband was an alcoholic who abused both her and her children. When he died, she became a foster mom and Mike and her daughter Betty were always the older brother and sister to the changing seas of names and faces and stories. I would visit Ruth each day after school and since she lived only a few blocks away, either her or Mike would walk me back home. Then one day, she invited me to church with her and her family.

"So where are you going all dressed up?" My father said as my aunt Loretta walked me down the stairs and into the kitchen.

"To church, Daddy," I answered.

"Why do you bother wasting your time?" was all that he said. "I'm sure you can find something better to do than hang around with a bunch of holy rollers thumping their bibles."

"Pammy, don't listen to him," Loretta told me. "You look beautiful, my dear, doesn't she, Ron?"

My father said nothing, just sat in his chair and picked up the paper. When Ruth came to get me, he had Loretta answer the door.

"See you both later. Love you!" I said as I left.

"Yeah, yeah," he mumbled. "Don't be too long."

Ruth told me the name of her church, *Yorba Linda Friends Community*, and when we got there, I was expecting it to be like that old Catholic church my grandmother took me to when I was little. Instead, there were drums and guitars and everyone clapping along to the music. And all of the people were really friendly. It was like no one noticed that I was unable to see and that my left hand didn't work. And the sermon, something about the "one lost little sheep" and how God would always go out of His way to bring it back home. I had to admit there were times that I cried, as if that one lost sheep was me and that God was trying to bring *me* back home.

I went to church with Ruth and her family every Sunday, then afterward, we'd go out to breakfast. No matter where we went, we would always pray before eating.

"Pam why don't you say the blessing?" Ruth asked as the server set the food on our table.

Then I bowed my head and thanked God for the first time in my life for everything that He'd given to me—friends who loved me, a whole new family, and even a second chance at life. I thanked Him for the doctors who made me better and for the paramedics who found my body lying in the street and did all that they could to save my life. But mostly, I thanked Him for my friend Ruth who had become like a second mother to me.

The next week, after the minister spoke, I felt something lifting me out of my seat as the band played "Come as You Are." I turned and looked at Ruth, then nodded my head when she asked me if I was ready. The next thing I knew I was standing down by the stage looking up at an old wooden cross and praying to receive Jesus into my heart. It was like the heavens opened before me and love poured down all around as the autumn light strained in through the windows and shined on my face. For a moment, I was no longer aware of my own disabilities and for the first time in my life, I truly felt whole. As I walked back to my seat, I could feel the embrace of what felt like a thousand arms all around me, everyone welcoming me into the family of God.

CLINGING TO LIGHT

When I got home, I couldn't wait to tell my father what happened.

"Dad, guess what happened in church?" I asked him.

"I don't want to hear it," he said. "You know that I don't believe in that shit."

"Well today, I got saved!" I told him, my face still beaming. "I got saved and now I'm going to heaven!"

"Well that's nice," he said. "Send me a postcard."

Things didn't go much better at school.

"So not only is Pam in the retard class, she's now hanging out with all of the holy rollers," I heard some girls in Drama class saying.

"Well you can all go straight to hell!" I told them. "It's the perfect place for bitches like you."

Back at home, Susie and Michelle were doing everything that they could to make my life miserable. Sometimes we'd be at the table eating and one of them would throw something at me.

"Hey, knock that shit off!" I'd tell them as a dirty napkin would land on my plate.

Other times a pea or a carrot would hit me on the top of my head and stick in my hair then fall to the ground when I stood to get up. I told Loretta, but both girls denied that they did anything.

"Pam doesn't know what she's talking about. Besides, she can't even see!" Susie told her mom when she asked her what happened. One day, I finally got up and smacked her, but Michelle and Susie snitched to my dad and he got really pissed then sent me upstairs to my room. Then there was the constant smell of weed in the house when my father and Loretta weren't there.

"Smoking that shit will send you to hell!" I would shout as I'd bang on their door while both of them just sat there and giggled.

I also tried to get my dad to stop drinking and going out to bars to meet women with similar threats of eternal destruction.

"You know the bible tells us not to get drunk," I told him when he came home late on a Saturday night.

"Yeah, and didn't *your* Jesus also turn water into wine?" he mocked.

"But he didn't tell them to drink it then get in a car!" I scolded then walked up stairs to my room.

Other times when I talked about God, he would stick his fingers into his ears. When that didn't work, he would just sit there and hum until I was finished. Once, he got so mad that he threatened to have me committed.

"In my house we do not *ever* talk about God!" he warned me. "You keep this up and I'll have you locked up in Fairview!"

"So I can't even say 'God bless you' if you sneeze?" I asked him.

"No!"

"But the bible says—" I tried to respond, but he kept on shouting.

"The bible is just a collection of fairy tales. Just like Santa Claus and the Easter Bunny."

Then Susie and Michelle both chimed in. "Not to mention the tooth fairy."

"Shut up, Sue!" I shouted back. "Both you and that drug addict whore!"

"The next thing I knew, there was a loud smack and a brief flash of light in front of my face as the sting of his hand throbbed on my cheek.

"Now look what you went and forced me to do!" my father shouted then he started pacing and taking deep breaths. "Goddamn it, I can't fucking believe it!" Then he walked to the kitchen, got himself a drink and sat down in his chair. "It's not you, it's not you okay, it's what you've become after that nosy old bitch started taking you with her to that cult she's a part of."

"But, Daddy, Ruth is my friend." I objected.

"Friends wouldn't turn you against your own family! He got up and started screaming again. "You tell her next time you see her that she is not to set foot in my house!"

The next week that she took me to church, Loretta had to walk me outside to meet her in front of our garage. Then when I told her what had happened at home, it didn't surprise her.

"You know, the bible says, those who will live godly in Christ Jesus shall suffer persecution." She said. "Pam, this means you're on the right track."

"Well I still don't like it!" I told her.

"No one does, honey. But remember, darkness cannot comprehend light," she said, then quoted some verse in the bible.

"There's still so much that I don't understand," I told her. "It's like I've not only lost most of my friends, but I'm starting to lose my family as well."

"Then you need to make new friends," she said, then thought for a second. "Hey, why don't you come with us to the Harvest Festival next week in the park? There'll be lots of new people for you to talk to."

It was the Sunday morning before Halloween. The day was crisp and bright, but by the time Ruth and I got to Craig Park over in Brea, a cool autumn chill had begun settling in. We took a seat by the lake, then Ruth returned to our table with hot dogs, chips, and two tall glasses of lemonade. Then she spent the next hour or so introducing me to all of her friends and apologizing that Mike and Betty were unable to make it.

The people seemed nice, but there weren't that many my age and the ones who were had boyfriends and girlfriends. When I started to tell them about my accident, most of them would tell me "how sorry they were" and that "God has a plan" then get up and leave. Then when Ruth excused herself to go to the bathroom, no one else even bothered to come to our table, just the trees all around and the sound of the ducks waiting for everybody to leave. I picked up my cane, got up from the table, and tried to find my way to the car.

As I looked up, the sun was sinking beneath the hills and the wind grew cold against my face. Soon, I started losing my breath, then braced myself against one of the trees and fell down in the grass and started to cry.

"I don't want to do this no more!" I wailed to everyone and no one at all. "Look at me! My God, will you look at me now? I'm a cripple, a fucking cripple! My God, why did *you* do this to *me*? I was always supposed to be a dancer, a dancer and maybe even an actress, but fuck that idea! What, am I supposed to dance with a cane in my hand or act when I can barely see the director? Not to mention I'll never be able to learn how to drive!" Then I pulled off my wig, threw it down on the ground, and used it to wipe the tears from my eyes. "I'll always need to rely on others to do *everything* for me, to help me get dressed, get me to school, and walk me to class. Poor little handicapped girl! A bother! A nuisance! A pain in the ass! My God, I just can't take anymore!" And there, under a cathedral of trees, no family or friends and a God who seemed as remote as the cold western sky, I imagined that I was abducted by an Indian chief whose family lived on this land before the Vaqueros chased them away. He gave me a knife that I had put on my keychain and kept it hidden inside of my purse. Running my hand along on the ground, I pulled open the zipper, flipped open the blade, and started making cuts on my wrist, releasing my bondage with each drop of blood. Within minutes I could hear their voices as the grass under my arms was splattered in small beads of red that fell down like drips from a faucet. "There she is! There she is! Somebody get her an ambulance!"

"I'm okay! I'm okay!" I insisted. "Just leave me alone."

Then the paramedics came and bandaged both of my wrists as Ruth stood beside us and talked to our pastor.

"The cuts appear to be superficial ma'am," One of the paramedics said as he explained to Ruth what had happened. "She said that she wants to go home."

"Well I think she still needs to go to the hospital." Ruth disagreed.

"Ma'am we can't take her without her permission. That is unless you're her legal guardian."

"I'm just a good friend," Ruth told him. "I'll make sure that she gets home safely."

"One more question, ma'am." The paramedic asked her, a troubled expression etched on his face. "Has she ever done this before?"

That night I stayed with Ruth then went back to my house the next morning when my father had already left for work. Susie, Michelle, and Loretta hadn't noticed what happened, nor did they ask. Later that day, I told them I fell when they saw the bandages on my wrists, but nobody asked me any more questions. When I talked to Ruth, she told me our pastor had said that she shouldn't bring me to anymore functions until I got some professional help. But I told her that I no longer wanted to go, since nobody there even gives a shit anyway.

"It's all like my dad used to tell me," I said. "All of those people are nice to you when you're in church, but as soon as you walk out the door, they couldn't care less."

I didn't see Ruth for a while after that. Sometimes she'd call me, and we'd talk for a while, but I no longer went with her to church every week. That year before Christmas, I started hanging out with my friend Christina, and soon she invited me over to her friend Fred's apartment where he, his wife Carol, and their friend Bob had weekly bible studies.

"I didn't even know that you were a Christian?" I asked her.

"I'm trying," was all she would say.

"Anyway, I tried going to church, but there's so many cliques. It's like high school all over again."

"Well Fred and Carol are really cool," she assured me, "and Bob is a cop right here in Placentia. Their fellowship is really small, so everyone gets to know one another. Why don't you just come by and hang out?"

The first night when I showed up at Fred's, there was only a handful of people, but everyone there was so friendly. Each meeting would start by each of us giving our testimony, and when I told them my story, they all got up and embraced me. There was also another young man who was legally blind and went through a lot of the same shit as me. After the study, Darren and I spent the night talking, then before we left, he gave me his number. Each night before Christmas when school let out, he'd call me at night, and we'd pray on the phone. That New Year's Eve we went over to Fred and Carol's apartment and we prayed and sang hymns as midnight approached while the TV in the other room showed the large white ball slowly begin to descend on Time Square.

WHERE IS YOUR GOD?

On a cold and rainy afternoon, I was upstairs in my room having stayed home sick from school that day. Then Darren called and asked me if he could bring me some soup. He told me that his roommate could have him there in less than ten minutes.

"Sure," I said, then minutes later I heard a knock at the door and him introducing himself to Loretta and her taking him up the stairs to my room.

"Here eat some of this," he told me as he held the cup under my mouth then wiped my chin with a napkin.

"Mmm... *Chicken 'n' Stars*!" I said. "How did you know that it was my favorite?"

"Let's just say that God told me last night in a dream just like Joseph."

"Well I don't recall them having *Chicken 'n' Stars* back in Egypt," I smirked.

"They probably did, only theirs had quail and manna," he said as we both sat and laughed.

"Thank you for caring," I told him as I finished the soup then reached over and gave him a hug.

"My pleasure," he said.

We both sat down on the edge of my bed and talked for a while before I finally told him that my dad would be coming home soon.

"Well then why don't we pray?" he finally said.

"Good idea," I answered then held out my hand as he took it in his.

We both closed our eyes, then he began speaking in some unknown language, "tongues" he called it. Then he moved his hand up to my shoulder and started messaging the back of my neck. "That feels good," I told him as his words were soon interrupted by shallow gasps and long deep moans.

"You know, the bible said that prayer always works better with the laying on of hands," he added.

"Really?" I sighed. "Where does it say that? First or second 'Balonians?'"

"It's in James," he answered as he began removing my shirt, then he stopped, and he chuckled. "At least I think it's in James."

Soon all of my clothing was thrown on the floor and he removed his pants then lowered his body down onto mine. The room was filled with the sounds of breathing and moaning and the thump of the bed against the wall— *thump, thump, thump...* yes!... *thump, thump, thump...* oh God, yes!... *thump, thump, thump,* louder... and louder... and louder... until I realized that it wasn't the bed but the door busting open and my father was standing inside of my room.

"So, who's your friend?" he finally asked me.

I'm not sure if I ever did tell him. After that, Darren stopped coming over for some odd reason, and pretty soon I no longer saw him over at Fred's apartment. Then sometime later, he called me and told me that he had just gotten back with his ex. At first, I was hurt, but then I just felt really pissed off. One night, I was sitting up in my room when the telephone rang, and I waited a while before finally answering.

"Look, why don't you just go fuck yourself!" I shouted. But the voice on the other end didn't seem to mind what I told him.

"Feisty little vixen aren't we?" he said.

"What do mean by that?" I asked him, sounding perplexed. "If you were standing next to me now, I'd kick you right in the balls."

"Wow, I like you! How long have you been working this line?"

"Wait, you think this is some kind of sex line?"

"Well isn't it?"

"No, you pervert!"

"Oh my God I'm so sorry," he said. Then we both just sat there and laughed. "By the way, did anyone ever tell you that you've got a really sexy voice?"

"Yeah," I answered. "Especially after the tracheotomies."

"The what?" he asked.

So, I told him my story, and after we talked, he soon convinced me that I could make lots of money doing this without ever leaving my bedroom. Furthermore, I never needed to meet anyone, all though most men would ask me to describe what I was wearing as they sat there and pleasured themselves by the phone. At first, I wasn't too sure, you know with me being a Christian and all, but it wasn't like I was some sort of prostitute since after all I wouldn't be having sex with these men. A week or so later, I told Loretta what was going on and she helped me open an account at Wells Fargo so I could walk across the street and get my money as soon as the checks were deposited. By this time, I figured that Susie and Michelle also knew, so I paid them off every once in a while if they promised they wouldn't snitch to my dad.

That year on Valentine's Day, I made a fortune as the phone kept ringing and a bunch of lonely old men would pour out their hearts before we got right down to what they were paying for. The next day, I walked to the bank and pulled out some money to give to my brother for his birthday.

"Holy shit, Pam, where did you get this?" he asked me.

"What does it matter?" I insisted. "Just take it."

"I can't take *that* much from you," he said.

"Then would you do me a favor instead?"

"What's that?"

"Go to Winter Formal with me?"

He looked at me then bowed his head unable to even look in my eyes. "Look, Pam, I really appreciate it, but you know that I've been out of work for a while. I don't really have any money."

"That's okay, Ronnie, I'll take care of it. Listen, bro, I love you. Is that good enough?"

"Well all right then," he said. "And, Pam, I love you too."

The following week, Loretta helped me get ready and walked me over to the limo that was waiting outside of our complex. "Be safe, honey," she said as she kissed my cheek.

"Auntie, do you remember I'm going out with my *brother*?"

"Well, have fun then," she said as she closed the door behind me.

I remember the look on Ron's face when we got to my mother's apartment and he walked out the door.

"My God, Pam, you really went all out!" he exclaimed as he sat down next to me in the back. "And by the way, you really look beautiful."

"And you look pretty handsome yourself," I told him when I noticed that he was wearing a suit.

"This is getting creepy." He finally said. Then we both laughed and sat there in silence until we pulled up into the Black Angus parking lot.

Ron was trying to flirt with one of the servers as she walked over to bring us our drinks.

"You better make sure and tip her well," he insisted, but I cut him off.

"Hey, you're supposed to be on a date with *me*!"

"Sorry, Pam. Can you forgive me?" he said, then he held up his glass. "Here's to my favorite younger sister."

"And here's to my favorite older brother," I said as my coffee and his tequila clinked together in an awkward but melodious resonance.

After dinner, the limousine took us to Casa Bonita in Fullerton, and I can honestly say that my brother was one of the best dates that I ever had. Aside from the fact that he mostly talked with all of the girls I knew in Drama, he was always the perfect gentleman. He even danced with me when I asked him despite not having very much rhythm.

"I'm more of a rock 'n' roll kind of guy," he said when I'd tease him about it.

"Yeah," I said but you're still a Vasquez!"

When the night was over, he leaned over and kissed my forehead and thanked me for a wonderful evening.

"Best time that I've had in while," he told me.

"Me too, Ron," I said.

"And besides," he added, as he pulled a napkin from out of his pocket, "if it wasn't for you, I wouldn't have gotten Heather's number!"

"You sly dog!" I teased him as he got out of the limo and made his way up to the door. "You really *are* a Vasquez!"

Later that year, things got even better as Susie announced she was moving in with Don and Veronica since they needed a babysitter now that their daughter Ashley was born. I don't remember what ever became of Michelle. I think she moved back in with her parents, or it could have been with some guy that she met, but anyway, they both were gone and out of my hair. Loretta stayed for a few more weeks, then she left to move in with some guy she was dating. She asked my dad if I would be safer if I stayed with my mother again because of the stairway and all.

"At least if she falls down the stairs, there's a better chance of her surviving than if she lived with her mom," he said.

I spent most of my days after school over at Fred and Carol's, then on the weekends, my friend David would pick me up and we'd go to "big" Calvary over in Costa Mesa for concerts. I was spending less and less time on the phone talking to men and more time rededicating my life to the Lord.

One night after I got home from church my dad was on the phone with Veronica.

"So where is she now? I see. Is she able to breathe on her own?" Then he held the phone away from his ear while my sister's voice screamed back through the receiver. "Calm down!

Will you just calm the hell down! Alright. Alright already! Look, I'll be right there. Yeah, bye."

"Daddy, what's up?" I asked him. "Is something the matter?"

"It's Susie. She's in the hospital," he said as he went to the closet to grab a jacket. "Your sister told me she thinks she OD'd."

"Oh my God! Is she going to be okay?"

"How the hell would I know?" he snapped. "Veronica's freaking out on the phone. I don't know what the hell's going on."

"Well tell my cousin I'm praying for her."

"Yeah, some good that's going to do," he retorted. "Just wait right here and don't go anywhere."

I never asked my father what happened, Veronica started telling the family about it when it was apparent that Susie would live. She said that she came home that same afternoon and found Susie passed out on the couch, heart racing, sweat running down all over her face. Then she explained how she'd pulled off her clothes, stood her up in the shower and set the dial all the way over to "cold." She told him that the paramedics said "that was what probably saved her" that and the IV they gave her of glucose and benzodiazepine.

As I sat in my room, I couldn't help thinking it was all my fault. Susie had remained conscious throughout the whole accident. Sometimes at night she would wake up screaming then her door would burst open and she'd step quietly into the hall, trying to avoid the severed heads that lay all around her blood covered feet. Sometimes, the Valium would help, and when that didn't work it was Xanax and weed. But this time, the doctors found toxic amounts of cocaine and tequila—"enough to kill an elephant" let alone a hundred-pound girl. Somehow, she made it through the night, then a few days later, she was released into a rehab facility where she spent several weeks before she enlisted into the Navy. Yet, that night, it was only a matter of seconds before the accident had nearly claimed its third victim.

Sometime after Susie's ordeal, my dad started going out with some girl that he met at the Foxfire. Her name was Karen, and she had a four-year-old son, Evan, who asked me if I would be his older sister if "your dad and my mommy were to get married."

Karen was also half my dad's age, not to mention really skinny. My mother and each of my siblings all thought that she was on drugs, but it wasn't like he paid it much mind. Before too long, my father gave her a key to our condo, and her and my dad would be up in his room while I played with Evan downstairs at the table. Sometimes, she'd leave him at home with her mother or drop him off to stay at his dad's when her and my father went out to the club. Then there were days when my father would take us all out for ice cream then out to the park to feed the ducks. On one of those days, Evan put his arms around my neck and told me he loved me.

"I love you too, punkin," I calmly assured, kissing him on the top of his head.

One day, my father was up in his room getting ready when I got back home after church. I went up the stairs, opened my door, set my bible down on the nightstand, then called out to him in his room.

"Hey, Dad, I'm home."

"I'll be out in a minute," he said.

I could already smell the cologne even before he opened the door. Then a deep musky vapor poured out in the hall as he grabbed a coat and walked out of his room.

"Where are you going?" I asked.

"Out," was all that he said.

"You know," I thought for a second. "Maybe Karen and Evan would like to come to church with me sometime."

"Fat chance," he said. "Karen doesn't believe in that shit either."

"I was thinking more about Evan."

"Don't bother," he said. "Karen's my friend and that's all. You need to stop trying to play house."

"Well just because you don't give a shit about him, doesn't mean I don't!"

"Look, Pam, you need to mind your own business!" he said, then turned and walked back in his room.

"So that's the way it's going to be?" I said as I followed him in through his door. "Every time I mention God or going to church, you just ignore me?"

"What? I can't seem to hear what you're saying," he said sticking a finger in both of his ears.

"I said," I began to explain myself all over again, but then he just started to hum until he finally accused me of acting immature until I pointed directly at him and laughed in his face. "Now look who's acting immature!"

With that, he began shouting and waving his hands, his veins nearly popping out of his head. "You're going to lecture me about God? You think I don't know what you've been up to? That phone sex line you've been running right here in my house? That guy who was fucking you right there on your bed? And YOU are going to lecture ME about God?"

"But, Dad, I already asked God to forgive me."

"Bullshit! I don't want to hear any more of your bullshit!

"But, Dad."

I never got to finish my sentence. The next thing I remember were his hands on my neck as my body lay at the foot of the stairs. His face was red, and his eyes glowed like tongues of fire as he stood above me, pushing my head down into the carpet.

"God help me!" I began to shout, then started to gasp as his hands closed tightly around me. "Please God, please..."

"Where is your God now?" he began to shout, his voice now quaking with rage. "WHERE IS YOUR GOD? Oh, I got it, he must be asleep! Or he just doesn't care! Or get this, MAYBE HE JUST DOESN'T EXIST!"

I looked up into the ceiling as the light above started fading to black, then back into a dim yellow blur as I momentarily regained my breath. "Angel of God, my guardian dear..." I began to pray to myself as each heightened gasp escaped through my lungs. For a moment, I believed I was going to die, until the sound of a doorbell tolled like the bells of Saint Mark's Cathedral born on the wings of my guardian angel.

"Ron, Ron, are you there?" My father's girlfriend called out as she turned the key and opened the door.

"Just stay right here and do what I tell you!" he warned me then stood up and called her over. "Honey, come here! Pam had an accident! She fell down the stairs and I'm trying to help her!"

I'm not sure if she really believed him, she had to see the marks on my neck reddened by the force of his hands, yet she did as he said and helped me to get back up on my feet.

"It doesn't look like anything's broken," she said holding my head in both of her hands. "Ron, please go and get her some water."

"I'm sorry, I'm sorry," I repeated over and over just like my father had told me. "I got really dizzy and fell down the stairs."

"You're going to be okay now, honey," she said, stroking the hair from out of my face. "God must have sent you one of his angels."

"He did. He did." I assured her. "And she just walked in through our door."

Karen insisted that my father take me with them to dinner that night and so both of us just sat there and talked. She told him, "what a brave little girl you have" and that "God must have been looking out for her." My father mostly just sat there and nodded while I managed to keep my thoughts to myself.

But within a few weeks, she stopped coming over and I heard from my siblings that she'd died in her home while snorting cocaine. I asked my father about it, but he shrugged it off. "They're crazy," he said, but he didn't deny it. I prayed to God to look after Evan and keep him from harm, but I never found out what happened to him.

Sometime later, my father came home singing an old Michael Jackson song. He said that it was also the name of a woman he met at the club and was starting to date. Within a month it wasn't just dating, they were already speaking of marriage. Yet after getting to know her, I soon came to realize the only reason he loved her was because of her name. But unlike the song, this *Billie Jean* was *no* beauty queen.

BILLIE JEAN

"**D**ad, I don't know. I just don't like her," I said when my father invited Billie over for dinner. "I mean, she was very nice and all, but it seemed kind of fake. And besides, who eats pizza with a fork?"

"Well that's just the way she was raised," he said. "Maybe it's something she learned in the military. Anyway, you better get used to her, since I plan on asking her to marry me soon."

I let those words hang in the air, then I walked back upstairs to my room. I didn't want another mom, well, maybe Karen, but that was because of Evan. Evan, my God how I missed him. Someday, I thought to myself, I'll have a baby of my own—maybe two or three—and I'll raise them in the church and love them more than anything else. I'd never run out on them like my mom did to us or leave them alone to hang out at clubs. My father told me to give Billie a chance, so I guess I needed to just do what he said. But I was never really going to accept her, let alone ever address her as "Mom."

The next day when I went to school, my teacher was gone, so she had her assistant Miss Jennifer take over the class. I hated that bitch, and I was pretty sure that she hated me too. She asked us all of the same stupid questions that we had been answering all through the year, and pretty soon I tuned her out and started talking to my friend Christina. The next thing I know, I felt a hand on the back of my shoulder and her bitchy voice calling my name. After that I don't remember what happened. I think that I may have blacked out or something. When Principal Blaylock pulled me off of her, I was pushing her head into the floor and there was blood all over her face. I sat in the office until my dad came to get me and they told him I was no longer welcome at Troy.

"Mr. Vasquez," the principal told him. "We've done all that we can here to help, but we just can't deal with this sort of aggression."

"Then maybe you should try challenging her." My father answered on my behalf. "She may have a head injury, but she's still pretty smart."

"I'm not saying that she isn't smart," He assured him. "Your daughter is still a very smart girl, that's not the problem."

"Then what *is* the problem?" My father spoke up, cutting him off.

"It's just that we don't have," he paused for a second then continued his thought, "We don't have all of the resources here to deal with her specific condition."

My father got up from his chair, gave me his arm, and we turned and walked toward the door.

"Good luck Mr. Vasquez," The principal said, but my father and I kept right on walking.

In June of that year, my father and Billie flew out to Vegas and tied the knot. Soon he was packing my things and telling me that we'd be moving from Placentia to Buena Park to live with Billie, her son Greg, and her daughter Gina. Both Greg and his girlfriend Tracy were really nice, but Gina was both a bitch and a skank. Unfortunately, we both had to share the same bedroom.

"Just make sure you don't touch any of my shit," she warned me. "And keep your 'fat clothes' on your side of the closet!"

Shortly after my father and I moved in, the real Billie began to emerge—the one I suspected all along—a Dionysian mask drawn permanently in the image of "bitch."

One day as I sat in my room, Billie came in and gave me a crash course in how to properly make a bed. "I should be able to bounce a quarter off of the mattress," she said. "Geez, didn't your father teach you anything? And those cassettes all over the floor? If I see that again, they're going straight into the trash!"

Then there was Gina, the aspiring model, her perfect daughter, and a total whore. Each night she and some guy would be having sex in the bed right next to mine. Sometimes it was two or three, or it could have been the L.A. Lakers as far as I knew, but every night it was thumping and moaning, thumping and moaning, it's no wonder that she always slept until noon. One day I finally told Billie, but that only got her angry at me.

"My Gina would never do such a thing!" she bellowed. "You're just jealous that not only is she a model, but all the boys around here adore her."

"That's pretty obvious," I snickered. "Since most of them are also fucking her."

"I should smack you for saying that!"

"Go right ahead and I'll beat your ass. You fucking evil bitch!"

Next thing I knew she told my father when he came home from work and he came in my room and gave me a smack.

"Next time it will be even harder!" she warned me. "Isn't that right, Ron?"

My father said nothing.

"*Isn't that right, Ron?*" she asked him again.

"Oh, yes, yes," he finally answered. "Pam knows better than to talk like that to her stepmom."

"You mean step-bitch!"

Next thing I know the back of his hand whipped across the side of my face and I could taste the blood in my mouth.

"That's what I mean, Ron. You need to teach her a lesson!" she said, then they both walked out of my room.

For the next few nights I fantasized about how I would kill her. Gina first, and then Billie. Gina I figured would be real easy. I could cover her face with my pillow when I woke up and she was lying spread-eagle across her bed. I was sure that I'd get away with it too, I'd just say it must have been one of her boyfriends who found out she was cheating, or maybe a night of rough sex gone awry. Now, Billie, that would be much harder. I knew that my dad had a gun, but I never knew where he kept it, not even at home in Placentia. Maybe I could get someone to help me, you know, hire a hitman or something? Then one morning, when Gina was gone and Billie and Dad were registering me for classes that fall at some adult learning center just down the street, I heard a knock at my door.

"Pam, can we come in?"

"Go away!"

"Pam, its Greg and Tracy. Can we please talk?"

For the next hour or so they told me that they knew what was going on, and that they would be willing to talk to Billie about it.

"The problem is not you, it's Gina," Greg admitted. "My mom has always protected her ever since our father left. Now she gets away with everything."

"We both like you, Pam," Tracy assured me. "We understand how hard this must be for you."

No, you don't, I thought to myself, but I thanked them both and gave them a hug before they got up and walked out of my room. For the next few days, however, things did get a little bit better, until one of the guys that Gina was with tried to reach under my blanket and touch me.

"This one seems pretty nice," he said as he rubbed his hands across my breast.

"Get your filthy hands off of me!" I screamed as I pushed him away.

"Damn it, Ryan, leave her alone!" Gina shouted at him. "She's only sixteen!"

I thanked her then pulled up the covers and tried to ignore all of the sounds going on in our bedroom. The next day when nobody was home, I called my sister Veronica and asked if she knew where Dad kept his gun.

"Pam, you're crazy!" she said. "You need to try just getting along."

"But, sis, I just can't take anymore! I think one day I'm going explode!"

Then on a really hot summer day, it finally happened. When my dad left for work, Billie walked into my room with a quarter in the palm of her hand and a really angry look on her face.

"Time for inspection," she announced as she glanced around at my side of the room. "Let me see here—tapes on the floor, and that bed, do you call that making the bed?"

"I did the best that I could," I told her as her quarter disappeared into the covers.

"That's two tests you failed!" she shouted. "And now I'm hearing you've been talking shit about my daughter to Greg."

"Oh, your precious Gina?" I mocked. "The one with a conga line around her vagina?"

"Let me tell you a thing about Gina," she said, her face now only inches from mine. "Gina's not only prettier, but she's also a better Christian as well."

"Well not unless you consider Jezebel a Christian," I calmly replied.

"How dare you! You little bitch! I should smack you right now for saying that!

"I dare you!"

"What did you say?"

"I *double-dog* dare you!"

She raised her hand and started to swing it, but I caught in mine then twisted it around behind her neck. Then pushing all of my weight up against her I threw her down on top of my bed and started banging her head up and down on my mattress like one of her quarters.

"Are they tight enough now?" I raged against her. "Your fucking sheets! Are they tight enough now?"

I kept on driving her head into the mattress, my hand now clenched around her throat. I could hear the sound of her breathing and gasping as she frantically tried to push me away. But I wouldn't let go, this time it was going to be me or her. Then I heard the sound of a scream and arms grabbing me around my waist desperately trying to pull me off her.

"Let her go! Let her go! You're going to kill her!"

It was Gina at first, then Greg walked in right behind her and they both held me down while my hands flailed wildly into the air.

"I told you she's psycho," I heard Gina say to her brother. "I want that bitch out of this house!"

The following week the doorbell rang, and I heard my father and Billie talking to a man with an accent that sounded like the guy on TV who put *shrimp on the barbie*. After a while, he knocked on my door and told me there was someone who wanted to meet me.

"Pam, this is Frank King, as in Frank-King-Stein, he's the director of NeuroCare down in San Diego. He'd like to speak to you for a while.

From what I could see, he was dressed in a blue blazer and had on a thin paisley tie. He was wearing circular glasses with leopard-skinned frames that made him look more like a comedian than a physician. Then he held out his hand for me to shake and started in on his whole spiel.

"NeuroCare is on the cutting edge in the growing field of head-injury rehabilitation that is in the forefront of helping survivors and their families regain a normal quality life," He began, then soon launched into his memorized script. "Located in the city of Ramona, our beautiful hundred-acre ranch offers scenic vistas, horseback trails, and an outdoor swimming pool. Our goal is the complete rehabilitation of all of our patients in a comfortable and safe environment."

"Whatever," I said, getting up out of my chair. "It was nice meeting you, Frank-King-Stein, but I'd rather go to Catalina this summer."

"Her reaction is perfectly normal," Frank told my dad as I got up and left the room. "One of the biggest problems is because these people may look okay after their accidents, we usually tend to think they're okay. But when they go back to school or work, they're not always able to readjust and that's a tremendous blow to their fragile sense of self-esteem. That's why they call head injuries the silent epidemic."

"So, what you're saying is you think you can help her," My father asked him.

"Mr. Vasquez, I don't think we can help her," he calmly assured, "I *know* we can help her."

The very next Monday, September 14, 1987, my seventeenth birthday, my father took the day off from work. He packed two of my suitcases while I got ready for school and loaded them into his car.

"You ready, Pam?" He asked me as he walked back into the house.

"I guess so."

When I got in his car, I could tell right away that something was wrong. Sometimes he would sniffle and dab at his eyes then ask me how I was doing.

"I'm fine," I would answer. "But why are we getting onto the freeway?"

That's when I knew that I wasn't going to school that day, or any day for that matter. I sat there in silence for more than an hour as the car made its way down the freeway then up in the hills before my father talked to a security guard and a large metal gate opened in front of us. He told me that he and my mom would come by and visit whenever they could and that I would only be there for a while until I was better. He got out of the car and walked me over to where I was staying, put my suitcases into the closet, then he wished me a happy birthday and tried to kiss me goodbye.

"Yeah, some happy birthday," I said as I pushed him away.

HIDDEN VALLEY

I spent the next year in a remote section south of Ramona in a place they referred to as Hidden Valley, and within days after I got there, I quickly learned why they wanted to keep it hidden. For one, there was no outdoor swimming pool and when I mentioned it to Frank when he came by to visit, he assured me that it was under construction and by next spring "you'll be dipping your toes right in." And as far as those vistas were concerned, well it really didn't matter how scenic they are when you're legally blind. But the biggest lie of them all was the "comfortable and safe environment" bullshit.

The day I moved in, my roommate Sue Martelli announced that "she hated all fat chicks" and "wished that I had died in the accident." The good thing, if you want to call it that, was that Sue was paralyzed from the waist down and confined to a wheelchair after a diving accident her senior year. So, every time she threatened me, I just made sure to stay out of reach of her wheels.

In many ways, NeuroCare was just like a prison. It was lights out at ten and we had to be up at six in the morning for breakfast. Then there were breakout sessions where we were put into groups and would talk about overcoming our struggles. As much as I hated it, I did meet some interesting people. There was Craig who had been there since the place first opened. He was a roadie for some punk metal band who was thrown from the window when their van rolled over and was found on the street, his body pinned underneath a pair of hundred pound speakers. And Kimo, a repo-man from Hawaii, who was shot in the head by some deadbeat when he went to go get his car late at night from right out in front of his house. Then there was Kristin who was sexually assaulted and beaten by her stepdad, the last time within an inch of her life. But perhaps the most tragic was Scott who blew out his brains when his girlfriend left him, but he missed and splattered the top of his head all over the walls of his parent's garage. He spent the next few weeks in a coma, then tried again with sleeping pills when he woke up and looked at himself in a mirror.

For the first two months, I didn't say anything, just sat there and listened, until Daniella showed up. Daniella's story was almost like mine, a cheating boyfriend, a joyride at night, a head split open on a dark stretch of highway, and a life draining out onto the pavement. Only she was riding on the back of a motorcycle when a pair of headlights appeared in the dark and drifted into oncoming traffic. Her boyfriend was killed on impact, and Daniella was thrown up against the windshield then summersaulted back onto the street. Her brain injury may not have been as severe, but when I met her, she was pretty fucked up.

"Hi," she said. "I'm Daniella." The words took like twenty minutes to get out of her mouth. Yet, she was always pleasant and kind and would always refer to me as her friend. She'd even sneak me some extra snacks that she redeemed with her "good behavior points." We also had something else in common, we both absolutely *hated* Sue.

"What do you say we both just kill her?" I asked Daniella when Sue told her she sounded just like Darth Vader. "We can just take her wheelchair out through the gates and leave her body for the coyotes or push her into the pool when it's finished."

"Now, Pam, that wouldn't be nice," she told me. "And besides, it wouldn't be very Christian."

It turns out I almost did it without her when I got back in my room and found my tapes crushed on the floor under her wheels. "Oh, I must not have seen them," she said when I noticed.

I don't know whether I threatened her life, but I remember I was kept under twenty-four-hour surveillance and lost all of my good behavior money. Two days later, during a therapy session, one of our counselors asked me why I was so angry.

"I don't know." I shrugged.

"Well then can you tell me who are you most angry with?" he asked me.

"Everyone, I guess."

"That's too bad," he said. "Such a beautiful girl like you deserves to be happy."

"Thanks," I said.

"Look, my name is Rick," he said taking my hand and holding a card with his number inside. "Call me if you ever need someone to talk to."

It wasn't like the way that things were back home when I could just pick up the phone and call someone whenever I wanted. There was only one phone in the room, and I didn't want Sue listening to my conversations. Sometimes I'd call him when Sue went to sleep before the monitors came in and turned out the lights.

"Bye, I gotta go," I'd say when I heard their voices out in the hall.

"See you tomorrow," he'd answer, then he'd hang up.

Rick also had a roommate who hated me, though I never could figure out why. One day during meal prep, we were both in the kitchen, and I started cutting some celery when he grabbed the knife from out of my hand and cut two of my fingers. After bleeding all over the counter, the attendant wrapped my hand in a towel and took me over to the medical building where I had to get stiches. The next day they asked us what happened, but he denied doing anything wrong. Then when I told Rick about it, he said that Alex was a really good guy, but sometimes his brain misfired, and he couldn't remember what he just did. "Such is the nature of his injury," he said.

"Well that's pretty fucked!" I told him. "I have a head injury too, but I don't go around cutting people."

"No two head injuries are ever the same," he said. "Do you mind if I ask, where were you injured?"

"The frontal and occipital lobe."

"So, you also have issues with sudden aggression."

"Not unless somebody pisses me off." I assured, then we both laughed together.

"Someday I intend to go on to medical school and study the brain. Maybe that's something that you should look into."

"We'll see," I said.

Sometime around Thanksgiving, my father came over to visit. The sun would go down behind the long row of hills sometime around three, so by the time he got there, the place was already covered in shadows. He sat down with me in the lobby and we talked for a while before they called us over for dinner.

"What happened to your hand?" he asked me, noticing all the layers of tape.

"Cut myself in the kitchen," I said. "But at least it got me out of having to do meal prep."

"Why in the hell are they having *you* doing meal prep? Don't they realize you can't see?"

"It's not like they care. No one really cares around here. All right, I take that back, maybe Rick and Daniella."

"Well I still care," he said taking a hold of my bandaged hand.

"Yeah right," I told him as I pulled it away. "By the way, where is your bitch, I mean wife?"

"Oh, Billie." He said as he lowered his head. "We're done. Billie and I are no longer married."

There were a lot of questions I wanted to ask, but I was pretty sure I knew all the answers. Billie never loved my dad, and I wasn't sure that he ever loved Billie. Maybe they thought if I was out of the picture, they'd be able to make it work, but that was neither here nor there. Still, my dad wouldn't admit that he'd made a mistake, and that included taking me here.

"So," I finally asked him, "when will you be bringing me home?"

"When the doctors say that you're ready to leave."

"When is that?"

"I don't know."

When Don and Veronica came to visit, I found out that my father moved back to the condo with Ron and his friends. They called it their "bachelor pad." That told me everything I needed to know. Sometime before Christmas, my mom and David took me to their place then brought me back the day after New Year's. They told me that they had planned to get married "If Ginny can keep herself sober a year," David added.

I wished them luck then hugged them goodbye in the lobby until one of the guards looked at his watch and said it was time, "Vacation is over."

The following night, I couldn't sleep, so I waited for all of the lights to go out then got up and walked out of my room. I started walking down through the hall until I got to a door, then I opened it up and went outside. I had no idea where I was, but I kept on going—a cold empty sky, an ocean of stars, the promise of freedom. The tall wet grass under my feet came to an end on a long stretch of pavement. *I made it!* I thought. *Now if only someone would find me.* The next thing I knew I was standing in front of a flashing red light and two guys getting out of a truck.

"Stop right there!" A voice called out through some sort of speaker. "Stay right where you are!"

When I got back inside, one of the counselors, I think her name was Carol—Carol or Candace—I knew her name began with a "kuh"—walked me back inside my room then took all of my "good behavior" money away.

"You will need to earn back our trust," she told me.

My friend Daniella lent me some of hers so I could go to the store and get soap and shampoo and toothpaste and mouthwash. She even smuggled me some of her snacks.

"Thank you!" I told her as she handed me a chocolate chip cookie.

"What are friends for?" she answered.

Sometime after that, Rick got permission to take Daniella and me to his church in Ramona each Sunday morning. After church, we went out to breakfast then out for a drive in the hills before we had to be back in our room.

"Promise me no more escapes?" he said, as he led me out of his truck.

"Promise," I said, fingers crossed behind my back.

"Good," he said. "Because my butt's on the line!"

So that's what we did every Sunday. We went out to church then we'd sit, and we'd talk for a while. Sometimes we went to a park and we'd feed the ducks and play on the swings, as long as we were back in our rooms before three. My mom was supposed to meet us that Easter, but David called and told me she was too sick to come and that she'd try to get out there on Mother's Day. My father showed up and met us for breakfast, but he declined my invitation to take him to church.

"At least will you pray with us for my mom?" I asked as we all joined hands at the table.

He shook his head as Rick, Daniella, and I bowed our heads and locked hands together. Then I heard him get up from his chair and walk through the door—his engine starting outside the window, wheels turning against the gravel. I asked God to not only heal my mom, but to touch my father as well.

As the temperature outside began its slow and steady climb toward the typical triple digit summer days in the Santa Maria Valley, the grasslands of the Laguna Mountains turned angry and brown, frequently casting its limestone boulders down onto the Julian Highway. One time, my dad couldn't make it to see me due to "some big fucking rock in the middle of the road." Then the following week, my sister Veronica drove up and brought me a recipe for chilequillas, then got stuck between there and Escondido on account of another massive slide. But that wasn't the only thing that was hot that summer. After several weeks of good behavior, I was finally allowed back into the kitchen. I remember it was the weekend when Frank King was there, and I wanted to make him my favorite thing to eat growing up.

"What do you call that again?" he said in his exaggerated Queensland 'strine.'

"Chilequillas," I said. "Just think of chili killers and you get the drift."

The trouble was that I made them so spicy they damn near killed everyone. In fact, no one was even able to eat them, no one that is except Frank King.

"What do you say I take this home and buy us all pizza?"

"Yeah!" Everyone in the room began cheering out loud including me.

"I would never have guessed that you like spicy food," I told him after dinner was finished.

"Love it!" he said. "If you grew up with the food in Australia, you'd like it too."

"So, what you're trying to tell me is that the food in Australia sucks?"

"Absolute rubbish!" he said. "Don't listen to that bloke on TV that all we eat are shrimps on the barbie. It's more like beetroot and vegemite sandwiches."

We both laughed for a while, then he asked me if things were better and I told him for the most part they were, or at least I hadn't threatened to kill anyone.

"That's good to hear," he said. "The staff tells me you're about ready to move on from here."

"You mean I can go home?"

"Not exactly," he explained. "But closer. You'll be doing part two up in Pasadena. We'll have you moved in before your birthday, and if things go well, you'll be home before Christmas."

As the day grew near, they finally got the swimming pool finished and we spent most of our evenings hanging out and talking around it. In the mornings, I'd go out and swim a few laps after breakfast. Then one morning, Daniella came out to greet me at the edge of the water.

"So, I hear that you're leaving," she said in a slow somber voice. "It would have been nice of you to tell me since I believed we were friends."

"Look, Daniella." I said as I grabbed a towel to dry myself off. "I was going to let you know eventually."

"When?" she asked me.

"Well, when the time was right."

She looked at me for a moment then started walking away, but I followed her out to the gate, then she turned back around and cried in my arms.

"You are my friend!" I assured her. "We'll always be friends. I promise that I'll stay in touch. I'll even come over and visit you when you get out of this place."

"Promise?" she pleaded.

"Promise," I said.

"Okay, then pinky swear."

"Sorry, but I'm not going to do that!" I told her. "It's a long story."

The following night, I started packing when I heard a knock on my door.

"Come in," I said. Then the door burst open.

"Rick?"

He didn't say anything, just held me close as tears rolled down both of our cheeks. Then he told me he "loved me" and that he loved me from the moment he saw me. We promised that we would stay in touch and that when I finally got out of my new place, he'd come up and get me and take me back home to San Diego where we would get married and start a family together.

"But Orange County has always been my home." I told him.

"Then I'll move up there when I'm finished with school. Just promise that you'll wait for me wherever you are."

He kissed my cheek then walked out of my room and closed the door behind him. I never did make him that promise, "we'll see" was all that I said as he cried on my shoulder, his hands running up and down on my back.

It turned out that my new place was only about a block away from the parade route on Colorado Blvd. Each year when I was a child, I had wanted to go see it in person, but this time when New Year's Eve came, I wanted to be back home watching it all on TV. The rooms here were smaller but I had my own, so I didn't mind. After breakfast, they put us in classes to teach us things like cooking and cleaning and tending the garden they kept on the premises. There were also lots of books to read, but I still couldn't see well enough, so they started giving them to me on tape. We also had a weekly class on public speaking, and before too long, I not only got pretty good, but they couldn't seem to shut me up. Soon one of the counselors had an idea.

"Look, we're right down the street from your favorite station," he told me.

"Really what's that?"

"KROQ."

"KROQ, rock of the 8o's!" I interjected. "So, what about it?"

"Well, they're always looking for interns, you know someone to answer the phones and take requests. I know some people down there and I can put in a good word for you."

That's how I got started in radio. Twice a week after I had finished my chores, one of the counselors would take me down the street where I'd work at the station for a few hours, then he'd pick me up and bring me back. After a month or so, one of the producers suggested that because of my voice, if I worked really hard and learned all the ropes that someday I could even get on the air.

"It would just be a few commercial spots here and there, but who knows," he said. "You certainly have a voice for radio."

I told my dad when he came over to visit that week, but he just smiled and nodded his head. "I'm proud of you, honey. I really am. But this weekend I'm taking you over to David's."

"Why? What's the matter?" I asked.

"It's your mom," he answered. "She's in the hospital and it doesn't look good. I told her you would be coming to see her."

I walked in through the door that I had been wheeled into three years ago—the smell of the halls and the outstretched arms of its patron saint on every statue. I was taken up to the Oncology ward where my father helped me put on an apron and gloves then was led by the hand around to her room where my siblings were already sitting outside.

"Pammy!" she said when I walked into see her. "I know, I know, it's Pamela now."

"Hi, Mommy," I said as my dad walked me over to the side her bed.

When I leaned over to give her a hug, I could sense that she wasn't doing too well. Her hands were brittle and rough, and from what I could see, her skin had turned from light beige to a sickly dull yellow. Underneath her sheet was a thin black gown like the kind that she wore when she was at home.

"I asked the nurses if I could wear this today," she said, her voice now barely a whisper. "I wanted to be in your favorite colors, black and yellow, just like that band that you like."

"You mean Stryper?" I said.

"Yeah, you know when I first saw the name on one of your tapes, I thought it was 'Stripper'." She said and we both started to laugh. "Anyway, it's so nice to see that you're doing so well."

"It's good to see you too, Mommy," I said taking her hand in mine. "You need to get well so you can spend Thanksgiving Day with us."

"I don't think so, Pammy," she said, slowly shaking her head. "I'm in so much pain. I can't even get out of bed." Then, freeing her hand from mine, she turned toward the wall and started to cough.

"I'm sorry, Pammy. I'm sorry for everything. I wasn't very well back then either."

I wanted to ask what she meant, but since I already knew I just said nothing.

"Mommy, remember what you used to tell me when I was in therapy? No pain, no gain. That's what you said to me right? No pain, no gain?" I said as tears started streaming down on my face. "So, I get it. What you're telling me now is it works for me but not for you?"

I could see my mother beginning to cry, then a pair of hands reached over to pull me away, taking ahold of each of my shoulders.

"Come on, Pam," my father insisted. "You're upsetting her."

"I love you, Mom!" I wailed as he led me out through the hall. "I love you so much!"

My dad took me over to David's then picked me up on Sunday night to take me back to Pasadena. He told me that he'd talk to the staff and try and have me back for Thanksgiving weekend. He said he'd let me know as soon as he could and that he'd give me a call for me to be ready. The following Monday, the phone rang inside my room and I rushed over to pick it up.

"Daddy," I answered. "I see. I see. Tell me you're kidding! No! NO! OH GOD, OH GOD NO!"

A REQUIEM FOR MOM

My mom passed away that Monday morning, November 19, 1988. She was just forty-six.

When I say my *mom*, I mean the person who tucked me in bed and made cookies for me on my first day of school. It was my birthday that year, and she'd made enough for the entire class. I remember it got everyone to like me and I think she knew that would happen so that's why she did it.

My mother was actually two people, the one who was drunk and the other who wasn't. The one who wasn't was the most beautiful person I'd ever met—kind and gracious, she'd give you the shirt off her back and if she ran out, she'd make you a new one. You see, my mom loved to sew. When her and my father got married, she was always making clothes for her nieces and nephews. My sisters told me when they were little how she used to make dresses for them and when their friends asked where they had got them, my mom made dresses for them as well.

And my mom loved to cook, boy did she ever love to cook! Every day our house was alive with the smells of gourmet meals or freshly baked pies. And not only did she make enough for the family, but at times she would invite some of our neighbors to join us for dinner. That's who she was, generous almost to a fault.

And who could forget those parties each summer? My mom was always the perfect hostess, warmly greeting each of our guests then cutting the rug all night with my dad—the starlet and her leading man—his Ginger Rogers and her Fred Astaire.

My grandma once told me it wasn't always that way. She said at first, she didn't want her to marry my father. Of the eight girls and four boys that she raised, "Ginny" was always her favorite, "her princess" she called her. She was talented, pretty, and did well in school, so well in fact, that she could have gone to any college she wanted. My dad was the rebel, the bad boy from the wrong side of town, the Jim Stark to her Natalie Wood. Yet those who knew them, thought they were perfect together. They got married in 1960 when my mother had just turned eighteen, then had their first child, my sister Marie, three weeks before Christmas. The following year, they had another girl, my sister Veronica, then three years later my dad had a son, his junior, his "Ronnie." That's when they moved from Compton to Bellflower and got their first home right down the street from the church where my mom volunteered, and for a while, everything seemed so perfect. That is until that warm summer night when my mom got the call that Loretta's three kids were killed in a fire.

It had happened during the summer of Manson, four days after the fourth of July and twelve days before Neil Armstrong's "one giant leap"—a year and two months before I was born. My mom was always concerned about her sister Loretta—her boyfriends, her drinking, and her partying lifestyle. And now she had kids to take care of, all three by her husband who'd recently left her.

My mom didn't like the guy she was currently living with, he was ten years older and "looked like a cholo," she'd tell my father. So, the kids mostly lived with her and my dad in the Bellflower house. You see, Loretta was not only her sister, but also her twin. Born only minutes apart, she was bound to her not only by family, but every second they shared in the womb. And my mom loved those children just like her own. She would bake them cookies and make them hot chocolate and my siblings would let them play with their toys. In fact, her and my father even talked of adopting them.

But that weekend was the Fourth of July and Loretta begged my mother to let her take them back home. Besides, Julie, her oldest, was turning four on Tuesday and they wanted to have a party for her. Then a night of drinking, a house full of friends, and a lit cigarette lying dead in a sofa that smoldered for hours before erupting in flames when everyone slept. Then there was fire and smoke everywhere and the sound of three little voices that screamed out loud from their room—"Momma! Momma!" they cried until a wall of thick acrid smoke filled up their lungs and drowned out their screams.

Loretta and her boyfriend were both pulled to safety, but when the firemen came, they found all of the children crumpled against their bedroom door unable to breathe. They were taken to Long Beach Memorial where they all were pronounced dead on arrival. When the sun came up on the smoldering hull of what once was their home, all that remained was a tricycle left out on the patio, a stuffed toy panda propped up beside it, a melted red bow still adorning the top of its head.

That's when everything changed with my mom. By the time I was born, she was already drinking—yet a bottle of wine and a shot of tequila could never make all of those screams go away. So, she cleaned the church as an act of penance for some terrible sin that was not even hers, like Martin Luther ascending her own *scala sancta*, blistered hands kept the pews of St. Linus perfectly polished each day before mass. When we moved into our Anaheim home, she still would return on the weekends until my father had to remind her that she now had four kids of her own to take care of.

I don't remember her ever sleeping. It either seemed that she was always at work, or making dinner, or cleaning the house. Even on days when I'd wake up at night, I'd see her out on the living room sofa watching TV or reading a book.

"Get back to bed, Pammy!" was all she would say. "You've got school tomorrow."

Then she'd be in the kitchen the first thing in the morning making us breakfast.

Of course there were times she'd pass out then wake up screaming and thrashing around as if she was trying to reach through the smoke and run out through some wall of invisible flames that locked her forever inside of a nightmare that only another bottle of wine could make go away.

I finally forgave her. I could now understand all of the pain and the nightmares and the PTSD—the loss of those who died far too soon, and the guilt of never saying goodbye. They didn't have any drugs back then for all of that stuff, and therapy was out of the question, so she was left to carry it all on her own. And all things considered, she probably did the best that she could.

My father was never a spiritual man, but when I was with him that weekend after Thanksgiving when we laid her to rest, I knew that he had forgiven her too. We drove up to *Loma Vista Cemetery* over in Fullerton, our family all dressed up in black, and under a tall shady tree, we laid her to rest. As the first ladle of dirt tumbled over the top of her casket, I saw him kneel and bow his head, and lifting a pair of dark glasses up from his eyes, he emptied his heart in the form of a prayer.

"Ginny, you were always and will always be my first love. Thank you for the time that we had and for the beautiful and talented children you gave me. I know that we had our problems there at the end." Then he took out his hanky and dabbed at his eyes. "And I know that it was probably my fault as well, even though I would never admit it. I... I... I... just wanted to be good enough for you. Ever since the day we first met I never believed that I was good enough for you! But Ginny," he said. "Ginny, I loved you. I've always loved you. And... and..." He began to stutter as the dam finally burst and poured out from him like a fountain that ran from his heart then out through his eyes. "I hope that you now finally have peace."

PAM 2.0

After Mom's funeral I never did go back to Pasadena but drove to a house in Buena Park to live with my sister Veronica. It turned out that on my eighteenth birthday, the settlement money came in from my accident and since my father was now my conservator, he'd decided that the best thing to do was put her and Don and her kids and I under one roof. The situation was strained from the start. Veronica was eight months pregnant with my niece Amanda, and Don had just gotten out of rehab. To make matters worse, she was already raising a four and a two-year-old and had to keep an eye on me too. Not that I helped matters any. I kept getting out at night and going for walks while Veronica slept, and Don was at work. Sometimes I'd get lost somewhere in the neighborhood, while once I ended up all the way over by Knott's Berry Farm, when the phone rang, she had to go get me. "What the hell are you doing out here!" she screamed as she grabbed me and pulled me into her car.

It went on like that for the first few months before she decided to put a lock on my door and I only got out when I had to go see Dr. Katz or go to my classes at Cypress College since they let me record all of my lectures. I tried going to the Braille Center in Anaheim first, but after only one day I decided there was "no fucking way" I could ever learn braille. Dr. Katz was some shrink that the program I was in recommended and every week he would come over to visit and sometimes take me out for some ice cream. He was also costing me an arm and a leg, but since the bill went straight to my father, I didn't care. He put me on some new medication to help me deal with what he called my "black moods" and told me that for things to get better, I needed to keep myself occupied.

"So, let's see, in addition to all of my pain medication, and the shit that I've been taking for seizures, you want me on *this* stuff as well?"

"I put you on the lowest dosage, just give it a try. If you don't feel any better in a couple of weeks, we can try something else. But mainly, you need to find something to keep yourself busy."

So, true to my word, I signed up for classes during the week, then went out to some of the clubs around town on the weekend even though I was only eighteen. Every week, my dad would come over and bring me some of my settlement money, so every time I wanted to get out of the house, I'd just pick up the phone and call me a cab. Sometimes, Veronica tried to get me to come out of my room to eat dinner with her and her family, but I usually just stayed inside and called out for pizza. By that time, Trey was working at Dominos and they'd let him drive out to see me even though I lived outside of his delivery area.

"So how is Tatania?" he'd ask me when my sister let him into my room.

"All right I guess," I told him. "Care to join me for dinner?"

"Uh, no," he answered. "If I told you how they made that shit, you'd never order a pizza again!"

"You still hear from Erika?" I asked pulling a slice from out of the box.

"I still see her sometimes."

"Can you give me her number?"

"I'll have it for you next time I come," he paused. "That is if there is a next time."

"Of course," I answered, then took another long deep bite and dabbed at the grease on the side of my mouth. "How about Randy?"

"He and Cindy are married now. But it's pretty fucked up since after the accident he can't have any children."

"You mean?"

"Yup. His gonads. Crushed like a pair of grapes." He said clapping both of his hands together.

"Ow!"

We briefly hugged, then I walked him out through the front door. When he came back later that week, he handed me Erika's number, so we started calling each other again. She said that her and Jeff were "on again, off again" and that she was thinking about going to beauty school. But I noticed as we hung up the phone, she no longer called me her BFF. Then one morning, Dr. Katz called me with an idea.

"So, let me get this straight." I asked him. "You want me to work for you at St. Jude's?"

"I really think it will do you some good," he said. "And besides, I think your story would really help others. It would only be as a volunteer, so I can't pay you or anything, but I'm sure it will help you get some experience if this is what you decide to do with your life."

So, the next week I went back to the place where I'd spent the last day with my mom, and eight months of my life learning to live all over again. Only this time, I was wearing a badge and had my own office. Yet it wasn't all sunshine and rainbows. The first person that they gave me to work with was a little girl who was only eleven. She had a head injury similar to mine when her mother got drunk and crashed her car into a tree. When she got there, she wanted to fight everyone, hitting and spitting at all of the doctors and nurses. I remember she tried to hit me as well but one of the nurses who was standing there with me reached over and grabbed her hand.

"Hello, young lady," I said, "my name is Pam."

"Fuck you!"

"Ok, let's try this again. My name is Pam. What's your name?"

"Go away!" she screamed, then threw a glass of water at me.

Then one of the nurses finally spoke up. "Amber honey, this is Pam. She was in a bad car accident too."

The next time when I came over to visit, she didn't try hitting or spitting at me. I told her how pretty she was and that no matter how bad things were now, they were going to get better.

"But my stepfather died, and my mom just got out of the hospital! Not only that, they had to shave off all of my hair!"

"My boyfriend died in the car I was in." I told her. "And they shaved off all of my hair as well."

"So?"

"So, look at me now." I said shaking my head all around. "Grows like a weed. And from what I've been told, your step-dad is in heaven with God."

"But I don't want him in heaven, I want him down here!" She screamed and then started to cry. I walked over and bent down and held her, then we both cried together until one of the nurses came in to get me.

I went to see Amber every day until she was transferred. One day, her mother came in and gave me one of her pictures from school. From what I could see she was very pretty—long blonde hair and piercing blue eyes. She'd be okay, I thought to myself, but I couldn't be sure. Everyone there that I saw had scars on the outside that one day would heal, but the scars on the inside, that would be harder.

One day, when I got home from the hospital, Erika called. She said that she was moving to Vegas and that her and Jeff were going to get married. We called each other every day, then one day I got a message that her number had been disconnected, then my sister came into my room and handed me a letter from her.

"Should I read it?" she asked me.

"Sure," I said.

Then she took the letter out of the envelope, put on her glasses, and carefully unfolded the paper.

"Dear Pam. I'm starting my life over in Vegas. You know, getting the hell out of here. [smiles]." Then there were a few lines about our friends and our teachers from high school and even one about Marty before she continued. "So, what I'm trying to say, is that I don't want you trying to contact me. I need to forget what happened, and as long as I keep on talking to you, I can never forget." Then there were a few more lines about Randy and Trey, but still no apologies about what happened with Marty, and then one final conclusion. "So, while I wish you the best, I need to ask you not to call me again. In fact, I'd rather you just forget about me altogether. Good-bye. Sincerely Erika."

I just sat there, too stunned to speak, let alone cry. So, I called up Trey and asked if he had Randy's number. But when I tried to call him, he just blew me off. The same thing with Diane and Lisa and all of my friends from Troy. I had become *persona non grata*.

That night, I went out to one of the clubs where they'd let me in without any questions and decided to have a few drinks—well maybe more than a few. On my way home, I got lost in one of the parks, then sat down on one of the benches until a police officer came and took me back home.

"Next time, I'm taking her down to the station," he told my sister as they both stood outside the front door. And when she got back in, my sister was *pissed*.

"You need to stop all of this shit right now!" she screamed as she walked in the door. "With all of the meds that you're on and you're going out drinking? What, are you *trying* to die?"

When I shrugged back at her, the screaming erupted all over again until her kids started waking up in their room. "Now look what you've done! You've gone and woke up the entire house!"

"But Veronica," I tried to say.

"Don't but Veronica me!" she shouted back, her face now reddened and glowing with anger. "I'm sick of your bullshit! All of the shit that I'm dealing with and you're becoming my biggest problem!"

"Oh, I see," I told her. "But of course it's no problem when Dad sends you my money each month to pay for this house!"

"Shut up! Will you just shut up!" she screamed as her kids were now crying and the oldest was getting up out of his bed.

"I wonder if they know that your *baby* sister is paying your rent?" I went on.

"I have no baby sister!" she screamed and got right in my face. "It's just your fucking head injury talking again. My baby sister is dead! You're just someone that they sent to replace her!" Then she turned and put her kids back to sleep then walked into her room slamming the door.

The next day, I asked myself if she was right. Was Pam really dead, and if she was dead, then who was I? Was I dead as well? Was I just someone who God sent back to play some cruel joke on my family, not to mention on me? *It all made sense now,* I thought. No wonder my friends wanted nothing to do with me. *No wonder my family treats me like shit! I'm just a burden, a bother, a girl who should have died in the accident!*

The next morning when my sister left for work and grandma came over to get all the kids, I went into my sister's bedroom and opened the closet. Then I moved around some of the clothing, and there it was standing straight up in the corner. I remember the long steel embrace and the smooth wooden handle that sat on the linoleum floor. I picked it up, took it over into my room, then slowly began to feel for the trigger. A few more seconds it would all be over, I'd never bother anyone again! As I leaned forward, I opened my mouth and a metallic tang filled up in my throat and rang out in both of my fillings. I prayed for God to forgive me, then I closed my eyes and reached for the trigger. The next thing I knew a piercing clangor blared in my head and cut through the room with an earsplitting din. *The phone!* I thought. *Goddammit, the phone!*

I put down the gun for a second then went over to make the sound go away.

"Hello?" I said in a voice that was almost a shout.

"Pam? Pam? Are you okay?"

"Trey?"

"Yeah, what the hell's going on? You sound like someone's pointing a gun at your head!"

I couldn't help but laugh a little. Then we started to talk and to joke with each other. The next thing I knew an hour had passed and I almost forgot about the gun on the floor.

"Trey, you're never going to believe this," I said. "But God must have a sick sense of humor. That thing you said about having a gun to my head? Well I don't, *anymore*."

When I hung up the phone, I put the gun back into their closet then moved all of the clothes the way I had found them. The irony was that if Don or Veronica ever found out, they'd probably want to shoot me themselves!

The next week, when my father came over to give me my money, he was with some woman who I don't remember seeing before.

"Pam, this is my girlfriend, Betty. Betty, this is my youngest, Pam."

"Nice to meet you, Pam," she said as she tried to give me a hug until I pushed her away.

"She's been through a lot," I heard my dad whisper putting an arm across her shoulder.

Then he counted my money and invited us out to lunch with them, but I not so politely declined.

"So, what you're saying now, Dad is this is soon going to be my new step-bitch?"

"Look, you're getting too far ahead of yourself, and besides, Betty is nothing like Billie," he said. "Why don't you just give her a chance?"

The following week she came by herself, did all of my laundry, and cleaned up my room.

"So, this is where they're having you stay?" She asked me as she tucked in my sheets and fluffed up the pillows.

"Yup," I answered. "How do you like it?"

"It's so small," she exclaimed. "It looks like the smallest room in the house."

For the next few months, she started coming over twice a week to clean up my room and take me to lunch. Then one day, she came over and said that she had some sort of surprise.

"Let's get you dressed, I'm taking you shopping!" she said, as she walked in through the door.

First, she took me to her beauty salon where they cut and styled my hair. Then she took me out to the mall, and we spent the day trying on clothes.

"This would look so nice on you!" she said as she held up an outfit and walked with me into one of the fitting rooms.

"It's awfully bright." I told her but still she insisted on buying it for me.

"Every time I see you, you're all in black," she said. "You need to start looking more cheerful."

When we sat down in the food court and started to talk, I looked at her from across the table and just asked her, "Why? Why do you want anything to do with me since no one else does?"

"Well, maybe it's because I'm not anyone else," she insisted. "Maybe it's because I want everyone to see what a beautiful girl you really are."

Then, slowly, I began to not only trust her, but I looked forward to her coming to visit. When we went out shopping together, I asked her if I could buy her something, but she always refused. *Well this is different*, I thought. But I still insisted each time we went out.

That year for Christmas my father went out to get her a ring that he hid inside the smallest of five boxes like one of those Russian dolls you see at a gift shop. So, the following year it was official, I had a new stepmom and also a younger stepbrother.

I didn't have much time to notice. Starting right after Halloween, I was spending five nights a week at the Crystal Cathedral acting in the *Glory of Christmas*. It was Dr. Katz's idea that I try out, but after the audition went well, they decided to put me into the show. The week before Christmas, my family came out to see me. They all sat down in the front on either side of my father and

Betty. The night they were there, I was a shepherd, and as the angels announced their "tidings of great joy" I couldn't get my sheep to be quiet. "Shish!" I whispered. "Shish, the angels are talking." But my stupid sheep kept bleating away. Then I noticed that people were starting to laugh and some even uttered "ah, isn't that cute?" So, I just stood there and smiled and took it all in as the "glory of the Lord shone all around."

After the show, all anyone talked about was "that pretty young lady and her sheep." Some of the attendants even asked me for my autograph. As a shower of light echoed between the lofty crystalline towers and spilled at my feet in a bright rainbow prism, I could hear my dad's voice beaming with pride, "That young lady right over there," he said then pointed over to where I was standing, "that's my daughter!"

SECOND DEATH

At the start of the year, it was too cold to go out at night, so I spent a lot of time in my room. Betty would come over on Tuesdays and Thursdays and help me organize all of my things, then we'd go out for lunch. Sometimes she'd take me into a store where we'd look at gowns for when her and my father got married. She would try one on then go back to the rack and try on another, attempting to find the one that was perfect. Each time I told her that she looked beautiful, but she just laughed and told me it was because I still couldn't see very well.

One night, after one of my classes, I stopped to eat at a Mexican place on the corner of Holder and Ball. As I sat alone at one of the tables, waiting for my food to arrive, a man walked over, sat down beside me, and asked if he could join me for dinner. He introduced himself as Bobby then told me that it pained him to see "such a beautiful girl eating alone." So, I moved over and we shared a bowl of chips and salsa, a taco salad, and a pitcher of unsweetened tea.

"So, do you come here often?" he asked me.

"Now that's original," I answered. "Do you say that to every strange girl you meet in a restaurant?"

He laughed for a minute, then we just sat there and talked. When I told him I had to get going, he motioned over to the waiter and told me "I got this," then asked for my number. Soon after that we started dating and he'd come over to see me at the house that I shared with Don and Veronica.

"Who's that?" she asked me one day as he walked out the door when she got home from work.

"Oh, that's my boyfriend, Bobby," I told her.

"Your boyfriend? So now he's your *boyfriend*?"

"That's what he said," I answered back. "He said that he was my boyfriend and I was his girlfriend. And then he told me he loved me."

She stopped and stared at me for a second then walked away shaking her head. "That's what every man tells you at first."

Throughout that spring, Bobby and I were always together. He'd pick me up after school and on the days when I volunteered to work at St. Jude. Then one day he had an idea that I should just move in with him.

"It makes perfect sense," he said. "Come on, are you really happy living there with your sister and all of her children and her husband who when he's not in rehab, he's there with his friends drinking and partying?"

"But I love those kids," I told him, recalling the times when I told them stories at night before bed and when their grandma would drop them off after school. "Who's going to tell them what happened to 'Fluffy' and 'Meow Meow?'"

"Fluffy and who?"

"It's a long story."

Veronica wasn't too happy when I told her I was leaving, but my dad set everything up so that my estate would still be paying her rent. Then everything changed when Don was transferred out to the desert and she put in her own transfer shortly thereafter. In the meantime, I had soon come to realize that my sister was right, every man tells you "I love you" at first.

One morning, I was on the phone, when Bobby came home from work. He waited for me to hang up then he asked me "who in the hell were you talking to?"

"Oh, that was my friend Trey?" I answered. "We've been friends ever since middle school."

"Well tell him not to call here no more!" he commanded. "Same goes for any other of your male friends."

One day, he walked into our room when I was on the phone with Daniella. She had called me at Veronica's house, but my sister told her I had moved and then gave her this number. He walked right past me then he reached for the nightstand and hit the receiver.

"You bastard!" I shouted. "That was Daniella."

"Didn't I tell you no male friends?" he warned me again.

"Daniella! Her name is *Daniella*!" my God, you're an asshole!

It went on like that for over two months, then one day, when he was at work, the telephone rang and there was a female voice on the other end asking for him.

"Bobby's not home. Can I take a message?"

"Yeah, tell him that his girlfriend called."

"His girlfriend?" I said. "But *I'm* Bobby's girlfriend."

"Oh, I thought you were his roommate," she said.

From the sound of her voice she couldn't have been more than sixteen, and as I found out later, I was only off by a year. She told me that he'd go there each morning, shower at her place, then get dressed for work. When I confronted him about it, he told me that she was just some old friend whom he had been comforting while she was dealing with a death in the family.

"Comforting her how? With your penis?" I screamed. "Listen, Bobby, you are so full of shit! But I'm on to you now, in fact, we're *both* on to you!"

"Look, Pam, you know that I love you," he pleaded. "What do you want me to say? I'm sorry? Okay then, I'm sorry."

"No, I want you to get the hell out of here! Pack all your shit and get the fuck out!"

"But my name's on the lease. I can't just pick up and go."

"Your name's on the lease, but I'm still paying most of the rent! Hey, I got an idea," I snarled. "Why don't you ask your little whore to move in?"

The next morning, I called my dad and asked him if he could find me a place. So, he called up Regional Center and told me about this program where I'd be living alone but someone would come over to help me. Bobby stayed at our place for a while then moved back in with his parents. For the next two weeks, each of us came and went on our own without ever saying a word to each other.

I finally ended up moving into an apartment on Ball and Gilbert not too far from where I was living. The place was small, only one bedroom, but after so many years of sharing a room, then living in programs, then with my sister, not to mention all the drama with Bobby, it was nice to have a place of my own. Of course, every morning, someone from Regional Center would spend a few hours with me and try to teach me what they referred to as "independent living skills." But for the most part they all just seemed to annoy me and before too long it was starting to remind me of Neurocare.

And speaking of Neurocare, I wondered how things were going with Rick. So, one night I tried calling his number, but I got no answer. I tried again the following day, but his roommate answered and told me was going to UCSD and living on campus. I decided that I would just leave it at that then I told his roommate to tell him "hello" and "wish him the best" and if he should ever see him again, "to give him my number."

One morning when I got out of the shower I walked to my bedroom and turned on the radio. As the closing strains of *Enjoy the Silence* blared through the steam in one final spoken invocation, my attention turned to the commercial that followed. KROQ night at *Oscar's West*? Swedish Egil? Friday at eight? Sign me up! So, when the doorbell rang a little later and some girl from Regional showed up, I asked her if she could help me do laundry. "Not all of it," I said. "Only a few pairs of jeans and my lacy black tops."

"Well, Pamela, it says today were working on 'meal prep,'" she said as she walked over into my kitchen and slapped a fully skinned chicken down on the sink."

"So, what the fuck do you expect me to do with it?" I demanded.

"Now, now, such language!" she scolded. "I expect you to wash it and cook it for dinner."

After a while it became like some sort of joke—"meal prep, meal prep"—they'd say, but instead of raw chickens they began resorting to frozen meals that I only had to put in the microwave. It wasn't that they refused to do laundry, but instead, they insisted on standing around while I washed and folded all of my clothes. "So, I'm actually paying you guys for this?" I'd tell them as I put my clothes into the washer, selected the temperature, and added the soap.

"Well, Pamela, this is *independent* living skills," the girl would remind me.

When the night finally came, I was all decked out in denim and lace. I got there early and ordered a "produce platter" and a cup of coffee, since my program decided to test me for alcohol, and waited until the DJ went on. Then all the lights in the room went down and a spotlight shone down in the corner over the "Corona" and "Budweiser" signs and black light posters of 8o's musicians. Then an old familiar voice rang out through the club that sounded more like a middle-aged uncle than a world-famous DJ. Yet, his mixing skills were everything I remembered. When I wasn't dancing, I hung out near the booth watching his hands the best that I could as they skillfully moved over the boards.

"Pamela!" He looked up and said when he got to a break. "What have you been up to these days?"

"Learning from the best," I told him. "You don't mind if I watch while you mix?"

"Of course not," he said. "Why don't you come on and join me back here?"

The next few weeks, I went to see him on Friday at *Oscars* and on Saturday nights when he was at *Fashions*. Then sometime in October, the Crystal Cathedral called and asked if I'd do the *Glory of Christmas* again. Now I had my job at St. Jude's, my classes at Cypress College, my nights at the club, and the *Glory* shows. I rarely got any sleep, I never had time. "I'm sure that Dr. Katz would be proud." I'd tell myself. "After all, I'm keeping myself busy."

One night, I was walking back from one of the clubs when a voice called out to me in the dark, then a shadow emerged and started walking beside me. "Pam. Pam!" It began calling out after me. I remembered the voice. In fact, it sounded just like the one who had lied to me.

"Bobby? Bobby, is that you?"

"Pam, I haven't stopped thinking about you," he pleaded. "Please, can we talk?"

"No, Bobby. Just leave me alone!"

"Please, honey? I miss you so much," he groveled, putting his hand against one of my arms.

I yanked away, then slid my headphones over my ears, reaching down to my waist for my Walkman. There was a brief moment of crackling static and a thunderous boom that rang out in my head—the screeching of tires screamed through the night as the world went black all around.

"Some light-colored car," Bobby frantically told the police. "Shit I don't know! Yellow, white, maybe tan? I didn't really get a good look. My God, my girlfriend's been shot! Oh my God! Oh my God!"

They took Bobby over to the station and had him answer some questions, but every time they would ask, he just started crying. Finally, they decided that he really didn't know anything so they let him go home. For me there was no dark tunnel or bright shining light—no riverbanks or shallow green waters, or lost souls crying out for "one more chance." Now it was only a still small voice that spoke in my head like a thundering whisper. When my time came, I would be alright. No more waiting by the banks of a stream in a small wooden cottage, a whisper of oaks and a cool sullen fog hiding my face from all those who loved me. This time the voice smiled back through a mirror and told me that it "was not yet my time."

After a week at Anaheim Memorial, I finally woke up, this time with a half-shaven head. I heard a policeman talking to my father as he stood outside of my room in the hall.

"We're pretty sure it was only a pellet gun." The officer told him. "Probably doctored. Most likely some sort of initiation."

"Initiation?" my dad asked, nonplussed. "Initiation for what?"

"To get into a gang. You know, to see if some punk had the balls to actually shoot someone." The officer then took a sip of his coffee and exhaled deeply into the air. "Then next time they give them the real McCoy and instead of an ambulance, we're calling a hearse."

My dad just stood there in silence, now and then looking back in my room.

"Mr. Vasquez," the officer said to my dad. "your daughter is one lucky woman."

"Tell me about it," my father said shaking his head.

STATION TO STATION

Talk about luck! Almost five years after I died, I was once again back in the hospital. I was hit on the side of my head about an inch or so above my left ear. The doctors had decided to leave some of it in since that would risk further frontal lobe damage to try and remove it. So, in addition to a "new plastic" skull, I had a crushed silver pellet lodged inside of my head. But what really sucked was just when all of my hair grew back and I'd lost all the weight from walking so much, I ended up back here again—a week of sedation, my head all shaved on one side, ice cream three times a day, and a river of tubes sticking out of my arms.

When I finally got out of the hospital, my dad moved me out of my place and into one in a gated community. "I've got you in a much safer neighborhood," he assured me. "And don't you be walking around at night anymore!"

Of course, that still didn't stop me from going to clubs. I dyed the other half of my hair, the part that wasn't shaved down to the skin, black as the night and painted all of my nails to match. When I looked in the mirror and the blurry young female shadow standing in front of me came into focus, I saw what I thought was some kind of Goth—Morticia, Elvira, a female raven, sexy and cool, but most of all dead. Sometime later, I called up the Crystal Cathedral and told them I wanted back into the shows. That's when the director told me that Schuller himself wanted to see me. It turned out that he had found out about my settlement and asked me if I ever heard about tithing.

"What's tithing?" I asked him.

"You know giving ten percent of your income to God."

"So, in other words, ten percent of my income to *you*?"

"Well, no," he said, then his face broke out into a smile like the one that he flashed so generously each week on TV. "That is unless *this* is your church."

So that was when I stopped doing the shows, and for a while I stopped going to church altogether. On Christmas Eve, my father and Betty came over and brought me a tree, then decorated the inside of my apartment. I called and ordered KFC and we sat down to dinner as red and green lights blinked all around us. That night it got really cold, so cold that my dad had to fill up a bucket of water from inside of my bathtub and dump it out over his windshield to melt all the ice. But it stayed pretty warm inside my place as we all sat around the TV drinking hot chocolate and talking late into the night.

Sometime later, I got a call from my sister Veronica. "There's some guy named Jeff that keeps calling for you. He said he worked with you over at KROQ, so I gave him your number."

"Jeff? Oh, *that* Jeff," I said. "Thanks, sis!"

So, it turned out that one of the producers at KROQ was now an agent and he wanted to take me on as his client. Within weeks I was answering phones on KOST 103 and KIIS FM. I even interned for Rick Dees, or "Dick Sleaze" as I called him. It turns out that he taped most of his shows in advance then showed up each morning and had his board operator do most of the work while the rest of us were expected to get him whatever he asked for, or in other words, spend four hours kissing his ass.

Then one morning, Jeff called and told me that two KROQ DJs, Freddy Snakeskin and Swedish Egil, were leaving to start a new station, MARS FM, and that they would like to have me on board, not as an intern, but part of the staff. So, on May 24, 1991 "the new music invasion" was launched. I worked the overnight shift mostly as a production assistant while Mike Fright and Holly Adams showed me the ropes. Sometimes Egil would drop by and say "hello" and train me on some of the new equipment. Before too long, I was able to do my own mixes. Given that I had only one working hand, I learned to perfect my cross-fade technique by toggling beats across multiple channels, each one synced to a different track. One day when he came by the studio, I stopped him at the door and waved him inside.

"Here, check this out!" I said then handed him a pair of headphones.

"Wow, Pamela, that's intense!" he said, then he handed me back my receivers and before he walked out, told me I needed to watch all my levels.

Not long after that he was taking me out to some of his gigs and as I got better, let me have some time on the board. Then he'd introduce me over the mike as the room broke out in a round of applause. Things went well for me that year, my work at the station, doing live gigs—even taking a class in Mortuary Science. Of course, that left me no time to work at St. Jude's so the last day when I walked through the doors there were plenty of hugs and tears all around.

"So, *you're* the famous DJ!" one of the children came up and said before I took off my apron and gloves. "Would you please come over and sign my cast?"

So, I took the Sharpie from out of his hand and wrote down the words, "To Brandon, my hero! Get well soon. Love Pam." Then I bent down and kissed the top of his head as we both just stood there and cried. Later that year, when Jeff drove me out to the station, I noticed that all of the DJs and even the Program Director were standing outside in the lobby.

What's going on?" I asked him.

But he just put an arm around me when the owner's wife came in to tell us that the station was going to be playing "smooth jazz" starting next week and that all of our services were no longer needed. For a while everyone stood there in shock, then someone, I think it was Freddy, said "bummer" and threw up his hands. One by one, everyone just walked out to their cars. We stayed on through the weekend and like dead men walking managed to go through the motions until *James Brown is Dead* by L.A. Style rang out one last time before all of that elevator shit took over.

For the next few weeks, I did practically nothing, just sat in my apartment as one final hot breath of summer torched all of the walls in my room and kept me awake as the streetlights below blared in through the window. About a week after my birthday, I went out to see Trey who had joined the Air Force and was now stationed somewhere out in New Mexico. He took me out to the bars with his friends and even I had a beer, it was the first and last one that I ever had. At first, I didn't like the taste, but the sandstone mesas, wide dusty plains, and the testosterone laden fraternity of airmen made it seem right. And Trey was always the perfect gentlemen. He said it was to show me what a real relationship was supposed to be like, "Unlike all of those losers that you seem to find."

"So, Trey, what is it that you're trying to tell me?" I asked him as I threw back the rest of my beer.

"Holy shit, Pam. Slow down a little!" he chuckled. "I didn't know you were such a drinker."

"I'm a *Vasquez* remember?" I laughed. "Now back to my question."

"Well maybe," he said. "Maybe if you lose a little more weight." Then he smiled and put his arm around me. "Come on, you *do* know I'm kidding?"

I stayed with him on the base for the weekend then he drove me out to the bus station somewhere out on the outskirts of town.

"Don't be a stranger," he said as he gave me a hug. I turned around and got on the bus as the airbrakes blew a long deep sigh into the air. Somewhere under the dying warmth of the New Mexico sun, I watched him disappear in the shadows, his monogramed cap standing stately over a pair of dark mirrored aviator shades.

When I got back home, there were several messages on my phone, each one from my agent Jeff.

"Hey, Pam, I'm not sure if you'll be interested, but I've got a gig for you if you want it." Please call me back." Beep.

Then another.

"Hey, Pam," Jeff again. Just wanted to say I've got a gig. Pays pretty well, and besides its local. Give me a call." Beep.

Then a third.

"Hey Pam. Okay, okay, it's Gay Radio. I know, I know, but like I said, it pays pretty well. Goodness Pam, where the fuck are you?" Beep.

I picked up the phone and decided to call him. There were other messages, all from him, but I decided to erase them without even listening. When my dad found out that I took the job, he asked if I was a dike, or if I had gone "lez" and some shit like that. But I told him not to worry and that I still liked guys, then offered him a sticker to put on his Bronco.

"Uh, no!" was all that he said. We both stood there and laughed at the thought of the looks my father would get as he drove down the street.

The studio was located on some nondescript parcel of land about a mile from Disneyland, and when Jeff picked me up, it only took us all of ten minutes to get there.

"See, I told you it was local," he said as he drove into the lot. "We don't need to drive to L.A. anymore."

Any misgivings I'd had about taking the job were also dispelled right away—well maybe not *right away*. The Program Director was some guy named Chris—*Chris Cream*, to be exact. Besides that, he had a boyfriend named Harry who worked with him at the station.

"Pleased to meet you, uh, Mr. Cream," I said.

Pleasure's all mine," he said. "And please, call me Chris."

"All right, Chris it is."

"And this strapping young stud over here is my partner, Harry," he said to the man in the skinny black jeans.

"Nice to meet you, Harry," I said as I held out my hand. "Is that Harry with two 'r's' or one with an 'a' and an 'i'?

"I like her already!" Chris laughed. Then he took me into the studio to meet the rest of the staff.

"You'll be doing the 'six-to-nine' with Annie, or *Sega the Sex Goddess* as she likes to be called.

Then he walked me over and introduced us. "Pam, Sega—Sega, Pam."

"Sega the what?" I asked somewhat confused.

"The *sex goddess*, bitch!" she said with a smile. "And your name is Pam? Is that it, just Pam?"

"Well, no," I said. "It's actually Pamela. But you can call me Pam if you like."

"We need to work on something better for you. You know, something that makes you really stand out," Chris said as we sat down in his office.

"Well I ain't gonna be no *Nina the Nympho*, or *Susie the Slut*," I assured him.

"Let's see now, Pam, Pam, uh, Pammy..."

"Don't even go there!" I warned him.

"Sorry, just thinking out loud. Hey how about Spam? DJ Spam?

"You're fucking kidding!" I said.

"OK, we'll think of something. In the meantime, just hang out with Sega and do whatever she asks you. Well, maybe not *everything*!" He said with a long hearty chuckle.

It turned out, working with Sega was pretty chill. Since it was mostly a talk show with some interviews, news, and music thrown in, she let me break in whenever I wanted. One time, this guy called up expecting to hear some of the easy listening shit that the station had played before he had moved. Imagine the shock when he heard some *sex goddess* chick talking about things like condoms and lube and "coming out" to her folks. So, he calls in when we're both on the air and reams us a new one, calling us every name in the book, before he asks me if I too was a dike.

"Well no, sir, actually I'm 'bi,'" I answered politely.

"Oh, you mean as in *bi-sexual*? He snarled back into the receiver.

"No as in bye. Good-bye!" I calmly replied then I hung up the phone.

"Shit, Pam that was awesome!" Sega exclaimed. "Made an ass out of him right on the air."

"*All* of that went out on the air?" I asked her.

"Damn right!" she said then added a "high five" for good measure.

Things went well for the next few weeks, then one day, Chris shows up right before my shift began.

"I got it!" He said. "You're Pam like the cooking spray, right?"

"Uh, yeah. I guess."

"So, from now on, you're non-stick Pam—*DJ Non-stick Pam!*"

"I like it!" I said. "Besides, who needs Crisco, when you've got Pam?"

From that moment on, I was *DJ Non-stick Pam*, and I used that name at every other station I went to. I remember telling Trey about it, but he didn't seem to get it at first.

"Let's see here, you're working at KWIZ, or it that K-*whiz*? And your on-air title is some sort of cooking spray?"

"It's not K-whiz, Trey. It's KWIZ like in *quiz*."

"Well, I'm happy for you, a cooking spray now working at K-whiz." Then we both started laughing.

Sometime before Christmas, I started taking some art classes and one of the instructors, some Asian guy, immediately took a liking to me.

"So, you tell me that you cannot see very well," he told me. "Then how do you learn how to paint?"

"This is actually my very first class."

"Then it looks like you've got some natural talent," he proudly assured. "What did you say your name was again?"

"Pamela," I said. "Pam, Pamela, DJ Nonstick Pam, just don't call me Pammy!"

"Hey, aren't you that lady who works on the radio?" he asked, as his voice began to rise in excitement.

"That would be me."

"I'm Piasha," he said. "And Miss DJ Nonstick Pam, someday I'd like to take you to dinner."

So, for the next few months, Piasha and I were an item. I knew that he still looked at men, but I didn't mind. One day, on his birthday, my family came over and took him to dinner at some local Asian place that he liked.

"I have to warn you," he told my father, "the food here is *really* spicy."

"By the way, in case Pam didn't tell you, we're all Mexicans," he proudly proclaimed. "So, bring it on!"

Those were words that my father soon learned to regret. After each, bite he gulped down most of his water then asked the server to just leave him the pitcher.

"Damn! How do you people eat this stuff?" he asked.

"My family is from Thailand," Piasha told him, "so we're kind of used to it."

And Piasha was always so kind and so sweet. Before we'd go out, he would come over and put on my make-up then turn my head toward the mirror and say, "I'd like you to see the most beautiful girl that I know."

But that was the problem, I was a girl, and Piasha, I don't think that he ever knew who he was. The bottom line was that he was an artist, and as an artist his first love was beauty, regardless of gender. Before too long, I let him move in so that he could save up the money to buy his own studio. Most of the time he slept on the couch, but sometimes he didn't. But mostly we'd just sit in the living room watching a movie and cuddling together sharing a bag of popcorn between us. I knew in my heart that it never could last, but I still didn't expect it to end like it did. One day after work he came home, and I could tell that he had been crying.

"Pam you know that I love you," he said, "but I still can't seem to get over Eric."

"I see."

"Last night he called me, and I realized that I still have these feelings..."

"So, what you're trying to say is you want to break up," I cut him off.

"Not break up, just maybe separate for a while."

I still went to his class every week and we both pretended that things were okay. Then on the final day of class, I ripped off the cloth that concealed my canvas. Standing before him, a Shukra warrior clad in a blue, almost indigo robe. On his hip, a gleaming sword of chromium steel holstered beneath an uncertain hand—an Excalibur forged in the aisle of Avalon, a ring that the Dark Lord Sauron had fashioned. On one side of him, a deep dark abyss, a sea of hands rising in waves reaching out from under his feet. Above him was a cathedral of light, a shower of stars, and a host of angels singing together. Standing between them, a thick red curtain that could only be rent with the sword in his hand.

"This is for you," I told him. "I hope someday that you conquer your struggle."

I never did see Paisha again after that. I heard somewhere that Eric was killed while riding his scooter on Garden Grove Blvd. He was crossing the street and a car ran the light, and well, you know how that goes. Then later that year, I found a new church, one over on Anaheim Blvd.—the one where all the bikers went. I didn't know about all of the bikers before I went there, I just liked the sound of the name—*Set Free*—as I knew there were still so many things in my life that I needed to be set free of. It didn't hurt that the first day I went there,

I met some guy with dark wavy hair that hung down to his shoulders. He was wearing one of those muscle tees that exposed a set of rippling biceps, like a pair of pistons gleaming down from the bright chrome engine of a Harley Hog, one of many that stood in the parking lot. He wasn't too bright, in fact he seemed sort of slow, but he was really into me like no one else had ever been, and I felt like I would always be safe within the make-believe fortress of his embrace.

MUSCLE AND BLOOD

Things moved quickly with Robin and me, perhaps a little too quickly. He asked me if he could come over and make me dinner then he'd always ask to stay for the night.

"I'll just sleep on the couch," he promised, but then he always seemed to wake up in my bed.

And he always carried a bible with him wherever he went. He told me stories about his life and that when he was young his parents kicked him out of the house and he got into parties and drugs, until, he would say, "Jesus Christ came into my life."

My dad had no problem with Robin and me living together. At least he never told me he did. I know that Betty didn't seem to mind, seeing that he was a body builder and all. Besides, he promised my dad he would do all of the cleaning and laundry when I was away at the station or in one of my classes. Not to mention he'd always be there so I didn't have to go out walking alone. Of course, at the time, he wasn't working, but every now and then he'd do some odd jobs and make a few bucks so it wouldn't be like he was mooching off me.

So, we stayed there in Anaheim for a while until the shit hit the fan with Pastor Phil who had a problem with me working at Gay Radio.

"You do realize that homosexuality is a sin," he would tell me, then let me know that if I really wanted to be "set free" I would leave the station.

But there were other sins going on right under his nose that he didn't seem to have much of a problem with. There was drinking and drugs and under-age girls having sex right there in the houses he rented. Of course, most of the people who lived there were really trying to follow the Lord, but it wasn't too long before the city of Anaheim "had their fill" of Pastor Phil. The following year, the group dispersed with branches springing up all the way from El Cajon to Visalia. I also was growing tired of living in Anaheim and so one day I called up my dad and told him that I wanted to move.

"Shit, Pam, you must think I'm a real estate agent or something!"

"No, but you do love me!" I said in a voice that I always used when I was trying to charm him.

"All right then. Where is it that you want to live?" He finally conceded.

"Brea sounds nice."

"It's also expensive!" he said, sounding more like a conservator and less like a father.

"You will if you love me," I pleaded.

"All right then. I'll find you something in Brea. Geesh!" He let out a breath then he hung up the phone.

And soon, before the end of the summer, Robin and I were living in Brea.

In many ways, Brea reminded me of Yorba Linda, only much more developed. From State College to Brea Blvd. then from Lambert to Imperial Highway it was shopping malls, restaurants, and movie theaters—in other words, Irvine without all the yuppies. We lived right in the middle of everything in the Town and Country apartment complex. Across the street was Bobby McGee's, where I used to go dancing, and the 24-Hour Fitness were we went to work out every day. The day after we moved in, I paid for both of our memberships and Robin spent most of his time over there when I was at school or working at the radio station. When I got home, he'd have dinner waiting for me, some kind of Mexican dish that his mother would make, it wasn't that great, but I ate it with him and then we'd both take a shower—usually together—watch some TV then go to bed. For my birthday that year, he bought me a ring—some little number he got from a parking lot vendor—it wasn't that much, but it showed me he cared.

"Someday I'm going to ask you to marry me," he promised as he slid the gilded brass band down on my finger, "then it will be all diamonds and gold."

But within a few weeks, the gold started coming off on my finger, leaving behind a dull green halo, then the bloom started coming off of the rose altogether. For one, he didn't like me working so much. And since he didn't drive, my agent Jeff had to come out each day and give me a ride to the station, and that soon began to rile him up.

"But Jeff's engaged to be married!" I told him.

"Yeah, but he's still a guy," he reminded me.

"So, what are you saying? *All* guys are cheaters?"

He said nothing, just stormed out of the room.

"I'll be at the gym," he said as the door closed behind him.

He also didn't like me working at Gay Radio either. After all, "how did I *know* they were gay and wouldn't just 'ungay' themselves if the moment arose."

"Seriously, that's the most stupid fucking thing I ever heard in my life!" I said as I threw up my hands and walked out the door.

Then I started noticing some of my things turning up missing. Like some of the jewelry my mother had left me and a few of the signed CDs I got when there was a promotion at KROQ. But every time I'd confront him, he'd just deny it.

"You must have misplaced them," he'd tell me. "And besides, I'm a Christian. Doesn't the bible tell us not to steal?"

"It also tells us not to have sex before marriage, but that doesn't seem to bother you much."

"Well, we're gonna be married someday," he'd assure me, "so, in the eyes of God you're technically already my wife."

Then there was the time I got to the station and both Chris and Harry noticed the bruises on both of my arms. I didn't tell him that the night before, Robin had grabbed me and held me down when I wanted to go outside for a walk. I could tell that evening that he had been drinking and was probably on something as well.

"Girlfriend, you need to get out of there!" Chris warned me. "Things are never going to get any better."

"But he says that he loves me," I told him.

"Love doesn't leave these kinds of marks!" Harry said, lifting up both of my arms.

The following week it all hit the fan. Not only were more of my CDs missing, but a birthstone necklace and few gold bracelets. When he got back from one of his workouts, I confronted him when he walked in through the door.

"So, what are you doing with all of my shit?" I demanded.

"What shit?" he objected.

"Don't play fucking dumb with me, Robin! I know that you've been stealing my shit then probably selling it to buy drugs!"

"But Pam," he objected, "as a Christian..."

"Christian my ass!" I screamed cutting him off. "Take all your shit and get out of my house!"

He ended up not leaving that night but begged me to let him sleep on my patio until he asked his parents if he could move home. Then a few days later I came back home and found him in the living room watching TV.

"So, when are you leaving?" I asked him. "Weren't you supposed to talk to your parents?"

"Look, Pam, I'm sorry. You know that I love you," He pleaded. "I promise I'll change."

"I hope that you do," I calmly assured him, "but it won't be while you're living with *me*. I'm going out for a walk, and when I get back, you had better be gone."

I opened the door, took a right, and walked down the hall and pressed the "down" button on the elevator door. The next thing I knew I could see this ominous shadow approaching as the floor thundered under his feet. I hit the button again, and again, *and again and again*—nothing.

"Help! Help!" I banged on the door until two strong calloused hands started closing around my throat.

"How dare you! You fucking bitch!" he snarled, his face twisted into that of a monster straight out of one of those horror movies I watched with my dad when I was still little. "I should just kill you right now!"

Then he heard some sort of noise that caused him to briefly let go of my neck, then the large metal door slid open behind me and I fell back into its waiting arms and pressed number one. The door seemed to take forever to close as my heart felt like it would soon burst out of my chest. Slowly, I watched the narrowing crevice of light disappear closing off the flood of rage that began to wash up against it.

"Fuck!" I heard him screaming as he frantically beat on the walls—then the slamming of a large metal door and the pounding of stairs, like Hannibal's army descending the Alps. When the door finally opened, I ran outside and hurried out through the gate, breathing and gasping, screaming for somebody to help. The light outside made it hard to see so I held out my hands to feel my way along the edge of the building then braced myself for the stairs that I knew were just up ahead. Four, three, two, one... suddenly I was out on the sidewalk in front of the complex, when the space under one of my feet made me turn back around as I heard a car blasting its horn. I started running down Brea Blvd. through a sea of faces that sounded like soldiers but were dressed like men sweeping the ground before them in loafers and flip-flops, khaki pants and worn out Chuck Taylors.

"Help! Help!" I cried to anyone or no one at all.

I got to a parking lot where I remembered some stores, a nail salon, and a dental office. I tried to get to one of the doors when I felt a pair of strong sweaty arms grabbing me from behind.

"Going somewhere?" He growled in a voice that was less of a man and more like a monster. I tried to scream but no sound came out. He clamped one of his hands over my mouth so I couldn't scream anymore. I began to shake my head back and forth but the more that I moved, the tighter he held me. In a moment of terror, I finally bit him.

"You bitch!" he screamed. He threw me down on to the ground and stepped on one of my legs. Pain shot through my leg like a bolt of lightning then out through my body. But before I could scream, he twisted my arm behind my back, pinning me down to the ground. Then maybe he heard somebody coming, or maybe it was a vision from God, but I saw him look up for a second as his dark eyes briefly met mine. He let out a grunt that turned into a roar as he ripped off my fanny pack then ran out across Brea Blvd., horns blasting and tires screeching till he disappeared over the street. Then there were sirens wailing like banshees, men dressed in white, and a cold steel prick in one of my veins. At some time, I may have passed out, because I woke up in the ER at Anaheim Memorial. The same place I had ended up when I'd been shot. Only this time, it was a broken leg and a few fractured ribs concealed behind a bag of morphine that hung on a stand over my bed.

"What, what happened?" I said to a man dressed in blue who stood at the side of my bed.

"We got him," he told me. "Nailed his ass."

Then one of his partners who was standing behind him filled in all the rest of the details.

"Dumb ass ran right behind the Mortuary. We found him trying to bury your purse."

"You mean my fanny pack," I corrected.

"Yeah, whatever it was," he said, then continued. "He got up and tried resisting arrest. That was when we tased the shit out of him. I mean *really* tased the shit out of him!"

"So where is he now?" I asked him.

The other cop, the first one, the older of the two, told me that he they took him to jail, before the younger one spoke up again.

"We let the guards know why he was in there," He said, then he started to chuckle. "I'm sure that he's having a *real* fun time."

He continued to snicker to himself for a while, until the other cop finally shot him a look.

"You get well now, young lady," The older one said then he paused for a second. "And next time make sure that you choose someone better."

The day they released me was six years to the day when my mother had died. My father had Betty stay at my place to look after me while my leg healed up, then a few days later he knocked on the door.

"Daddy, what is it?" I asked when I answered.

"It's David, he said. "He passed away last night in his sleep."

The following week, after Thanksgiving, they laid him to rest beside my mom. Ever since my mother had died, I found out that he was drinking again and all that he talked about was how much he missed Ginny and how hard it was for him to go on without her.

"Well at least now they're finally together." I heard my dad say to one of his kids as if he ultimately came to the realization that David was the only man who had been able to do something he couldn't.

MIXING QUEEN

hristmas that year really sucked. For one, I was still in a cast, so it was hard for me to walk anywhere. Then, later that day, it started to rain, so I ended up staying inside. My father and Betty had come over the week before and put up some lights, but all that did was make me depressed as I watched them blink on and off in the window's reflection as the rain outside spilled colors like tears made of paint. *Screw this, I'm going to bed*, I thought to myself, when all of a sudden, the telephone rang.

"Collect call from *Chino State Prison*. Do you accept the charges?"

I was too stunned to say anything, so the message repeated itself. Then for some reason I decided against my better judgement not to hang up. But the voice on the other end wasn't Robin, but his mother instead.

"Pam, my son wants to tell you he's sorry," she told me.

"So, what now? He's sorry?" I said. "Tell him it's too fucking late! Oh, and tell him that I hope he gets butt raped tonight!"

Then I heard some talking going on in the background then his mother's voice again on the phone.

"He understands how you feel and he's not asking you to forgive him." Then came another series of whispers before she continued. "He just wants to wish you a Merry

Christmas and he prays each night for God to watch over you."

"And Merry Christmas to you," I said to his mom as I put the phone back on the receiver.

At first, I wanted to scream, "How dare him! That bastard! That pile of shit! Damn him to hell! I hope that he's rotting in there!" Then I walked over and turned on the TV and some children were singing *Silent Night* somewhere outside of *Rockefeller Center*. As the rain beat harder against my window, the furnace went on and lifted the chill from out of the room. When I awoke the next morning, the TV was on, but by that time Christmas had come and gone.

All through the winter, the rain never seemed to stop falling. Early one morning, Betty came to take me to the hospital to remove my cast, so it was nice to be able to get out of my apartment. Then one day, the telephone rang just as the sun broke in through my window.

"Who the fuck is trying to call me so early?" I mumbled to myself as I reached over to pick up the phone. But the voice on the other end seemed so excited that I didn't have the chance to stay angry for long.

"Pam, this is Jeff. Can you hear me?"

"Yes, yes, go ahead," I muttered.

"Pam, I've got some good news and bad news, which do you want?"

"The good news I guess."

"OK, here goes. KWIZ has leased some time at night to start a new show."

"Go on."

"It's a techno format called *Renegade Radio*, you know the same kind of stuff that they played when you were at MARS. It's hosted by Egil and DJ Mike Fright and they wanted to know if you would be interested. You know, doing some mixing and on-air promotions."

"Hell yeah, I'd be interested!" I said as I sprang out of bed. "When do they want me to start?"

"Next Sunday night, or Monday morning, what have you. The show goes from midnight to six."

"So, before I start, I can say hi to Chris."

"Well," Jeff demurred as he lowered his voice, "that sort of leads me into the bad news."

"Shit, I forgot there was bad news."

"Uh yeah, Gay Radio went off the air."

"Really? When did that happen?"

"A while ago when you were still injured. They didn't seem to get enough advertising. You know how that works."

"Why didn't you tell me?" I asked now raising my voice.

"I didn't want to upset you. Besides," he said changing the subject, "now you'll be doing remotes throughout L.A. and Orange County. How cool is *that*?"

"Okay, I guess. But I'll still miss Chris and Sega. If you hear from them, can you please tell them to give me a call?"

"I will," he said with his typical half-assed assurance. "You know the problem with you, Pam, is that you're too goddamn sentimental!"

"But that's why you love me," I told him.

"Uh, yeah," he said, "that's one of the reasons. Anyway, I'd better get going. I'll see you next Sunday. I'm sure you can't wait to get started!"

So, by Easter that year, I was now doing two shows on KWIZ—*Renegade Radio* Monday through Friday from midnight to six, and a *Roots Reggae* show that they did on Sunday. When I wasn't at the studio mixing, I was off in some remote location on Hollywood Blvd. or out in the Valley. No to mention, the money was good since I was able to sell my mixes through the deal that Egil had landed with EMI records. Sometimes, on the weekends, Jeff would set me up in some swanky hotel right off of Sunset and Vine. There was The Hollywood Roosevelt, The Dixie Hotel—even the Downtowner Inn was nice. And before too long, I had a new nickname. Of course, I was still *DJ Nonstick Pam*, but now I was known by a more royal moniker—*The Queen of Mixing*.

Of course, what good is having money if you can't spend it? Ever since I was out on my own, it was Taco Bell or some "hole in the wall" restaurant somewhere in a strip mall. Now it was shopping on Melrose and getting to eat at some of the nicer places in town. One night after work, I found this little Italian joint off of La Brea—*Frankie's*—so I sat down inside, ordered a drink, and that was when I met Tony.

"You're first time here?" he asked as he walked over to greet me.

He was kind of short with thick dark hair that he wore in a bun. He also liked to speak with his hands, so I guessed that he was probably Italian. Then he offered me a glass of wine—Pinot Grigio—"it's on the house" he told me, "we offer it to our prettiest guests."

"So, how long have you worked here?" I asked as I raised the glass to my lips and took a small sip leaving a dark red stain on the rim.

"About five years now," he answered politely. "The owner Frank is my uncle."

"So, hence the name Frankie's!" we both said as we laughed together.

Then he sat down and suggested I get the Sicilian Clams.

"I get it," I interrupted, "you want me to order an aphrodisiac!"

"You got me!" he said throwing up both of his hands in the air. "Guilty as charged!"

Tony and I started seeing each other on and off when I wasn't working. Then one night, he brought me home to his parents for dinner.

"We're gonna show you some *real* Italian cooking!" he promised. "Like the kind of food we used to have growing up in New York."

When we sat down to eat, it was just like the dinner scene from *Saturday Night Fever*. Tony's dad was also named Tony, and his other children were Peter and Paul, "good Catholic boys," he told me "unlike that one over there" he said pointing at Tony.

"Come on," his mother Rose Mary said as she brought in a huge plate of Chicken Parmesan and set it down next the bowl of Pasta Faggioli, "the boy's brought his girlfriend over for dinner. Let's show the lady a little respect. What did you say your name was dear, Pameline?"

"*Pamela*," I politely corrected her.

"So, Tamela, welcome to our home!" She said as she sat down at the other end of the table. "Who wants to say grace before dinner? How about you, Pamalina?"

"Sure," I replied. I said a quick prayer, thanking God for all this good food, then we all concluded with a resounding "*amen.*"

Tony Sr. looked toward his son who was already digging into the pasta. "I don't remember seeing you crossing yourself. Or did you forget after so many years of not going to church?"

"I'm sorry, Dad, it's just that I've been so busy with school and work."

His dad cut him off. "And that nice lady over there," he said waving his hand in my direction, "shouldn't you be serving her *first* rather than stuffing your face?"

"It's all right," I assured him, but he was still not impressed.

"I taught him better than that. You know Frankie's boy, uh..."

"Little Frank," his mother broke in.

"Yeah, little Frank," he continued. "He's a priest now back in New Jersey. I always had hopes that that would be Tony. But Tony would never listen to me."

"Anthony was once an altar boy." His mother reflected. "Just the sweetest little thing. I mean him handing the bread and the wine to the priest, then wiping off the edge of the chalice. Ah, my little Tony!"

She got up from the table and went back to the kitchen. "Who wants seconds? Come on Paloma, a young girl like you has got to eat!"

"I'd love to Mrs.—"

"Please, call me Rose Mary," she insisted.

"Well, Rose Mary, I'd love to, but I'm way too full!"

After dinner, she brought out some chocolate cannolis and I somehow found a way to make room. When dinner was finished, I thanked my hosts, then Tony got up and walked me outside.

"You be good to her now!" his father demanded. "And tell her she's always like family to us, isn't that right, Mama?"

"That's right, Patricia, you're always like family. So, don't be a stranger you hear?"

For the most part, Tony did treat me well. It was just that we were both way too busy for anything serious. He always mentioned how "Mama wants us to get married someday and start a family and all, but me, I don't know."

"What don't you know?" I asked him.

"I don't know if I'm ready. I don't know if I really want any kids."

So that was one red flag, I guess. But that still didn't stop us from seeing each other when I was in town.

DARK RAVE

On June 21, 1996, Egil was promoted to Program Director at KDLD and *Groove Radio* appeared on the map. He not only brought over the staff from *Renegade Radio*, but some of the DJs I worked with at MARS like Holly Adams and Joe "The Boomer" Cervantes, not to mention me as well. The only problem was now that instead of working just down the street, Jeff would need to give me a ride each day to the studio in Santa Monica.

"I don't know Pam, every day?" he bemoaned.

"You would if you loved me!"

"Yeah, but now I also have kids and a wife that I love." Then he told me that he had an idea. "I'll give you a ride Monday through Wednesday, but Thursday and Friday you'll need to take a cab or a bus."

"A cab or a bus?" I complained. "Do you have any idea how much that will cost me?"

"Then I'll bring you a schedule," he promised. "If I'm correct, there's only one transfer. You take the 47 from downtown Fullerton, then you get on the 7 once you get over to Union Station.

And then," he assured me with a wave of his hand, "it's a straight shot right on down to the station."

The first three nights, Jeff picked me up at my place and gave me a ride out to Santa Monica. We got there around ten, and he would drop me off at ether Johnny Rockets on the 3rd Street Promenade or Joe's Pizza down on Broadway, then he'd point out to me how get to 11th and Pico where the station was located. Either way, I only had to walk a couple of blocks.

Now Thursday's and Friday's, that was trickier. Union Station itself was not so bad, but a few blocks in either direction was a world where only the brave, the homeless, or the addicted would even dare enter. In the shadows of the B of A Tower, The Disney Center, and Museum of Contemporary Art—the dark ravines of dirty sidewalks, storefront hostels, and empty syringes littered a dead and forgotten world. To the north was Twin Towers where just released inmates would line up to board a bus out of town to start a new life somewhere beyond the outstretched arms of the Santa Monica Freeway that ringed the city's decaying intestines. One time, when my bus got there early, I took a walk over the First Street Bridge and ended up in some housing development over on Mission. When I turned around, I could see all the lights in the distance—faraway reminders that the Tech Boom had swept up only part of the city, leaving the rest to scrape by in its wake. Window fronts were girded in cast-iron bars, graffiti sprung from the sides of buildings and crumbling walls that separated the street from a soulful abode of adobe-style bungalows, taco carts, and sidewalk vendors still plying their wares late into the night.

A wave of terror welled up inside me, not only was I lost, but I was going to be late for my bus. I saw two large windows with lights that were still glowing inside. I could hear the voices of children and could make out a light burning brightly above a large wooden door. So, I walked over and rang the bell, then I saw a middle-aged woman walk up to greet me.

"Bueno," she answered, "que puedo hacer por ti?"

"I don't speak Spanish," I answered, "but can someone please help me. I think that I'm lost."

"Espara aqui," she said stretching a hand out in front of her body, then she went back inside to go get her husband. "He speak good English. Esta mujer necesita ayuda."

"I need to get back to Union Station," I pleaded. "I'm lost and I can't see very well."

"Follow me," he said as we walked around to the driveway and got in his car.

"Thank you, sir! How much do I owe you?" I said as he dropped me off by the curb.

"It's okay." He answered. "Just next time, promise you'll be more careful. Here at night, es mui peligroso—I'm sorry, I mean it's very dangerous."

"Well, God bless you, um..."

"Oscar." He said and held out his hand.

"Oscar, I'm Pamela. And again, God bless you!"

Then there was the time when I sat on a bench waiting for the train, listening to some mix I had done on my Walkman, when suddenly, these two punks ran over and snatched my purse right out of my hand. The next day when I told Jeff what happened, he got me a beeper, a cell phone, and some pepper spray to put on my keychain.

"Make sure you only use it if you are in danger," he cautioned. "I don't want to hear about how you assaulted somebody for pissing you off."

"You know me too well." I smiled when he handed it over.

"Okay, and here's my number. Just send me a page if you get into trouble."

But downtown L.A. wasn't the only place that was dangerous. One night, I had to go out to a rave way out in San Bernardino. I kept asking Jeff "how much further" as the city lights disappeared all around us and the warm desert wind blew in through a half-opened window.

Soon, when we got off the freeway, it was like we were in some faraway outpost of potholed streets, crumbling houses, decaying palms, and abandoned warehouses—not to mention the downwind cul-de-sac for some of the worst smog in the nation.

"My God, how this place has all gone to shit!" He exclaimed as we drove into what looked like a ghost town. As he made a left from Baseline to Vernon, trash and tumbleweeds piled up against rusty chain-link fences that revealed four-digit address that shamefully leaned against the battered remains of modest clapboard ranch style homes. Then he pulled a paper out of his pocket and rolled down the window.

"We're getting close," he said as he slowed down his car in search of the mailbox that contained the address to the rave.

"Are you sure that you'll be alright here?" he asked as he got back in the car and unfolded the postcard he got out of some tattered old drop box "You know, I can call the station and drive you back home."

"I'll be fine. Besides, I'm not a baby."

"Well okay then. Just give me a beep if you need anything."

So, there we were at a place they called the *Nocturnal Wonderland* down in the city's West Stadium neighborhood. I could already hear the voices inside and feel the energy locked up behind those tall metal doors. Loud and unsettled, they seemed to arise from a pit of depravity—a teenage wasteland of music and drugs. When I knocked on the door, I was asked for a password, but I told the large Samoan man with braided dreads and arms covered up in tattoos that I was the DJ.

"*Nonstick Pam.* The girl you've been waiting for," I said with a smile as he led me inside.

But once the music began, all of the fear inside went away. My name was announced to the roar of the crowd as the pulsating rhythms of *Renegade Soundwave* tore through the room. That night I was at my best, as if I literally mixed for my life, realizing that one missed segue or the lapse of a beat would turn their rivalrous glee to disdain and these drugged out vipers would swallow me whole. But that night, when I ended my set, all I got was a standing ovation then offers of drinks and of sex. When DJ Mike Fright came up on stage to kick off his show he announced to crowd, "Let's hear it again for *DJ Nonstick Pam!*" the room erupted all over again.

When I walked off the stage, some guy who looked about twenty—blonde hair shaved off on one side and painted green on the other—asked me if I wanted a drink.

"Sure," I told him, then added because I was technically working, "unleaded, no bubbles."

"Somebody get the DJ a drink!" he shouted waving to where the bartender stood. "Unleaded, no bubbles. By the way, I'm Tyler," he told me. "I help set up these events."

After a few hard swallows, the drink was gone, then somewhere under the swirling lights, the desert moon, bending branches, and sandstorms sweeping over the street, the room began spinning inside of my head. There were all of these voices, most of them male, and a crush of hands pressing against me. I heard the slamming of doors and the sound of denim when it tears at the seams. Then all I could feel was cold all around then the dank musty smell of sweating bodies, everyone shouting and gasping, waiting their turn. Then as another crashed down on my chest, the music stopped, and the world went black.

"Again, can you tell me what happened?" The man in blue asked as the sunlight outside filled up in the room.

"I don't know. I don't know," I insisted. "All I remember is he gave me a drink."

"Who? Who, gave you a drink?

"Tyler," I said. "He said he was Tyler. Tyler or Skyler."

"I don't know," he maintained. "We asked some of the people who were there last night, and I don't remember a Tyler."

"Then Skyler. Do you remember a Skyler?"

"I've never fucking even *heard* of a Skyler. Or, is that just some name you made up?"

"Now why would I try and make up a name?" I questioned.

"Let me see here," he said, "to cover for somebody maybe? You know that you guys shouldn't be out here doing this shit. Busted several last night for underage drinking, and others for possession of drugs."

Then there was a knock at the door, and I heard a voice saying "she's clean, no booze, no weed, and no coke. But", he added. "It appears she was roofied."

It turns out that when the cops broke up the rave soon after midnight, no one could find me since I was locked inside of one of the rooms. Then the next morning they showed up again and found me covered in bruises and blood. Oh yeah, it also turns out that while everyone danced, I was brutally, and repeatedly, sexually assaulted.

The next day when I got out of the hospital, I called Jeff and not my father to come out and get me. The entire way home he tried to ask me what happened, but I just turned my head to the window and looked out over the hills now dressed all in brown having long since died under the sun.

EVERYTHING BUT THE GIRL

"What's wrong with Pam?" Everyone asked that week at the station since I barely spoke. It also didn't help that two weeks later I was sick every morning and hardly could keep anything down during the day.

"Pam if you need to go home, I understand," Egil told me when I showed up the Monday after Thanksgiving and passed out in the studio.

"Look, I'll be fine," I insisted, but he called up Jeff and told him to get me.

The next morning, I decided to visit my doctor and he put me through a series of tests, then he told me to sit down and wait for a while. In what felt like forever, I sat there and stared at the walls, the Ansel Adams wilderness prints taking me back to those family vacations up in Yosemite. Then the door burst open and the doctor walked back inside.

"Well Miss Vasquez, there seems to be nothing wrong with you."

"Nothing wrong? Then why do I wake up sick every day?"

"Let's see here," he said as he looked through the stack of notes on his clipboard. "Temp is good, urine looks fine, eyes, ears, nose, and throat all look okay. Oh, by the way", he said then he let out a hint of a smile. "Congratulations!"

"Congratulations?" I said. "For what?"

"You are with child," he answered. "Miss Vasquez, you're pregnant!"

I wanted to tell my family, but I decided to save the announcement for Christmas. Then when my siblings and I went to my dad's, I handed him a card with snow covered gables on the front and a hundred-dollar bill tucked neatly inside.

"Merry Christmas, Daddy!" I said as he walked over and hugged me. "And wait, there's still one more thing."

"What is that little girl?" he asked me.

I stood before him, then slowly turned toward my family gathered round by the tree and let out a breath. "I'm pregnant!" I said.

My dad just about shit a brick. Same thing for the rest of my family.

"What kind of a sick joke are you trying to play?" My father asked me, his expression now stern and his voice growing angry.

"It's not a joke, Dad, I'm having a baby!"

"I don't want to hear it!" My father railed waving his hands through the air trying to make it all go away. "In fact, right now I'm going upstairs."

As soon as my dad disappeared from the room, the whole house fell into a deafening silence until my sister Veronica finally spoke up.

"What do you mean you're fucking pregnant?" She said grabbing my arm. "You'll never even live through the pregnancy, let alone try and raise a baby yourself!"

"Well I don't give a fuck what anyone says, I'm having this baby!"

I pulled out my phone and called up a cab while all of my siblings just stood there yelling at me.

"Merry Christmas to all, and to all a good night!" I told them as I walked out the door.

When I got home, the telephone rang, and my stepmother Betty wanted to talk.

"Oh Pam, they're just worried," she said. "If you want to have this baby, then that's your decision. But everyone is just worried about you."

"Well, I *do* want to have this baby."

"Then that's your choice and not theirs. So, don't let them make that decision for you."

"So, you're not angry with me?" I asked her.

"Of course not," she said. "And I'll be there to help you if that's what you want."

"I love you, Mom!"

"I love you too, Pam. And Merry Christmas to you!"

Sometime after New Year's, I was up in L.A. doing a gig when I stopped over at Frankie's.

"Tony, you're not going to believe this!" I said after he hugged me and sat down at my table.

"Believe what?" he asked, pulling the cork from a bottle of wine.

"I'm pregnant!" I told him.

In the space of an instant, I watched all the color drain out from his face.

"Is it mine?" He asked in a voice that barely arose from out of his chest. "Are you planning on keeping it?"

"Of course I plan on keeping it. What kind of stupid question is *that*?"

"Well, you do remember," he said, "you do remember that I told you I don't want any kids. You *do* remember that, *right*?"

"Of course I remember. I just wanted to tell you. Please understand I'm not asking for anything."

"I see," was all that he said. Then he got up and walked away until somebody else came over to wait on me. It was the last time I saw him. He never bothered to call after that and when I went back to the restaurant on certain occasions, he would never be there. So I just stopped going back.

Later that month, the telephone rang in the morning, and my father's voice was on the other end. It was the first time the two of us had spoken to each other since Christmas.

"I'll be over there in less than an hour," he told me. "I'm coming to take you to have an abortion."

When he got to my place, it sounded like he was trying to break down the door. Then he finally put in his key and walked right inside.

"Come on are you ready?" he asked me.

"I'm not going anywhere!" I told him.

"We'll see about that!" he insisted, "or don't you remember that *I'm* your conservator?"

"You're only the conservator of my estate!" I corrected him. "But *not* of my person! You cannot legally make me do anything!"

"Then I'll take you to court if I have to!"

"Go right ahead," I dared him as he turned and walked out the door.

For the next few weeks he came over and tried to get me to sign some papers, but since I knew that he was probably up to something, I'd politely refuse. Then he would break down and tell me he loved me and that he couldn't stand to see me risking my life. By then I figured he had already talked to his lawyer and was informed that he did not have a case. Once he even tried using God to convince me.

"If it's some sort of religious belief, I'm sure that God would forgive you," He assured me like some sort of priest absolving my sins.

"Look, Daddy," I told him, "you know that I love you. But I am not aborting this baby!"

Later that evening, I called up KOST 103, a station my father would always have on in the kitchen when him and Betty would sit down to eat and made a request.

"*Papa Don't Preach*," I said to the voice on the phone.

"And who would you like to dedicate this to young lady?" The gentleman asked me.

"To my father Ronald, from his youngest Pam."

"And is there anything you would like me to tell him?"

"Yes," I said, "tell him I love him."

I'm not sure if he heard the request, but sometime later he seemed to back off. When my sister Veronica came in from the desert, she would bring me a plate of her chilequillas and a bowl of menudo just to make sure I was eating all right.

"You know these babies will try to take everything out of you," she would warn me.

At night, before I would lay down in bed, I would hear her thumping inside of my tummy, like she was giving herself tap dance lessons. I would reach down and cradle my belly and rock her to sleep. I promised God that when she was born that I would always try to do what was best for her.

"She will always be my whole world," I told Him. "I swear, I would lay down my life for this child!"

The winter rains dried up early that year, and by March, I was now able to walk wherever I needed. One day when I was walking home from Pepe's, I crossed Brea Blvd. and waited for the light on Acacia. When it finally turned green, I slid my cane down off of the curb and started to cross. The next thing I knew, I felt the crush of thick metal chrome driving into my side, throwing me down to the pavement below. I saw some guy getting out of his car, then turning around and trying to take off.

"My baby! My baby!" I screamed as a crowd started to form all around me.

When the paramedics arrived on the scene, they heard me screaming and one of them asked if my baby got hit.

"You idiot!" another one said. "Can't you see she's pregnant? We better get this one to the hospital."

I saw the police talking to the person who hit me. As he'd tried to get back into his car, two young adults, a guy and a girl, had run over and restrained him then called the police.

"I didn't see her!" he kept on saying shaking his head. "I thought that I still had the light. My God is she going to be okay?"

"You better damn well hope so!" one of the cops told the man as he sat down at the curb and started to cry.

They rushed me over to Placentia Linda where they were already waiting for me as the police kept talking to some of the witnesses. A few of them followed me to the hospital and waited outside of my room. After drawing some blood and taking some x-rays, one of the doctors walked up to my bed.

"Miss Vasquez you are one lucky lady," he told me. "It doesn't look like you broke anything."

"My baby!" I shouted. "How is my baby?"

"Your baby's just fine," he assured me. "Now you get some rest."

After a while, they started letting in visitors. A man who worked at one of the restaurants I went to, the guy and the girl who stopped the driver, and some guy that I don't remember seeing before.

"My father's a doctor," he told me. "And I'm doing pre-med studies over at Fullerton. I was just coming home from one of my classes when I saw what happened. You certainly are a living miracle."

"You don't know the half of it!" I told him then I listened as he introduced himself.

"My name's Steve," he said, "and you must be Pam."

"Wait, how did you know that?" I asked him.

"Is says so right here on your chart," he said pointing at the clipboard that hung by my bed.

A few minutes later, the curtain tore open and my sister Veronica was standing at the foot of my bed huffing like she had just run a marathon.

"I better be going," Steve told me. "See you again?"

"Sure," I said.

"Who was that guy?" Veronica asked as she walked over and put her hand on my forehead.

"Oh, that's Steve," I answered. "He was one of the people who witnessed the accident. How the hell did you get here so fast?"

"Dad called me from work, and I drove like a maniac. Must have been doing a hundred the whole way."

"You need to be more careful, sis."

"I need to be more careful? What about you?"

Then we both laughed for a while before she left to go to my dad's to wait for him to get home from work. Her, my father, and Betty came back to see me that evening. Then the next morning before I was released, Steve came over to visit as well.

"Brought you some soup—chicken noodle," he said, moving my tray over my chest. "I heard somewhere that it makes everything better?"

"What is it about you guys and soup? I asked him, shaking my head.

"What's that?" he asked.

"Oh nothing," I smiled. "It's just every guy that I've ever dated has always tried bringing me soup."

"So, we're dating now?" he asked.

"Not really," I said.

"But would you like to? I mean, one day when you're better?"

I didn't answer him right away. But that still didn't stop him from coming to visit me. On the day that I was released, Veronica came to take me back home, then just like that, Steve and I started dating. I'm not sure that he was ever my type, but he cheered me up and made me laugh. No to mention, him and his family were Christian.

Later that spring, the weather changed from cool to hot as if somebody flipped the switch on some giant outdoor thermostat. After that, both of my legs started to swell like a pair of purple Kevlar balloons.

"You look fine," Steve assured me as he came over to take me to dinner.

"Either you have a crush on Barney, or you're blinder than I am!" I laughed.

The following weekend, he took me over to meet his family. Both his mother and father liked me a lot, but after our meal, his sister Christina pulled me aside to give me a warning. But unlike most of my past boyfriend's sisters, it wasn't about me hurting him, but rather him hurting me.

"Pam, you seem like a really nice lady," she said, "but Stevie, don't get me wrong cause I really do love him, but Stevie can be a bit of an asshole."

"Why do you say that?" I asked her.

"I don't know. Maybe it's because with Dad being a doctor and all there's a lot of pressure for him to succeed. Anyway, he always finds a way to sabotage everything that's good in his life."

"Well, thanks for the warning," I told her.

When the day started getting closer, I could barely get out of bed. By that time, I must have weighed over three-hundred pounds and to make matters worse, I was no longer able to work. Egil assured me there would always be a place for me down at the station, but Jeff seemed to be growing more and more distant and I soon came to realize that me not working was costing him money.

One day, Veronica called me to discuss what we needed to do when I got ready to deliver. She would take some time off from work and come over to stay with me the week before I had to go in. By this time, Steve and I had already thought of a name. For a girl it would be Aimee Elizabeth—he insisted it be spelled with an "i" and two "ee's"—and Austin Christopher if it was a boy. Before we hung up, she asked me one final question, one that we had often discussed but as that day was approaching, I tried not to think about. I thought that if things worked out between Steve and I, that maybe he could help raise the baby, but he was still working and going to school. So, I kept it inside and tried not to think about it until that moment she brought it back up.

"So", Veronica asked me, "do you still intend on having Don and I raise the baby?"

I couldn't answer her right away, knowing that it would probably be the most difficult choice I would make in my life. For one, I knew that with my visual impairment I would never be able to raise a child on my own. Second, my father wasn't going to provide any help since he never wanted me having this child in the first place. And lastly, since I didn't really have a man I could count on, my baby would not have a father. I know that Ruth would be willing to help, but she was already well into her fifties and recently got a new foster child, a four-year-old boy, she was raising. Let's see, I could always call Tony, since the baby may even be his—ah fuck Tony, he never wanted to have kids in the first place so what kind of father would he ever make? I guess Veronica would probably be my best option, maybe even my only option. I know she lives out in the desert, but at least my child would have brothers and sisters, not to mention a mother and father. Yet inside I felt as though I was dying, like something was about to be disconnected. After more than eight months I was going to be losing a part me, a little life that depended on my every breath, my every meal, and my body's ability to protect it from that asshole driver who hit me. At night when I felt the baby starting to kick, I would cradle my belly and sing it a lullaby until the kicking stopped and both of us started dreaming together. If it were a boy, he would be a musician just like my brother, or maybe an actor. I wouldn't want him playing football or anything like that, since not only did I never like football, I'd always worry that he would get hurt. If it were a girl, she would always be my little princess, and with all of the kicking at night, most likely a dancer. What do I do? *Please, God, tell me what should I do?* I could hear myself starting to cry as my sister, now growing impatient, asked me again. Then wiping away the flood of tears that were starting to pour down my cheeks, I finally answered her quietly, "yes".

On the morning of July 28, I was rushed over to Placentia Linda for an emergency C-section. I remember the pain and all of the blood—blood *everywhere* like in one of those horror movies I used to stay up and watch with my friends—and the needle, it felt like it must have been ten feet long as they slid every inch of it into my spine.

"Keep breathing! Keep breathing!" Veronica said as she pulled back the soaking wet strands of my hair from off of my forehead. "We're here for you, baby!"

There was an intense pressure across my abdomen then a tearing sensation inside of my uterus. I don't remember if I stopped breathing, but I heard the doctor scream at the nurse for an oxygen mask and everyone almost chanting in unison, "breathe! breathe! Come on, Pam, just breathe!"

Feeling dizzy and close to passing out, I asked Veronica if the doctor had finished cutting me open.

"Cutting you open?" she screamed with excitement. "They're stitching you up! Pam, you just had a baby!"

Then I heard a loud crack of a hand upon skin and a loud cry rang out through the room—a baby, my baby! The newest member of the human race.

"It's a girl!" the doctor exclaimed. "A beautiful little baby girl!"

"Not to mention, she's also a Vasquez!" Veronica said as the baby let out another long cry.

The doctor held her up so I could make out her face, her deep dark eyes, and full head of hair. I started to cry and Steve, who had just arrived in the room, walked over and gave me a hug. One of the nurses came to pick up the baby and take her to stay in the nursery. The next day when Steve came to visit, I asked if he had the chance to go see her.

"So, what do you think?" I asked him.

"She's ugly!" he said.

I reached out and slapped him.

"Ow!" he exclaimed. "What did you do that for? All babies are ugly when they're born, all that blood all over their bodies. They look just like..."

"Just like what?" I asked him.

"Like little baboons," he said.

I reached over and smacked him again.

He asked me what I'd decided to name her.

"Arielle Breanna," I said. "My sister's idea."

"What happened to the name we decided on?" he wondered. "You know Aimee Elizabeth, or did you forget?"

"Well since my sister is going to raise her," I started to say, but he never let me finish my sentence.

"Well to me she will always be Aimee Elizabeth! That's what I'll call her if," then he paused for a moment while shaking his head. "That is, if I ever see her again!"

Then he turned and walked out of my room.

The next day I woke up late and asked if I could go to the nursery and see my baby.

"I'm sorry Miss Vasquez," one of the nurses told me. "But your sister came and got her this morning."

"What do you mean she got her this morning?"

"Her and her husband." The nurse informed me. "You do remember when you signed all the papers that both her and her husband would be raising the baby?"

"Just go away! Will you please go away?" I shouted, then I laid back down and started to cry, the tears spilling down all over my pillow.

I was released from the hospital a few days later and when I got home, my sister and her family were gone along with my baby. For the next few weeks, Steve would come over when he got off from work and we both sat down and ate dinner together. Then around the time of my birthday, Jeff came over to my apartment and handed me an envelope with a ribbon on top.

"It's from all of the guys at the station," he said.

"What is it?" I asked him.

"Why don't you open it and see for yourself?" he insisted.

I tore open the envelope and opened the card and two tickets fell out onto my lap.

"What's this?"

"See for yourself. I made sure to have them blow up the print."

"Dear Pam, Congratulations to the youngest member of our Groove Radio family and to the future 'Princess of Mixing.' Can't wait to have you back at the station, in the meantime, enjoy the show! Sincerely, The team at Groove Radio."

Then he picked up the tickets from out of my lap and read them to me: Everything but the Girl live at the Hollywood Palladium November 13, 1997.

"Oh my God!" I screamed.

"And check out the seats!" he said, holding a ticket in front of my face. "Section two, row three!"

"Holy shit!" I kept saying over and over and over again.

The next day, I called up Steve and asked him if he wanted to go, but he blew me off like he didn't even know me, much less the man I was dating for nearly six months.

"Everything but the what?" he asked me. "Come on, Pam, you know I don't like all of that techno shit."

"But it's not even techno," I argued, but that still didn't matter.

"Maybe some other time" he said. "I've gotta get going."

Just like that, he hung up the phone. So, I ended up going with one of my neighbors, some girl named Natasha who had just given birth a month before me. The night was cool, and the music swept over us in corpulent waves as the crowd began to sway back and forth in time with the beat. But as the lyrics to *Missing* boomed out all around, its images of deserts and rain, and my baby rocking to sleep next to my sister unaware that *I* was her mommy, I never felt more alone in my life.

LONG DISTANCE MOM

Later that year, about a week before Christmas, Steve called and told me that he wanted to take me out on a date. I got all dressed up like I did before I was pregnant, a denim top, leather leggings, and a white mesh shawl draped over my shoulder. By that time, I was already working out at L.A. Fitness trying to lose all of my baby fat. Each morning my trainer—some clipper-cut former WAC—I think that her name was Nancy—would spend a whole hour busting my ass.

"I don't think he's ever seen me like this," I said to myself as I looked in the mirror and dabbed on some lipstick. It turned out I was right by the look on his face when I answered the door.

"My, don't you look nice!" he said like a teenage boy witnessing his first Playboy centerfold.

When we got in his car everything changed.

"Where are we going?" I asked him.

"You'll see," he said.

He removed a CD from inside of his console, pushed it inside of the player, pulled the car over and before he hit "play," he told me that it was "my song to you."

"My God, I can't wait to hear it." I cooed, then pushed myself over to get closer to him. He pressed the "play" button and turned up the volume and I slowly began shrinking away as the venomous lyrics poured out through the speaker descending into an ear-splitting self-revelation—"cause I'm a liar! I'll tear your mind and burn your soul!"

"Take me home!" I shouted. "Goddamn it, take me home *now*!"

"What's the matter, Pam? Can't handle the truth? Did you really think that I wanted to spend the rest of my life with some chick who can't even care for herself?"

"Well that still didn't stop you from sleeping with me, did it now, Steve?"

"Well you were a good fuck, I have to admit," he smirked, as he turned his car back into my complex.

"You asshole! If I ever see you again, I swear I'll kick the living shit out of you!" I shouted through a gale of tears, clenching my fists and raising them up in front of my body. Then I kicked the door shut with one of my tall black boots and the side of his car with the other. "Fuck you!" I shouted as he pulled away then rolled down his window and tapped on the brakes.

"Oh, you'll call me again," he snickered. "The next time that you need some of this!" He opened the door, grabbed at his crotch, then slamming it shut, he hit the gas and sped down the street.

"You want me to go over there and kick his ass?" My brother asked when I told him what happened.

"Naw, don't waste your time, bro," I said as I thanked him for making the offer. "Besides, you don't even know where he lives."

The odd thing was that his sister Christina and I still kept in touch. "You were always too good for my brother," she'd tell me whenever we'd talk, but then she would add, "Well don't say I didn't warn you about him."

Another thing that helped me get over Steve was I was now back to working full time at the station. So, the next few months, it was the station at night and the gym in the day. Sometimes when I got home in the morning, I'd play my new mixes on the stereo my father had got me for Christmas. Needless to say, that didn't always sit well with the neighbors.

"Turn that shit down!" the lady next door would say as her and her husband would take turns banging on the side of the walls. "Goddamn it, we're both trying to sleep!"

So, I moved the dial from "nine" down to "seven" but if the banging continued, I'd turn it back up to "ten".

"*That* wasn't loud!" I shouted back. "This, *this* is loud!"

A few weeks later I found a paper stuck to my door. The letters were big enough so even I could read them: *EVICTION NOTICE* it said right at the top.

I called up my dad and he got me some little rinky-dink joint on Laurel and Birch that looked more like a glorified studio. I think he was trying to do it to punish me. Not that it mattered, since I didn't last that long over there anyway.

"What the hell am I going to do with you?" He shouted as him and my brother showed up on the weekend to get all my things. "This is your last chance," he warned me. "Then I'm sending you back into a program!"

He found me a place in Birchwood Village right across the street from the mall. Less than a month after I moved there, some assholes broke in and stole all my stuff when I went out to the desert on Mother's Day weekend.

And speaking of Mother's Day, it was the first time I had seen my daughter since Christmas. Don picked me up at the Greyhound Station in downtown Indio and drove me out to their house in the cove. My niece Amanda ran to the door, let us inside, and gave me a hug.

"Where's Arielle?" I asked her.

"In the kitchen with Mom. I'll take you to her," she said grabbing me by the hand.

The words first hit me like a slap in the face—"in the kitchen with Mom"—but wasn't *I* Arielle's mom? Then I saw those eyes, so deep and so dark, and a face so innocent and bright—hands outstretched looking up from her chair, she reached out to me and I bent down and hugged her like I never wanted to let her go. Yet even then, her eyes seemed so distant, like a maidenhair fern deprived of the sun—a past life regression concealed beneath a lifetime of shade, it seemed as if she knew so much more than she wanted to tell us.

After dinner, I sat down beside her on the couch and now and then she'd stare back at me, but not once did she put her arms around me the way that she did with my sister and brother in law and all of their kids.

That night when we all went to bed, I could hear Don and my sister arguing inside of their bedroom and it didn't take me that long to realize that the fighting was all about me.

"So now every holiday, your crazy fucking sister is expecting to visit?" Don asked Veronica. It sounded like she was trying to defend me before he started yelling again. "We'll then you go and get her. I don't have time for this bullshit!"

I lay on the couch and pretended to sleep as I quietly tried to hush all of the sobs back down inside of me. The next morning, I kissed my daughter good-bye then Don threw my suitcase into his truck and drove me back out to the Greyhound station. When I got back home, most of my stuff was missing, not everything, mind you, just most of the things that mattered like the rest of the jewelry my mother had left me, and CD's and tapes with all of my mixes.

"I think that I know who it was." I told the police when they finally got there. "He must have come looking for me when he got out of jail."

"We'll check into it, ma'am." The officer promised, then took a report and walked out the door. But from that moment on I knew that I needed to get out of Brea.

The next day, rather than calling my dad, I called up the guy who I sometimes worked with from Regional Center, Larry Wilson, or "Larry the fairy" as my father had called him.

"He's not gay, Dad," I told him the first time after they'd met at my place and I sent them out for lunch. "You just don't like him because he's a vegan."

"Well I'm sure that he doesn't refrain from *all* forms of meat." My father said as he laughed to himself.

So, a few days later, Larry and I drove around and looked for a place.

"Here's one that's renting!" he said as he pointed to a complex on Yorba Linda Blvd. on the Placentia and Fullerton border. "You want to go look?"

We walked into the office and the girl who worked there showed us a place on the third floor overlooking the pool. It was only one bedroom, but it had lots of space and an outdoor patio if I wanted to start painting again.

"I love it!" I said. "Can we go and get it right now?"

"Pam, remember that you're under a conservatorship," Larry reminded me. "First we're going to need to talk to your father. Do you want me to call him?"

"Sure. He gets home from work about five."

"All right then I'll call him tonight after five," he told me. "And, Pam," he said, "you need to let me talk to him first—promise?"

But when six o'clock rolled around and there was no word from Larry, I decided to renege on my promise.

"Absolutely not!" My dad shouted into the phone. "What, do you think I can just stop everything whenever you need something?"

"But, Dad..."

"But nothing! Good-bye."

Click.

Sometime later, Larry must have called to convince him, but not before my dad called my brother and asked him if he minded having me living right down the street, but I guess that it was cool with Ron because on the first of the month, I was living in Fullerton.

Early that summer, it was still really cool outside, and to make matters worse, the angle of the street that I lived on made the sun appear to go down where it did in the fall, so it was like a place without summer, which was fine with me since I *hated* summer. So, every night for a couple of weeks the clouds would roll in and absorb all the light from the streets then rain it back down like a sea of shiny gray mirrors.

At the end of July, I went out to the desert for Arielle's first birthday. That night after dinner she got cake all over herself, and my sister picked her up and gave her to me and told me to give her a bath since after all "she is your kid."

"My kid?" I asked. "Well I guess so, when it's convenient for you."

In order to get her to stop crying, I had to take off my clothes and sit next to her in the white creamy frosting-filled water. Then we stood up together and I turned on the shower—sheathes of warm water cascading against us cementing our bond.

A week after I came back home, summer decided to return with a vengeance, as the temperature soared to a hundred degrees and the sun's angry face not only melted the clouds but seemed to follow me wherever I went. It was even hot out in Santa Monica where the station was at, and one night we were all afraid that the power would go out since some of the lights kept going off in the neighborhood as the air-conditioned upscale stores on the Boardwalk welcomed stragglers in from the heat but soon began to slow down the grid. But a few weeks later the plug was pulled, and it wasn't due to a shortage of power. After more than a two-year run on KDLD, Groove Radio was replaced by World Class Rock, and once again we were looking for jobs.

"What do you mean that's everything?" I objected when Jeff showed up at my door to give me my paycheck.

"Well you forget, Pam that twice this summer you went out to the desert to see your daughter instead of doing remotes, so that's one part of it."

"And what is the other?" I asked him. "Or are you trying to tell me that lately you've been ripping me off?"

"Ripping you off?" His voice now rising in anger. "So, after seven years of working together, *now* I decide to start ripping you off!"

"Then where is all of my money going?" I demanded to know.

"Well let's see now, there's the traveling expenses that I never bothered to deduct for when I had to drive you all the way out to *bum fuck Egypt* and back. Then there was the time that you dropped an 'F' bomb on Mike Fright's show. Cost the station five thousand bucks, and guess who paid it?" Then he answered his own rhetorical question. "I fucking paid it, that's who! But you never thanked me for that, oh no, and now that I'm only trying to get what you owe me, you accuse me of ripping you off!"

We argued for a few more minutes before he literally invited me to take him to court and told me never to call him again. I guess I could have ended up suing his ass, but by that time it didn't matter. His wife just had a baby that summer, his third, and I didn't want to take food off their table. Besides I still had an estate, my rent and my utilities were paid every month, and I was getting two hundred dollars a week from my dad, so I didn't really have anything to complain about, moneywise anyway. My personal life was a whole different story.

WANDERING SPIRIT

When Groove Radio went off the air, there was a part of me that also died with it and since I didn't want to do love songs, smooth jazz, or God forbid *dinosaur rock*, my options were limited.

"So, you want me to play Stairway and *Free Bird* every fifteen minutes?" I asked when my brother suggested KLOS.

But none of it mattered since Jeff and I were no longer speaking. So, with nothing else to do every night, I decided to go out and check out the clubs in the area. There was Club 369 on Placentia Ave., but they were mostly into heavy metal. Then there was some sports bar across the street at the Albertson's shopping center, but that seemed more like a biker hangout where greasy white men in tattoos and leather would go every night to shoot pool and drink. Then I found a place that my friend Angela suggested, Off Campus, right across from Cal State Fullerton. I remember at first we were both disappointed, with such an obvious name one would expect the place to be brimming with college aged men, but instead it was mostly Foxfire veterans seeking new prey, shaved headed hooligans in crisp ironed Dickies, and burned out door-to-door salesmen in cheap Walmart suits. Then soon after we got there, *Sweaty Palm Phil* came over to buy us a drink and remind us "ladies" that "the night was still young." I politely thanked him then slammed down an unusually weak Kamikaze and waited for the night to get better.

Soon after that, DJ Kevin showed up and an occasional song encouraged us to get up and dance, and when I wasn't dancing, or talking to Angie, I was hanging out behind the booth chatting with Kevin.

"It must be nice," she would tell me when I sat back down next to her at the bar.

"What do you mean?" I asked her.

"I mean everywhere we go all the men just adore you."

"Yeah that must be why I'm still single!" I said as we laughed.

When I wasn't out dancing, I was talking to guys I met through a dating line I recently joined. Sometimes if they interested me, we'd go out for dinner or meet up at Starbucks. And there were those times it went further than that and we'd end up back at my apartment sometimes until morning. It's not that I was looking for love or some sort of commitment, in fact I would warn them as they kissed me good-bye, "don't call me, I'll call you."

One thing I noticed was, the absence of love removed most of my selective restraints—most any guy, or if none were available, even a woman would do. The first time it felt pretty awkward, but their warm soft lips and smooth firm breasts, made me feel as if I was loving myself. There was even a man who was technically married, but recently separated—some guy named Jeff, not my agent, but some guy that I met on the line—he was kind of fat and smelled really bad so I would insist that before we would do it, I "get on all fours."

Then there were nights when I was alone, and the walls of my room closed in all around me. Sometimes I would call one of the men on the *prayer watch* at Calvary Chapel, other times it was *new hope* at Crystal Cathedral. It wasn't like I abandoned my faith, but my light had grown dimmer—like Peter following along at a distance, moving in shadows, warming himself at the enemy's fire.

If it was before eleven o'clock I'd go out to Thirty-one Flavors for a Mint Chip Cappuccino Blast, come home and take all of my meds, get undressed, get into a bath, and pick up one of my toys from the side of the tub—the one's without batteries, as those were the ones I kept by the bed—then a symphony of water and plastic would rush up against my G spot like the torrents of an underground geyser seeded through an adjoining volcano. Closing my eyes, I would cast aside all of my morals—those that I learned as a child, and those that were soon and later undone—and fell into a dream as the walls began swaying in rising towers of lavender steam— *"I asked him with my eyes to ask again, yes! And then he asked me would I, yes! To say, yes! My mountain flower and I, first I, put my arms around him, yes! And drew him down to me so he could feel my breasts all perfume, yes! And his heart was going like mad and yes! I said, yes, I will. Yes!"* (Joyce, 1305).

One night as I was walking home from the club, dressed all in black and barely visible along the dark deserted streets of my neighborhood, some middle-aged man in a white minivan pulled over and rolled down the window.

"Pam, what the hell are you doing out here?" he shouted. "Get in and I'll give you a ride."

Terrified, I kept on walking, then he crept alongside of me blowing his horn.

"Pam, it's your brother. Come on, get in."

So, he helped me inside and we just sat there and looked at each other before he spoke up.

"Are you always out this late?" he finally asked.

"Not always, and you?"

"Just got back from the store," he said, but I wasn't sure if I believed him or not. "Come on, I'm taking you home."

When we walked in the door, the light above the dining room table was still on like it usually was, then looking around, he noticed two straws and a mirror sitting next to an unwashed cup.

"What the fuck is *this* all about?" he asked, lifting up one of the straws. "You doing coke? Or is it meth?"

"Dude, it's not even mine!" I protested to no avail. "One of my friends must have left it there. You know I can't see very well."

"One of your friends?" he said as he grabbed ahold of my arms and stared a hole right through my eyes. "Bullshit! What the fuck is the matter with you?"

Then he kept right on swearing at me as he went to the kitchen, reached under the sink, and pulled out the trashcan.

"Well you can tell your *friend* that your brother who actually cares about you, just threw all of his shit away!"

"Look, Ron, I'm sorry," I tried to tell him, but he wasn't having any of it.

"Sorry? You're sorry my ass!" he scowled. "With all of the meds that you're on, this shit can kill you!"

"Ron, you don't understand," I told him as he tied up the bag and walked to the door.

"What? What is it that I don't understand? I did some of that shit myself! Damn near ruined my life! Tell me what is it that I don't understand?"

"Ron," I said then I looked in his eyes still reddened with anger but starting to soften at each of the edges. "You don't understand, that I'm *already* dead."

A week before Thanksgiving, almost ten years to the day of my mother's death, I found out that Don and Veronica were no longer together. He left her for some skank named Victoria, who Veronica let move into their home when she claimed that her husband abused her. Now with Don out of the picture, she was in danger of losing the house.

"Dad, its Pam." I said when he answered the phone.

"Didn't I tell you that you're not allowed to call here no more?" he shouted back loud enough to tingle my ear.

"Dad, please you've got to call your lawyer we need to do something."

"What kind of shit did you get yourself into now?"

"It's not me, Dad," I calmly explained. "Veronica's going to lose her house."

So, he called up his lawyer and requested an ex parte hearing to see if I could use some of the funds from my estate. It turned out that since Don and Veronica were in the process of adopting my daughter, she never asked me for child support. But now that her marriage was over, I asked the judge if I could not only pay her to be Arielle's guardian, but that she be paid retroactively dating back to the day she was born.

"I don't need your fucking money!" Veronica said when I told her about it. "What, are you trying to tell me that I'm not able to raise Arielle on my own?"

"No, sis, I'm just trying to help," I assured her.

A few weeks later, right before Christmas, we went into court and the judge ruled in my favor. When the hearing was over, Veronica ran over to me as I got ready to walk out the door with my dad and his lawyer.

"Look, thanks, sis," she said, reaching out and touching my arm. Then she turned and went in the other direction out to the structure to look for her car.

That year, we all got together at Marie and Roger's house for Christmas, and since Betty insisted on me being there too, I was formally invited. The day was cold when we made the drive out to Bakersfield in my father's Bronco and once we got over the pass, the wind started picking up dust as the car shook back and forth on the road. Not only would most of my family be out there, but so would Ron's friend Jim, his wife Lisa, and both of his daughters. Last year I had stayed home at my apartment and Don and Veronica showed up with Arielle for a couple of minutes, then just like that they had to be going. But this year I would finally get to spend time with my baby. I went to the store to buy her some clothes and a stuffed golden bear like the one that lived in the big blue house on the show that she liked on TV. I also bought her a pair of white Doc Marten boots in a toddler's size. "You're fucking kidding!" Veronica said when I told her about them. I also decided to write her a poem and read it out loud in front of the family. It was a verse that I'd heard in a song—one from the seventies—but I made it my own, a heartfelt sonnet of love to a son that I changed into a song for my daughter.

"Hey, Pam you got a booger," Jim said pointing to the mole on my face as Roger let us in through the door.

"Merry Christmas to you too." I said as I gave him a hug. "So how is life in Tehachapi?"

"Pretty damn cold," he chided. "But the scenery's nice and the property's cheap so I can't complain."

"So, are those the little ones?" I asked him, pointing at the two little girls toddling around on the living room floor.

"Well, one of them is." He nodded. "The other one's yours."

Then I heard Veronica calling me over, as she stooped to the floor to pick up the baby.

"Say Merry Christmas, Pam. Arielle, can you say Merry Christmas?"

After a couple of tries, she did manage to say my name, but it was still "Pam" and not "Mom," so that kind of hurt. Then after I held her awhile, Veronica's son Andrew came over and snatched her away. When we finally sat down to dinner, I was all the way over at the end of the table next to my father and Betty while Arielle squirmed in her seat next to Veronica, saying my name over and over and trying to join me.

"Sit down, Arielle!" Veronica scolded as Roger who was dressed in a white chef's hat and a matching apron set a plate of prime rib, fresh baked rolls, and scalloped potatoes down on the table.

"All right, who's going to say grace?" He asked as he took off his hat.

With all our heads bowed, and what seemed like several minutes of silence, my father finally spoke up, "Good bread, good meat, good God, let's eat!"

After dinner, Veronica served us all a slice of "pink pie"—a recipe she learned from our mother—then we gathered all around by the tree to open our presents. While most of us got cards and money, my father surprised Veronica with a present that was, considering him, quite neatly wrapped. It was some sort of sweater that looked like the ones that your grandma would knit when you were a child. It was the ugliest thing, but it still made her cry when she opened it up. Then I gave Arielle the presents I got her and while she didn't know what to make of the boots, she sure loved the bear.

"Wait everybody," I said as Marie and Roger started gathering up all of the paper and boxes and Veronica piled up all of the dishes into the sink. "There's still one more thing."

"What is it Colombo?" My father chuckled.

"It's a poem that I wrote for my baby."

At first, I heard a few groans, then Roger told everybody to "listen up" as Arielle's eyes set softly on mine.

I took a deep breath and read it out loud in front of the room:

JERRY KUZNIK

The season is upon us now, a time for gifts and giving;
As the year draws to its close, I think about my living;
The Christmastime when I was young, the magic and the
wonder;
But colors dull and candles dim, and dark my standing
under;
Oh, little Arielle, shining light, you've set my soul to
dreaming;
you've given back my joy in life, and filled me with new
meaning;
A savior king was born that day, a baby just like you;
And as the wise men came with gifts, I've come with my gift
too;
That peace on earth fills up your time, that brotherhood
surrounds you;
That you may know the warmth of love, and wrap it all
around you;
It's just a wish, a dream I'm told, from days when I was
young;
Merry Christmas little Arielle, Merry Christmas everyone;
Merry Christmas little Arielle, Merry Christmas everyone!
(John Denver, 1975)

For a moment the room stood quiet and still, the
glow from the tree warming my face in cascading pixels of
light. Then I looked at Arielle, her face agleam, her mouth
slightly opened and two small hands reaching over in my
direction. I smiled back and for a moment our eyes locked
onto each other, suspended in the seasonal radiance that
held us together in a distant embrace until shards of

uproarious laughter rained down on me like showers of blood.

"Thanks, Pam!" Andrew stood up and bellowed, "for ruining Christmas!"

Then gales of laughter swept through the room as I tried to hold back the tears in my eyes.

"Pam, that was beautiful!" Betty exclaimed. "All of you should be ashamed of yourselves!"

"Look, Pam, you know that we love you," my brother assured me when all of the laughter finally subsided. "It's just that you were *so* serious!"

"There's no need to apologize, bro. I'm used to you mocking me." I reached in my purse and pulled out my phone. "I'm calling a cab. Andy, I'm sorry I ruined your Christmas!"

My father and Betty followed me outside with my sister Marie close on their heels.

"Just take her back to the motel," she told my father. "I don't need all of this drama at Christmas!"

We were all supposed to meet up the next day for breakfast, but the three of us decided to leave that night. On the way home, none of us spoke, as we climbed up into the darkening shadows and over the pass—the cold wind whistling in through the cracks of the white plastic cab.

When we got back home, my dad dropped me off at my place, without even saying good-bye let alone wishing me a *Merry Christmas*. I walked up the sidewalk that led to my building as glowing streams of white crystal bulbs still hung in the trees. I climbed up the stairs, opened the door, set down my purse, walked into my room, and laid down and cried.

I wanted to pick up the phone and call somebody. Let's see who out there still gives a shit? Trey, he's probably busy with family ever since he got married last year. My old friends from high school? Yeah right. My agent Jeff? Are you fucking kidding? Steve? What about Steve? Right now, I didn't care if he ever loved me, maybe he did and was too afraid of letting me know. Perhaps if I call him, he'll want to come over? I knew it was late, but maybe he was sitting alone in his room waiting for somebody to call him? Maybe he was feeling lonely as well, after all, Christmastime can be pretty lonely. Maybe he'd forget about all he had said, and he'll just want to come over and hold me. Don't we all need somebody just to hold us sometime? Feel some sort of human connection, a warm soft body to lay there beside us and tell us those things that make us feel alive, even if they turn out to be lies?

No, Pam! Don't do it! I said to myself as I picked up the phone and started to dial. Then I put the phone back on the receiver, picked it back up, and dialed the prayer watch. But then even after we prayed, I still felt like an uninvited guest to the party of the one whose birthday we all were celebrating.

For the next few days I stayed in my room and when I wasn't playing video games, I was writing poetry—really dark and personal stuff that if I ever let anyone see they'd probably want to have me committed. Then on New Year's Eve I was out on the couch eating popcorn and red vines, watching *Austin Powers* instead of Dick Clark, when the telephone rang, and it was my sister Veronica. And what was even stranger was that it sounded like she had been drinking.

"Hey, Pam, I just wanted to thank you again for saving my house. And oh, by the way, I'm sorry about what happened at Christmas, you know Andrew can be kind of an ass especially after his father left us."

"No sweat, sis. How's everything going?"

"I don't know if I ever tell you enough, but you know I'm not really big on emotions."

"Tell me what? I asked her then she started rambling again.

"You know that bitch, Vicki?" she said as she started to slur. "Vicki, Victoria, whatever her name is. You know what she said?"

"No sis I don't."

"She told me that Don never loved me! That's what she said. That home wrecking bitch!"

"Veronica don't listen to her! You need to ignore her."

"She's even got Don doing drugs again and drinking and shit. And you know what else?"

"No, no, what else, sis?"

"She said that she wants Don and her to adopt the baby!" Then she started crying so much that I could barely make out a thing that she said. Then choking back a new round of sobs, she regained her composure and boldly declared. "Over my dead body!"

"Mine too sis! Mine too! That fucking bitch!

"A whore! A fucking whore is all that she is!" Then she suddenly started to giggle and for some reason I giggled as well.

"You know what, sis?" I told her. "This year has *really* sucked!"

"Tell me about it!" she said. "Anyways I just wanted to wish you a happy new year and hope that things will get better and all, but I'm not really sure that they will." Then she started crying all over again.

"Well happy new year to you, sis! And by the way, I really *do* love you."

BIRTHDAY WISH

Early that year I found out that I was no longer welcome to even visit my father. "You just cause too much drama," he told me when he came over to give me my money. Though one time, Betty invited me there, since my new doctor was just down the street from his condo, but when he came home, he asked me to leave, but not before screaming at Betty.

"What's she doing here?" he shouted as soon as he walked in the door.

"I invited her, Ron!" she snapped back. "After all, she *is* your daughter!"

"You're always going against my wishes!" He screamed waving his hands and throwing his body into each raspy syllable. "Are you the one who has to find her a place when she gets thrown out of another apartment? Do you ever take a day off from work to go to court and talk to the judge to get her more money? I'm the one who is there every week, giving her money and... and... and... cleaning her manchas!"

Then he paced around and started to huff while Betty and I both sat and stared at each other. He eventually cooled down and let me stay for dinner, but he warned that I was *never* to show up again without calling him first.

"But didn't you tell me that you no longer wanted me calling you here?" I interrupted.

"You catch on quick!" he shot back.

It was then that I realized it was all about money and that my father didn't gave a shit about *me*. I was only a burden—a burden not only to him, but a burden to *everyone*!

"Oh God, why didn't you just let me die in the accident?" I asked him that night when I prayed. "Life would be so much better for everyone."

I swallowed my meds, brushed my teeth, took off my clothes and waited for the portals of sleep to mercifully enter into my room. I remember I saw this dark shadow emerging from out of the closet. I don't recall if it was a dream, I mean I never left my closet door open at night when I slept, it was something I learned as a child that if I cleaned up my room and shut my closet the "boogie man" would stay far away, so I guess that it *was* a dream—or was it? Do dreams have faces and names? Some do I guess, but since most of mine didn't I felt that this probably wasn't. Anyway, as the shadow grew closer, I could make out the hair, then its tall slender body moving slowly toward the foot of my bed. Any other time I would have probably screamed, but this time I wasn't afraid since I recognized both the face and the voice.

"Pammy."

"Mom?"

"It's okay, baby. Don't be afraid."

"I'm not," I said as my teeth were beginning to chatter.

"I just wanted to tell you I love you and how much I miss you."

"I miss you too, Mom."

"And your daughter, Arielle is it?"

"Yes."

"Beautiful name—*Lion of God*."

My mother always was very smart. Got straight A's in high school – *Pius X*, I think that was where she went— that was when she'd met my father and they started going out in her senior year. She always wanted to go to college, but then they got married that summer and later that fall my oldest sister Marie was born. As I looked up again, she was standing next to a man a few years older. He was big and tall with graying hair and a full white beard, yet his voice was so soft and so gentle as he stood in my bedroom next to my mother.

"I miss you, honey," he said in a deep husky timbre. "Remember when you would always come over and visit?"

"David?"

"She remembers you, honey," my mother assured him taking his hand.

"And do you remember Dillinger?" my mother asked me referring to David's hundred-pound pit bull that used to pull me and my friends on our skate boards then cuddle with me on the living room floor.

"Of course!" I answered excitedly. "Of course I do!"

"Well, he's up here with us," my mother insisted. "And you know what else, honey? All the pain in my body is gone! It's like I'm in a brand-new body! A body in which there is no more pain... no more pain... no more pain... no more pain..." then her voice slowly faded away and they both disappeared from inside of my room.

"The bible warns us to test the spirits," my old friend Ruth said when I called her. "And Pam, you need to start following God. From all that you've been telling me lately it sounds like you've drifted away."

For the next few nights, my mother and David came back in my room. Then one night, they showed up with Marty—at least he introduced himself as Marty and when he appeared, he was no longer a sixteen year old kid but a full grown man. Like my mother and David, he assured me that where they all were there would be no more pain.

"Nothing will ever hurt you again," he asserted, unaware of what he once did to me.

That morning when I woke up, I sat beside my computer and started writing a poem. It began with those words I heard in my dream—"*no more sorrow, no more pain, no more loss and no more gain.*" Then the phone started ringing and I hit the "save" button and walked over to answer it.

"Pam?" said a familiar voice inside the receiver.

"Steve?"

"Yeah, it's Steve. Please don't hang up," he pleaded.

"What do you want?" I asked him.

"I just wanted to tell you I'm sorry for being an ass. You deserved so much better than me."

"So *now* you're just finding that out?" I retorted turning his self-revelation against him. "And never mind me, do you remember what you said about Arielle?"

"Arielle?"

"My baby!" I reminded him.

"Oh yeah, I'm so sorry," he began to lament. "I'm sure that she's beautiful just like her mother."

"Well thank you, Steve. And thank you for calling."

"So, this is good-bye?"

"This is good-bye."

I hung up the phone, logged back onto my computer, and opened the file I'd saved with my poem— "*no more anger, no more rage, no more act upon this stage.*" Then resaving the file, I logged back out and started to cry. That night I set out all of my pills on the table wondering just how much I would need. Before I sat down and started to count them, I added another verse to my poem—"*no more fear and no more dread, come tomorrow I'll be dead.*"

"Goddamn it!" I shouted looking at all of the near-empty bottles next to my chair. "My father forgot to call them in the last time he was here! I fucking can't even do suicide right!"

Then I thought of my dad. He was getting older, a few more years until he retired. What would he live on? Say what you will about my father, but he was always a good provider. Not to mention his birthday was coming and I really couldn't leave him with nothing. Of course I'd have to look out for Arielle and leave something to all of my siblings. And let's see, Trey was always there for me too, I'd need to leave something for him. The rest, I decided, the rest of it could go to my father. "Happy birthday, Daddy!" I said to myself as I went back over to my computer, opened a document, and started to type.

"Are you sure that this is the way that you want it?" my lawyer asked me over the phone.

"That's what I said, Sheldon. Everything that I read you."

"Good. Then send me a fax and I'll file it for you."

"Thank you," I told him. "And Sheldon, my father's birthday is February 3, please make sure it gets done before then."

That night I sat up in my bed unable to sleep. I tried playing some video games, but since I ran out of all of my pain meds the 3D graphics and digital blips only caused my head to pound that much harder as if I could feel the blood as it coursed through each vessel. I began jerking my head back and forth trying to make the pain go away as now and then the white-yellow beams from a set of stray headlights shot through my window and onto the wall. Turning my head back to the screen, I started to feel this ominous presence standing behind me, its shadow beginning to swallow me whole as a cold wave of darkness brushed up against me like a blanket soaked in dark murky water. Then I heard a faint and distant female voice, like one trying to comfort a child during a nightmare, only in this case *she* was the nightmare.

"Pam. Pam," she called out my name as the screen saver flickered to life and the light from the computer screen faded to black leaving behind the sinister glow from bright red letters that flashed on the screen, "Pam is not here, will you please go away."

"Mom, Mom is that you?" My voice called out to her in the dark.

"No, silly," she answered. "It's your *friend* from Yorba Linda.

"Erika?" I questioned as another set of distant headlights outlined a tall slender shadow like a slide from a childhood nightmare shot through a circular movie projector. As the figure grew closer, dark matted ribbons of hair fell at her shoulder, and a black satin veil concealed her face.

"Erika's a bitch!" she exclaimed as she turned around, tore off her veil, and stared through me with dark empty sockets glowing with fire. "But *you*, my dear, were the one I desired!"

At first, I wanted to scream, but then as I began to feel her cool damp fingers stroking my shoulder, I almost felt a sense of relief as if she and she alone could make all of the pain go away.

"Honey, I know this sounds strange," she continued in a softer more mellifluous tone, "but I was also like you."

"Who are you?" I asked her. "You seem so..."

"Familiar?" She said as she finished my sentence. "Well the reason for that is because you are actually seeing yourself. Maybe not now, but in a few years after you take off some of that weight," she said, then she started to laugh.

"What do you mean?"

"Let's see here, born September 21, 1964 under a full harvest moon, long dark hair, really pretty, at least every man that I knew seemed to think so, even the ones who had raped me when I was a child."

Then I swallowed hard and took a deep breath as tears began to well up in my eyes. "What is your name?" I whispered.

"My mom named me Lilith."

"That's pretty," I said.

"But now everyone calls me "Lost Eyes" or "Empty Eyes" as if I'm some sort of freak!" She raged as her entire body started to tremble. "And then there was this young man, someone I believed who really did love me, who..."

"Who what?" I asked her.

"Who fucking cheated on me!" She cried out clenching her fists. "He promised someday that we would be married, even gave me his ring, and he ended up leaving for some skanky young blonde."

Suddenly, I was getting the picture.

"So, what did you do?"

"I killed her," she said in a voice that was as cold as a stone. "Held both of my hands on her throat as I looked in her eyes and recited the words, "What is thy sentence then, but speechless death?"

"*Richard II*," I said when she finished. "The murder scene in the castle of Pomfret."

"Precisely! You into Shakespeare?"

"Did *Midsummer Night's* the day of the accident."

"And you were?"

"Tatania."

"But of course," she said, grazing the back of my neck with her fingers.

Taking a breath, I began to intone "She was a vixen when she went to school," my expression now rising in the pain of remembrance. Then both of our voices cried out in unison. "And though she be but little, she is fierce."

"Beautiful, honey! That was so beautiful!" Lost Eyes assured me. "The best actors are always the ones who are able to channel their pain."

"You ever do any acting yourself?" I asked.

"When I was younger," she said. "Before my father died."

"I'm so sorry."

"Don't be. He wasn't always a very nice man."

"It sounds like you've had a pretty hard life."

"Like I said, we could almost be twins," she asserted. "Except, that I died in my accident."

"There are times that I wish I'd died too," I admitted.

"Then what's holding you back? Is it your family?"

"My family doesn't give a shit about me! Sure, my death might ruin everyone's day, but then they'll start counting my money."

"Is it your daughter?"

"How do you know that I have a daughter?"

"The spirits my dear, they tell me everything."

"I see," I answered then thought for a moment about what Ruth told me. "Arielle doesn't even know I'm her mother."

"Well what is it then, honey?"

"It's God. I don't think he'd want me taking my life."

"But would a loving God ever want you to be in such pain?"

"Perhaps it's his will."

"Didn't God say, 'I am come that you might have life, and that you might have it more abundantly?'" She stopped for a moment, clenching her teeth and asked me again. "*Didn't he say that?*"

"Of course," I answered.

"Then how abundant is your life right now? Just saying," she said then she put a hand on each of my shoulders as the flames in her sockets diminished into a warm amber glow. "Look, my dear, at one time I went to church every day, knew the bible forward and backward, and after it was all said and done, there's only one verse that you need to remember."

"What's that?" I asked her.

"It's 1 John 4:16. Surely, you've heard of 1 John 4:16?"

"Refresh me?"

She walked up behind me, wrapping me up in her cool, damp embrace and started stroking my hair with her hands. "'God is love,' my darling—'God *is* love!' No matter what you have done, or what you may do, remember that God always loves you. And not only that, God will forgive you!"

She set down her veil as it fell once again over her face. Turning around and facing the window, she started singing a song that I'd heard long ago—the summer we had first moved to Yorba Linda. Her voice was deep and resounding, but soft and beautiful like that of an angel just fallen from heaven—"you're a butterfly, and butterflies are free to fly"—recognizing the nefarious lullaby, I began to join her, our voices ringing out together as one—"fly away, high away, bye bye..."—then just like that she was gone from my room.

The next morning, I got a call from the pharmacy, "Ms. Vasquez, your prescriptions are ready." So, I got dressed, walked across the street to pick them up, and set the bag on the dining-room table—sixty of each Tylenol Codeine and Vicodin, not to mention thirty 25MG morphine tablets—that I decided would be more than enough. Then I remembered the bottle of tequila that I kept in the cupboard above the refrigerator that one of the guys I was dating had saved for when he came over.

"Well fuck him" I said to myself as I climbed up to get it on one of the chairs.

That evening I ordered pizza—pineapple and Canadian bacon—the same kind that Trey would deliver for me when I called him at *Dominos*. God how I wish Trey was here now! Or maybe I don't, cause he'd just end up trying to stop me again. When I was a girl, I always liked pizza. When my mom made something for dinner like liver and onions, or something else that I thought was gross, I'd go into my father's dresser, open up the drawer where he kept his money, pull out a twenty, and call out for pizza. At first, he got *really* pissed and threatened to ground me, but then he would just end up shrugging it off. I guess that he didn't much care for liver and onions since he always would steal a few of my slices. Now if any of my siblings would do that they'd end up beaten and sent to their room. But not me, I was the baby! And as the baby, I could do whatever I wanted.

I also had an affection for bears—well more like an *obsession* for bears! Every Christmas and for my birthday I'd ask my father to get me a bear. At first, he'd explain that bears were meant to live "out in the wild" where they could be bears. Then when we moved to Yorba Linda and had that backyard, he told me that they would eat Heidi and Skippy and also my cat.

Then he told me a story—I'm still not sure of its real or not—of this hunter who met a bear in the woods and as he pointed a gun to his chest, the bear told him "stop and let's talk for a while, what is it that you want?" "Well, I want a fur coat," the hunter said.

Then the bear answered, "And I want a full belly."

Then they both walked into the woods together and minutes later, the hunter had his fur coat and the bear his full belly.

He would tell me that story whenever I'd ask him to get me a bear. So, one year, I think that it was the day I turned four, he had my Nino dress up like a bear! The thought of hearing my uncle Tony trying to growl and not knowing whether to scare me or hug me still makes me laugh. Then when he finally took off the suit, he couldn't stop itching!

I was happy back then. But that was before all of the drinking, the rapes and the beatings. I was the one who was pretty and smart, the favorite of all of my teachers, the girl that all the boys wanted to date and who all of the girls had wanted to be. I got what I wanted, and usually I wanted it *all*. By high school I'd traded my Hessian leather for rockabilly socks, then "new ro'" pumps when the trend changed again later that year. My tight dark curls had grown down to my back and I looked just like that lady in *Heart*—the one who sang—the prettier of the two sisters. I was also an actor in training and studied to be a professional dancer. I was Phoebe Cates in every freshmen boy's swimming pool, and "carrot porn" in the high school lunchroom. And if anything, my upbringing taught me that I could use sex to get what I wanted.

Then came the fucking car accident! Goddamn it, why didn't I just listen to my father and stay home that night? Why did I put us on Carbon Canyon Road when my parents told me to stay far away from that place? And why was Edward Lepak even able to drive? If I only knew where he was buried, I'd go over there now and piss on his grave! And God, why didn't you stop it? Or could you? Or did you even bother to care? Maybe you wanted to get my attention since with the way I was living I probably would have been dead already. Perhaps Paul was right, him and Mike Hanning—*why don't you give up your life of sin, Pam? Why don't you start going to church, Pam? Why don't you stop snapping your gum, Pam? Why don't you stop having sex on the bleachers, Pam?* Okay, you were right, guys! And look where it got me? Anyway, I guess that I'll never know. What I did know was that when I first saw myself after the accident, I no longer even wanted to live—my head shaved, my left hand not working, my eyes a pair of darting black slits unable to focus for more than a second. I remember driving my head straight into a wall—*Kill the monster! Kill the freak! Kill the bitch who should have died that night instead of Marty!* Then I'd fall back crying onto the floor, my head now throbbing in torrents of pain.

And the pain—Oh, God, the pain! Every day my head and my back, the light in my eyes, the daily withdrawal from all of my meds, before each night when I'd lift my bottle up like a chalice, remove the cap and receive what has become my body and blood—three Vicodin, two Tylenol Codeine, and a tablet of Morphine. Then to keep me awake, I lived on caffeine. Was that the life I was expected to live?

This wasn't the way it was supposed to turn out. Fuck no, this wasn't the way! When I first moved to Yorba Linda, my friend Kelly and I would play this game where we'd pull a number from out of a bag and talk about where we would be at that age. We were both five at the time so how could we have known any better? *Sixteen*, I'd be starting my senior year, get elected Homecoming Queen and working on getting accepted to college. *Eighteen*, I'd be a professional dancer and just completing my freshman year. *Twenty-five*, I'd be finished with acting school and already starring in movies. *Twenty-eight*, I'd be married and have a couple of children, a boy and a girl, we'd have a big house with huge backyard and a dog and a cat, and maybe a horse, and did I mention a spiral staircase? Yeah, the house would have a huge spiral staircase leading up to all of our rooms. *Thirty*, fuck it, I'm already dead! In fact, I was always a dead girl!

I learned the night that my mother had beat me and pulled out all of my stiches that I was named for her niece, the youngest of Loretta's three children who had died in the fire. *Kristine*—Pamela *Kristine*! So, my entire life I was always the dead girl! And you know what they say, "from dust thou art, and to dust thou shall return".

It wasn't like I was leaving everybody alone. Marie has Roger and Sarah and Robyn, Ron has Shelly and Ryan and Nick, Dad has Betty and her son Aaron, and Veronica has Andrew, Ashley, and Amanda—oh, and I forgot to mention, Veronica also has Arielle, my daughter. Then there's my friends, most of who are married or moved or just don't call anymore. You think that *they* would miss me? Are you fucking kidding? If anything, all I was is a bother.

I took the bottle and I filled a glass I pulled from out of the cupboard up with the tequila, then I sat there and stared trying to make out what it said—"*We'll always be friends, we know too much!*" it said right on the front with a ladybug on it who was blowing a kiss. Erika! It must have been the same one that she sent me one year for my birthday after she was already living in Vegas. Well, my friend, if you only *knew*. If you read about this, I hope that you won't be disappointed in me. Same goes for Randy and Cindy and Diane and Lisa and Dexter and Jason and Neil and Jeff, and Christina and Michael and Trey—who I believed really liked me but could never convince himself to admit it—and especially *you*, Mr. Moore. Please know that you were always my favorite teacher! And Rick, I know that you'll make a great husband and father and I hope that you'll be the next Jonas Salk. Daniella, you were always so sweet and so dear. Keep up the good fight, my friend! And Ruth who was like a spiritual mother, and all of my friends who I met in church, I hope that you can find it in your heart to forgive me. And to all of my friends at the station, well at least those who are left, it looks like I'll be mixing with harps from now on! I hope that you can still hear my show each night in your dreams. And good-bye once again to Katie, and Marty, the old man who lived on my street, and to Mom and to David. Please leave the light on for me till I see you up there! And to my cousin Susie, even though we didn't see eye to eye you still always had my back—at least until that drug addict Michelle started living with us—anyway, I *do* love you, cuz! And lastly, to my father, you'll be taken good care of. I understand how hard it must have been for you to care for me all this time, coming over and doing my laundry and paying my bills and going to court and always finding me new apartments when I kept on getting kicked out of the ones I was in. I'm not sure if I ever said "thank you" but, Daddy, I'm saying it now. And despite how all this turned out I know that you always did your best and how much you loved me. And though you seldom ever put those three words "I love you" together, at least in that particular order, I always knew that you did. "I'm not a mushy guy" you would say, and I don't disagree, but when it came right down to it, you always had a really big heart. When the day comes and you find me, please don't ever blame yourself for what happened. Just know that I love you and that I'm always your "baby." And to anyone else that I may have forgotten like Bill and Tony and Nana and Grandpa and Betty and Aaron. When you think about me, please think good thoughts!

Walking into my bedroom there was just one more thing that I needed to do, one final verse to complete my epitaph, the one that I had been writing for weeks, if not for over the course of a lifetime, *with no more tears left to cry, the time has come for me to die.*"

FINAL CALL

By the length of the shadows closing in all around, I realized that I must have been sitting there for more than three hours. What had to be done, I had to do now. I got up and walked over to my window and looked outside before closing the curtains. There was a silver-white moon hanging just over the mountains, and for a moment, I couldn't remember ever seeing something so beautiful, as if both of my eyes were tapping my brain on the shoulder. But I was afraid to even say anything. I didn't know what might happen. I might even break out into tears.

I started thinking of Virginia Wolff, then Sylvia Plath. I wouldn't mind walking "head on into the deep end of a river," but sticking my head in an oven—a fucking oven!—God sakes, you'd have to be crazy, or brilliant, or was there a difference? Then there was Michael Hutchence and Ian Curtis, a snakeskin belt and a washing line, and they never needed to leave their apartment. I had a leopard skin belt of my own that I learned long ago how to tie into a noose, but the thought of me gasping for air would just bring back memories of asthma attacks that I had as a child. Or then there was John Bonham, not my favorite but my brother liked him. I could drink the entire bottle of tequila, pass out and ugh, *choke on vomit*. Or maybe I could pull an Elvis in the worst case of "here I sit all broken-hearted" in fucking *ever*! Goddamn you, Trey, there you go again making me laugh! Or Ron, or Roger two "wild and crazy guys" reenacting old SNL episodes while stuffing their pie holes full of pizza and *Jolly Time* popcorn. But my end would need to be different from theirs.

"Oh, happy dagger, this is thy sheath. There rust and let me die!" I started to laugh until I started to cry, walked into the bathroom, and turned on the water, now and again, dipping my hand under the faucet, making sure it was perfect. I carefully added some of the fragrant beads that I got at *Lotions and Lace* that I'd wanted to give out as a present but for some odd reason decided to keep them, and a cup full of lavender salt. Minutes later, my whole apartment was filled in sheathes of fragrant balloons.

I picked up my glass and a bottle of meds—enough to kill a fucking horse—and set it down on my sink under the mirror. Then I started taking off all of my clothes and just let them fall right down to the floor. First the dress, and then the bodysuit—my God, why was I wearing a bodysuit? Shit, Pam, you're making this hard! As I began stepping over my panties as they lay on the ground sitting on top of my feet, I remembered I still needed a knife. Or I could get one of my pizza cutters and rake my wrists in a vertical ribbon—four on each side just to make sure, like I was cutting a pizza, an orange-red river of blood spilling down from each arm—but at the last minute I decided to go with the knife. As the water got to the halfway mark, I began humming a song that I had learned when I first got into acting, the one from *A Chorus Line*. I used to always cry when I sang it, so now I just stuck with the humming, then at some point—mid-chorus I think—I said "fuck it,"

turned off the water and started to sing louder and louder
as if I no longer cared that my neighbors were hearing the
voice of a dead girl.

Kiss today goodbye
the sweetness and the sorrow
Wish me luck, the same to you
but I can't regret
What I did for love, what I did for love
Look, my eyes are dry
The gift was ours to borrow
It's as if we always knew
And I won't forget
What I did for love, what I did for love
Gone
Love is never gone
As we travel on
Love's what we'll remember
Kiss today goodbye
And point me toward tomorrow
We did what we had to do
Won't forget, can't regret
What I did for love
What I did for love
what I did for love
And I won't forget
what I did for love
(Kleban and Hamlisch, 1975)

***

"Oh, God, forgive me! God, please forgive me!" I pleaded as I pushed the faucet back into the wall and started to lower my body down into the water. "Shit, still too hot! I'll need to give it a few more minutes, fuck, what do I do, what do I do?" I began asking myself, as my heart beat so loud in my chest, I was afraid that the neighbors would hear it—*tha-thump... tha-thump... tha-thump...* Then I grabbed a towel, held it around my waist, and walked into my bedroom.

"Pam, we're waiting." I could hear their voices again through the vapor, stirring the water, calling my name. Then, for some crazy reason, I picked up my phone and dialed the number to the *Crystal Cathedral—Rrring, rrring, rrring, rrring, rrring, rrring, rrring...* "fuck it!" I thought as the voices grew louder and louder. "I'm coming!" I shouted to no one in particular, but the ones that I knew were impatiently waiting.

I tried calling one more number and by the time I got to ring number seven, I decided that like the Prophets of Baal in the days of Elijah, God must have been asleep at the switch, or like Jesus when he was asleep on the cushion as the waves crashed all around their boat and the disciples were certain that they all would drown. Well, *I'm* drowning! I'm drowning now and nobody cares! Right before I finally gave up and set the phone back on the receiver to mingle my blood in the angry white foam, somebody actually picked up the phone. It was the voice of a middle aged man who sounded much younger, but it may well have been the voice of an angel, and for a moment, the only voice I could hear didn't belong to those in my room, or those in my head, but the one on the phone—"Calvary Chapel Prayer Watch, how can I pray for you?"

EPILOGUE

Pamela and I were married on January 29, 2000—almost a year to the day after I answered her call. I'm not sure if it was love at first sight because after all she still couldn't see very well. I do remember when I first met her at Starbucks, she was dressed all in black, a denim shirt against a mesh see-through top. Her skin was pale, almost white, her long black hair swung side to side falling over each shoulder as she tried to keep it out of her face. Her lips were red like a black widow's belly leaving crimson stains on a long green straw. She was tapping her nails on a small wooden table when I walked up beside her and asked to sit down. "You're late," she said, then blew me off for the next few minutes. That was Pam, sassy from the very beginning!

Though we've been happily married now for almost twenty years, our life hasn't always been easy as the trials we've been through together would fill up a book—but now I'm getting ahead of myself. Yet through it all our faith has sustained us and "having done all to stand," we are standing therefore—a cord of two strands, an unbreakable bond, an ally, a partner, a lover, a friend, that's who we are to each other.

One day in April of 2012 my 1994 Jeep Wrangler, having nearly traveled to the moon and back, was going the way of all pistons and steel. So, after finding a newer one that I liked, I called the guy and asked him if I could go out and see it. He told me that he closed at six, but if I could get there in forty-five minutes he'd stay there and wait. Then I asked my wife if she wanted to go look at it with me.

"Sure," she said, then I told her it was out in Montclair.

"That's okay."

"But we need to get there in forty-five minutes."

"So, what is it that you're trying to tell me?"

"We'll need to take some kind of short cut."

"That's impossible, there's only one way to avoid the 91 freeway and that's..."

Then we both said it out loud together: "Carbon Canyon Road."

I watched for a moment as all of the color drained from her body as if she was reliving the day that was three days short of its twenty-seventh anniversary. Then she steadied herself and gave me a look like the ones that I've seen on her face many times before, the ones that had told me it was time for me to stand back and get out of her way.

"You know you can always stay home if you want." I offered. "You know, if you think that it's still too soon."

Clenching her fists, she looked back at me, snatched up her purse and said, "Fuck it, let's go!"

As Lambert Road started to narrow as it wound past the park and alongside of the golf course, I could see my wife sitting next to me, eyes tightly closed, her right hand locked onto the roll bar, and her lips moving as if reciting a prayer. After dancing along the side of an abandoned mineral hot springs, we crested the top of a hill then sliced through a forest of oak—twisted limbs of mangled trees dangling their threats along either side as I shifted from fifth down to third, weaving through spring colored hills painted green by a recent series of storms, my engine both whining and humming as we dropped for a moment only to climb up again as the road began bobbing and weaving in a series of turns. After a long steady rise, we finally made it into the hairpins. Stravinsky's *Rite of Spring* giving way to *Clair De Lune* as the highway straightened into a long gentle grade that carried us down to checkerboard streets and suburban homes laid out on a grid framed by distant rolling green hills as *Carbon Canyon Road* took on the less ominous moniker—*Chino Hills Parkway*.

"There, that wasn't so bad," I said as I looked at my wife still shaking and gasping as we took our place in a long line of cars that waited for the light at the 71.

"Would you please change the music?" she asked. "You know play something different?"

So I ejected my CD from out of the player, turned on the radio and flipped through the stations until a song came on that I remembered was really popular then, the one where the guy in the video fades into a painting and him and his girlfriend find themselves awash in a progression of green and brown slashes until the girl finally sets herself free and is standing there naked with her back to the camera.

"That's good." She said. "Leave it right there."

Turning her head toward the window, she slowly reached up for the zipper and with a mischievous grin, pulled it open and screamed out at the top her lungs, "Fuck you Lost Eyes! Damn you to hell!"

Then when the light changed to green, and the cars up ahead let go of their brakes, and the bright red wall that once held us back started moving forward again, she turned back around and looked out at the hills.

"You didn't get me! You hear me? You didn't get me! 'For greater is He that is in us'..."

She never completed her sentence. We made it in time and drove back home in a "new" 2001 Jeep Wrangler. I remember it was geared pretty low and it took me a while to get used to the shifting, but I got a great deal, and to this day I still have the car. We didn't take the canyon back home. By that time, the freeway was far less crowded, so there wasn't the need. In fact, neither of us have ever been back, having already reconquered that road— a cruel stretch of ungoverned pavement that forever altered both of our lives.

AUTHOR'S NOTE

Looking back, I clearly remember the day. A warm April morning, a strong cup of coffee, and the Sunday edition of the *Orange County Register* crashing up against my door. I always used to begin at the Sports page, then slowly make my way to the Calendar section, stopping sometimes to try my hand at the New York Times crossword puzzle. But that particular morning, something caught my eye on the second page of the Metro section—"Three people killed and five injured in two traffic accidents in Orange County." As I read on, I noticed that only one of the drivers' names was recorded, a seventeen-year-old Fullerton boy who was killed on impact and an unnamed thirty-five-year-old man from Chino who was also pronounced dead at the scene. The story then listed the names of the injured—a fifteen-year-old boy from Yorba Linda, a fifteen year-old girl from Placentia, and two other girls who were only fourteen. For some reason I was drawn to the names of the last two girls—my God, they were only *fourteen*! One of the girls had been taken to a hospital in Brea and the other was airlifted to Western Medical Center in Santa Ana. The one at Western was listed as critical.

The article went on to mention that alcohol may have been involved. *No shit,* I thought to myself as I put down the paper, walked to the kitchen, and poured myself another strong cup. Yet, I couldn't get the story out of my mind. I was twenty-one and by that time had driven drunk on several occasions. I'd been lucky, those kids weren't. I said a prayer, got on with my day, and lived my life for the next fourteen years before that story came to life when I met one of those girls. One year later, Miss Pamela Vasquez became my wife.

As I got to know Pam, I was convinced that hers was a story that had to be told. Her life was more than that of a typical north Orange County teen who'd been out for a joyride on that fateful spring night and happened to be out in Carbon Canyon when a drunk driver came speeding toward the car she'd been riding in. Her story was that of a miracle baby who doctors said should have never been born in the first place, and who grew up within a family pathology where a woman's life was lived through a child. It was also a story of unparalleled courage as she learned to live all over again—who tasted death but was sent back to earth to finally experience the fullness of love that would ensure she would never die twice. Far from being a tragic heroine, Pam is a fighter— passionate, loving, and unafraid. A woman who wears her heart on her sleeve, knowing full well that the worst that can happen already had.

As her story unfolds, Pam may not be everyone's hero, flawed and human though she may be, she is *my* hero— deep and devoted, a caring and gentle soul, yet willful and stubborn, and someone you *never* want to provoke. But God kept her alive for a reason, and I'm thankful He did. She may not be perfect, but she's perfect for me.

Throughout our marriage, we often discussed having somebody tell her story. But the more we discussed it, the more we realized that Pamela's story would need to be written by someone who knew her, someone who loved her, and someone who could bring her story to life. So, last year I began this labor of love as a huge "thanks" to the only woman who could ever endure twenty-plus years of living with me.

My hope, dear reader, is not only that Pamela's story inspires you, but that in the process of reading her story, you grew to love her as much as I do—or at least *almost* as much. After all she is *my* favorite dead girl. Hopefully she'll become your favorite as well.

Blessings,
Jerry A. Kuznik

ACKNOWLEDGEMENTS

I would first like to thank my wife Pamela for allowing me to tell her amazing and powerful story. She could have chosen any number of people to write it, but she chose the person who, apart from God, knew her best and loved her most.

I would also like to thank the following professors who encouraged me to pursue what they acknowledged was my gift for writing: Dr. Trudy Jo Naman, Dr. Bill Dogterom, Dr. John Sim, and Professor Dorothy J. Huson.

To Marni Macrae, my wonderful editor, who not only helped shepherd this manuscript, but cured me of a lifelong addiction to semi-colons.

To my father and mother, Jerry and Rose Kuznik, who adopted me as a child, raised me as one of their own, and who gave me the confidence to be the best I could be in whatever I did.

To my Lord and Savior Jesus Christ, whose death and resurrection assured me of eternal life in exchange for my sin.

And lastly, to you my dear reader, whose intelligence and love for a good story I swore to uphold. May you be encouraged by the words on these pages!

ABOUT THE AUTHOR

Jerry Kuznik lives in central Orange County with his wife Pamela and his dog and four cats. A former software developer and author of several short stories and poems, when he's not busy reading or writing, Jerry enjoys spending time with his wife, listening to classical and alternative music, taking long walks with their rescue dog Mowgli, and cuddling on the couch with their cats. He earned his Bachelor's Degree from Vanguard University, where he graduated *summa cum laude*.

A man of faith, Jerry and his wife Pamela want to use their time and their talents to reflect God's love to everyone that He brings into their life be it two legs, or four.

CPSIA information can be obtained
at www.ICGtesting.com
Printed in the USA
BVHW080149291120
594340BV00005B/374